# THE
# FOURTH OF JULY
# WAR

# THE FOURTH OF JULY WAR

## a novel by
## ALLAN TOPOL

WILLIAM MORROW AND COMPANY, INC.

NEW YORK   1978

Library of Congress Cataloging in Publication Data

Topol, Allan.
   The Fourth of July War.

   I. Title.
PZ4.T6796Fo   1979   [PS3570.064]   813'.5'4   78-15953
ISBN 0-688-03380-6

BOOK DESIGN        SUZANNE LOBEL

Printed in the United States of America.

First Edition

1   2   3   4   5   6   7   8   9   10

I dedicate this book to my wife, Barbara,
whose enthusiasm and encouragement were invaluable,
and to our children, David, Rebecca,
Deborah, and Daniella

# THE
# FOURTH OF JULY
# WAR

# CHAPTER

# 1

*Geneva, Switzerland, April 1983*

"WELL, WHERE IS HE?" THE IRANIAN AMBASSADOR ASKED impatiently.

He closed his lips tightly. There was a disgusted look on his thin face.

"Only a minute. I've told you," the Saudi replied. "Faisel is a busy man."

"And my time is worth nothing," Ahmad grumbled, walking over to the window of the Hotel Richmont.

The Iranian lit up another cigarette.

A spring snowstorm was brewing over the Swiss Alps. The first light snowflakes were already starting to fall on Lake Geneva. Soon the roads leading to the airport would become slick, slowing traffic.

"I'll be lucky if I get out today," Ahmad said, thinking about Maria waiting in Washington. Only the Shah's personal order had delayed his return. He had one thought in mind: to complete his assignment as quickly as possible.

A third man walked into the entrance foyer of the suite, dressed in a Saudi army uniform. He was tall and muscular with a pistol hanging on one hip and a gold curved sword on the other. Undoubtedly one of Faisel's personal security force, Ahmad thought.

"The Finance Minister will see you now," the third man said. Then he turned smartly and began walking down a marble corridor.

Ahmad followed two steps behind.

When they reached the large dining room at the end of the suite, Abdul knocked twice and opened the door.

Yaman Faisel, the Finance Minister of Saudi Arabia, sat alone at a huge octagonal table in the center of the room. He was an enormous rotund figure, immaculately dressed in a gray pinstripe suit from Bond Street and a stiff white shirt. A neatly styled mustache and beard, along with bushy black eyebrows, dominated his face.

He's eating, as always, Ahmad thought, recalling the dozen or so times he had met with Faisel during the past year.

A gigantic plate of oysters was sitting in front of Faisel—the largest that Ahmad had ever seen. Traces of red seafood sauce were visible around Faisel's mouth. The Saudi's eating habits contrasted sharply with his dress.

"Ahmad Zadak," Abdul announced formally. Then he left the dining room, closing the door quietly.

Ahmad walked forward and extended his hand to Faisel. The Saudi's handshake was limp. The palm of his hand dripped with perspiration.

"Something to eat?" Faisel asked.

He was speaking English with a mouth full of oysters.

"Nothing," Ahmad replied. "You didn't bring me all the way to Geneva to feed me."

Faisel was mildly amused by the annoyance that he detected in Ahmad's voice.

"I'll come right to the point then. I want to know whether the Shah has made a decision on the new proposal that I presented to OPEC?"

"No decision has been made."

"You discussed it with him?"

"In some detail."

"Then tell me the reason for the delay."

Ahmad had anticipated the question. He paused for a moment. It was important to phrase his answer carefully.

"Your proposal calls for drastic action," Ahmad said slowly. "It requires careful study."

"What about the increases in the price of oil that I proposed last year? And the reduction in production? Those were quickly approved by the Shah."

"This proposal is different. It may not be in our best interest in the long run."

Faisel speared two oysters with a small fork, dipped them in red sauce, and placed them quickly into his mouth. A strange man, the Shah, Faisel thought. With the passing of years, he was becoming meek and timid.

"Surely the Shah does not fear a military response," Faisel said, starting to laugh arrogantly.

Ahmad sat silently watching Faisel, trying hard to mask the contempt that he felt for the Saudi. He could recall the scorn and superiority that he and his army colleagues felt toward the Saudis—the jokes that they had made.

"He has not forgotten the lesson of 1973," Faisel continued disdainfully. "We instituted a complete embargo, and the Americans never even hinted at a military response. That was only ten years ago. Why has the Shah become such a coward?"

"I have nothing else to report. I will let you know when the Shah has made his decision."

There was a long pause as Faisel studied the Iranian.

Was he lying, Faisel wondered? Had the Shah made up his mind to undermine the new proposal? Maybe he had even disclosed it to the Americans? With the Shah, you could never be sure.

"I return to New York next week," Faisel said, concealing his concern. "You will find me at the Waldorf."

The Iranian left the room without uttering another word.

Faisel looked down at the plate of oysters. He had a marked frown on his face and deep furrows in his forehead.

As Ahmad's black limousine raced across slippery roads to the Geneva airport, the sun was just beginning to rise behind the Santa Ana mountains southeast of Los Angeles. Along the coast a twelve-story glass and steel building stood quite alone in the forbidding gray of the early morning hours. Encircled by a barbed-wire fence and closely watched by armed guards, the building resembled a feudal empire. On three sides large golden letters had been placed at its top. They spelled out the words GEORGE T. MORRIS ENTER-PRISES.

In the penthouse six men were seated at a large oak table in the wood-paneled conference room. Their white shirts were loosened at the neck and rolled up at the sleeves. They had a glazed look of fatigue in their eyes, the stubble of growth on their cheeks. Empty coffee cups and scraps of yellow legal paper littered the table.

"I will repeat my position one more time, Mr. Barton," Morris said calmly and dispassionately. "I am not prepared to accept forty million dollars in Global American stock in return for my stock in Morris Enterprises. I want cash. . . . And I want that cash deposited in my Zurich bank within forty-eight hours after we conclude this transaction."

Barton tried to keep himself under control while Morris spoke. But his face disclosed the corporate executive's anger. It was bright red, contrasting sharply with the mop of white hair that still covered his head.

When Morris was finished, Barton rose to his feet and began shouting.

"Ridiculous . . . Absolutely ridiculous. We have always traded stock for stock. I had no idea that you would insist on cash."

With a deadpan expression, Morris stared squarely into Barton's eyes. Morris had carefully guarded his demand for cash until the end of the negotiations—even keeping it from his lawyer and his accountant—Jordan and Armstrong.

He needed the full advantage that he could gain from secrecy and surprise.

"Don't tell me what you've done with other people," Morris said quietly. "I do things my own way."

Jordan was sitting with a scowl on his face massaging his forehead. It's impossible to represent Morris, he thought. The man never discloses a complete story.

Armstrong could barely conceal a smile. He had a strange admiration for Morris—the young tycoon who paid Armstrong a handsome salary. He was always amazed when Morris pulled the bold, daring move as he had so often in the last ten years.

Armstrong started as Morris's accountant when Morris owned two shopping centers and an apartment building in Torrance. When the real estate business grew tenfold, Armstrong expected Morris to sell everything and bale out. Instead, he had mortgaged the whole empire to buy the Bee Burger, a fast-food chain. Three years later, two hundred and fifteen Bee Burger restaurants went on the mortgage block for a software computer firm. Then there was the investment banking subsidiary.

Morris's drive for power and money was insatiable, Armstrong thought. His employer was either a captain of industry or a pirate. Maybe both. The accountant didn't make value judgments. He loved every minute of his relationship with Morris. When Morris built a twenty-seven-room mansion in Beverly Hills, Armstrong bought a large split-level with a swimming pool in Santa Monica.

"We don't have that kind of cash, Mr. Morris," Barton said, still shouting. "Certainly not on forty-eight hours notice."

Morris pounced on Barton like a predatory animal who had been lying in ambush for his prey.

"That statement is untrue, Mr. Barton."

Morris paused for a minute, making Barton wait.

"I know that you allocated a cash reserve of two hundred and fifty million dollars for taxes due on April fifteenth. I also know that your taxes will never exceed two hundred million because of tax credits from your new investments in Saudi Arabia. So you do have cash. . . . To be specific, you have it in short-term deposits at Chase Manhattan in New York—the Wall Street branch."

Barton turned white. The old man looked as if he would have a heart attack on the spot.

"How could you possibly know that?" Barton asked hesitantly.

He was shaking his finger at Morris.

"Only three men had access to that information."

"And one makes four."

Barton glanced suspiciously at his two colleagues.

The six men sat in complete silence for several minutes, waiting for Barton to regain his composure.

During the silence Morris's thoughts drifted back to that day in September 1971, only twelve years ago, when he left the scholarship office at Harvard University clutching the check for $3,000 in his hand. It was tuition for his last year at Harvard Business School. But rather than carry it to the Bursar's office at the Harvard Business School, as he had each of the three previous Septembers, he rode the "T" into downtown Boston, directly to the office of Winthrop and Merrill—members of the New York Stock Exchange.

There he invested the whole $3,000 in the stock of one company—a glamour issue that he had selected utilizing the computer at the Harvard Business School. Then he spent a frantic and neurotic September reading the closing prices on the stock exchange and throwing out "overdue" tuition notices that the Bursar's office fired regularly every Monday morning.

But the computer didn't fail him. By October 1 his $3,000 had become $23,000. Morris quickly sold, breathing a large sigh of relief when he paid his tuition and deposited $20,000 in a savings account. He had decided that $20,000 was what he needed to get started in building his empire after graduation. The $3,000 tuition check was Morris's only chance to get that sum. He was willing to take a calculated risk.

Morris could still recall those frantic weeks in September 1971. That was the only time in his business career that he had been without complete control of his own fortune. He had no intention of trusting the stock market a second time.

"Well, what will it be?" Morris asked, keeping the pressure on Barton.

"Be reasonable," Barton replied.

He was pleading.

"Take at least half in stock."

"One hundred percent in cash."

"You have to dispose of your stock before you're sworn in tomorrow. You don't have any choice."

"You're wrong again, Mr. Barton. If you won't buy, I'll place it in a trust while I'm in the government. That trust arrangement will satisfy the regulations, and Jordan here has already drafted the papers. All that I have to do is sign."

"You're bluffing," Barton said, staring at Morris. He wanted to look into his eyes, to read his mind. But Morris was wearing dark glasses as he always did in negotiating sessions.

A man's eyes could betray his thoughts. Morris wanted to be the only one who had that advantage.

"Don't count on it," Morris replied. "I'm leaving this room with Jordan and Armstrong. We'll retire to my office for the next fifteen minutes. You three can have your own conference here. When we return, I want your answer. Yes or no on the forty million dollars in cash. And no more bullshit. I just don't have time."

Morris got up and walked out of the conference room. Jordan and Armstrong followed two steps behind.

Barton watched them leave with a bewildered look on his face. He was trying to decide if the bastard really was bluffing.

When they reached his private office, Morris sat down in

the swivel chair behind the ornate desk—custom built to resemble the Shah's desk that Morris had seen in Tehran.

His cobalt blue eyes and his thick, wavy hair made him seem even younger than his thirty-six years. He was a trim 175 pounds, and there was no excess fat on his six-foot-one-inch frame. He looked alert and determined—very much like the financial genius and speculator whom *Time* had described as "The Boy Wonder of Wall Street for the 1980s."

Three weeks earlier the President had announced Morris's appointment as Director of the Department of Energy of the United States Government. Senate confirmation had followed quickly. Tomorrow morning Morris would take charge of the vast federal bureaucracy responsible for managing the country's continuing oil crisis.

Morris glanced at the communications panel in his side desk drawer. If he pressed one of those buttons, he could activate a hidden microphone in the conference room and hear the discussion that Barton was having with his associates. There was no need to do that, Morris thought, filled with self-confidence.

Morris leaned back in the chair and peered down at Jordan and Armstrong slumped in two of the plush velvet chairs that were scattered throughout the office.

"You two can relax," Morris said. "Barton will put up the money in cash. He wants control of Morris Enterprises so badly that he can taste those Bee Burgers."

Jordan rested his head on the back of the chair and closed his eyes. Armstrong leaned forward, cupping his face in his hands. The two men sat quietly waiting for their next directive. They knew that Morris had no use for small talk and that subordinates spoke only when spoken to.

Morris pressed once on the intercom connected to his telephone.

"Yes, Mr. Morris," a woman's voice said quickly.

"Miss Welch, get Janet Koch up here."

Two minutes later a twenty-five-year-old petite brunette

with large hazel eyes entered the office. Her hair was neatly tied with a blue ribbon. She was wearing a khaki pants suit.

Janet had a mildly enticing, sexy expression on her face that was completely at odds with her job as resident mathematical genius and Director of the Morris 6000—the world's most sophisticated decisionmaking computer. Two years ago Morris had lured her away from Cal Tech with the promise of unlimited funds to design her own computer and a personal charm that she was unable to resist.

Janet paid scant attention to Jordan and Armstrong lounging on the chairs. Her eyes focused only on Morris. She walked up to his desk and stood there apprehensively.

"You can go with me to Washington," Morris said.

Janet wasn't sure whether it was a question or a command. She didn't care. She had been praying that he would ask her to go. She had rejected the idea of a husband and children. Her total commitment was to Morris.

"I can go," Janet said calmly, trying hard to conceal her glee. She fantasized making love with Morris in the computer room of a large government office building.

"I want to set up a computer center at the Department of Energy like the one you have downstairs. I want you to direct it," Morris said without perceiving any of the lust that she felt.

"Do you intend to ship the hardware cross country?"

"No, we can't take any of the hardware out of this building." Morris was talking quickly. "Mr. Barton wouldn't like that. What I want you to do is duplicate the Morris 6000 in Washington. Make Xerox copies of all of your circuit diagrams and machinery plans. Take photographs of the whole operation. Then we'll order a duplicate for each piece of hardware."

Morris paused for a minute.

"Any questions?" he asked in a curt tone of voice that implied that there should not be any.

"No questions, Mr. Morris."

"Good. I'll see you in Washington at the end of the week." Morris walked over to the window facing north toward the City of Los Angeles. He enjoyed standing at that window watching the great metropolis unfold as far as the eye could see. Earlier in his life Morris had hated Los Angeles, the city of his birth. To the Okies, like his parents, it held no glamour —only poverty.

At the age of eleven Morris had watched his father being buried in obscurity—the victim of a premature explosion in the construction of a highway. It had been carelessly set by a co-worker. Just another accidental casualty in the great building of urban sprawl. It made no difference to the world that Horace O. Morris had ever lived. It made no difference that he was dead. But that violent event, and more important the obscure burial, shaped the life of George T. Morris. He vowed that it would not happen to him. People would know who he was.

When he was in high school, living with his older brother, Morris worked as a messenger at a Beverly Hills stock brokerage firm. Carrying checks and stock certificates from the firm to nearby banks, he cemented his conclusions about where he would fit into the economic spectrum.

As a scholarship student at Yale University and Harvard Business School, Morris had an outstanding record scholastically. But those were not happy years for Morris. They were lonely years. At first he was nervous that he couldn't make it academically, coming from an inner-city high school. But that wasn't his problem. He finished his freshman year near the top of his class. His problem was social. He was never accepted by the silver spoon boys in his class—the graduates from Andover, Choate, and Exeter, who spent their vacations on the ski slopes or in the Caribbean, summered at the Vineyard or Southampton, and casually wore tweed jackets from J. Press over frayed Levi's.

For the first two years at Yale, Morris desperately struggled for acceptance. He even entertained the hope that he would be tapped for Skull and Bones—the most prestigious of the secret societies that occupy large stone shrines scattered throughout the Yale campus. After all, his class standing warranted that result. But tap night came and went with Morris sitting alone in his room. Not a single secret society was interested. Perhaps he was unrealistic to think about Skull and Bones. But it was humiliating that none of the lesser secret societies had come.

After that, he redoubled his academic determination. He would prove something to those people. He would be better than they were. He became even more isolated, inward, and withdrawn.

During his last two years at Yale, Morris had no time for campus activities, dormitory bull sessions, or other nonsense. He left Yale with a magna cum laude degree, but without a single friend in the graduating class. He repeated this performance four years later when he graduated from the Harvard Business School.

Back in Los Angeles, Morris took his twenty-thousand-dollar nest egg from the stock market to start his real estate business. Six months later the business needed a large shot of capital to take off. By then, Morris was engaged to Marjorie. Her father, who happened to be the President of the San Francisco Golden Valley Bank, was standing behind Morris with his checkbook in hand.

Now Morris loved Los Angeles. It thrived on the modern technology that he had harnessed. He had made a fortune by capitalizing on three of its vital organs—the cheaply built shopping center, the fast-food restaurant, and the computer.

He was selling out because he was bored with business. He wanted a new challenge. But besides that, he was starting to worry a little about the company's future. He knew that every high one day becomes a low and that every rising curve one day turns downward. That was one of the immutable laws of business. The corollary was the faster the rise, the faster the fall. It was time for him to get out—while that curve was still rising.

Morris hated failure more than anything in life. He was afraid of it. He didn't know if he could cope with it. He associated it with his childhood, and those memories had been shoved into the furthest recesses of his mind.

Everyone just assumed that Morris had been born in Beverly Hills or one of the affluent suburbs. No one would have imagined that he was a product of the public schools in one of Los Angeles' jungle areas. And anyone who wanted to find out about his real background would have to dig hard.

This was what Morris wanted. He never pointed with pride to his humble origins—like so many self-made men. Believing that the American dream wasn't dead, he had pulled himself out—into the world of money and power—coupling his intelligence with drive and determination. He had no desire to look back.

As Morris studied the city below, he saw miles and miles of freeways weaving around the great metropolis like a spider's web. It was those freeways that were the veins and arteries of the city. Each morning and each evening they carried millions of tiny ants from homes to offices and factories and back home again.

But those freeways were becoming less congested from day to day. More and more people were being forced to forego the luxury of driving alone. There simply wasn't enough gasoline in the Los Angeles area to satisfy the thirst of the millions of internal combustion engines even if people were prepared to pay the prevailing price of $3.00 a gallon.

As Morris thought about the sharp increase in the price of gasoline during the last year, the adrenaline began racing in his body. That was his next challenge—the country's great oil crisis.

Morris glanced at his watch.

"Let's go. They've had their fifteen minutes."

Back in the conference room, Morris and his colleagues took their old seats opposite the Global American trio.

"Well, Mr. Barton, what's your decision?"

"The absolute best I can do is seventy-five percent in cash and twenty-five percent in stock. That's it. Take it or leave it." Barton's voice was firm, absolutely determined.

There was silence in the room. It was an eerie silence. Barton stared harshly at Morris.

Morris was surprised by the look on Barton's face. It was even more determined than before. For an instant, Morris was worried. Maybe he had misjudged. Maybe he was wrong.

Jordan sat nervously on the edge of the chair. If Morris had asked his advice, Jordan would have said, "Take it. Don't be a fool. Thirty million in cash due in forty-eight hours is far more than you had a right to expect."

But Morris never asked Jordan what he thought. Instead, he rose with a look of disgust on his face and began gathering together his papers.

"Let's go, Philip," Morris said to Jordan. "Get your stuff together. Mr. Barton has just passed up the best deal of his life. I'll sign those trust papers in my office."

Morris started to walk calmly and dispassionately from the room. Jordan and Armstrong were three paces behind. Just as Morris placed his hand on the doorknob, he could hear a voice behind him.

"Okay, you bastard. Get back here. You win."

Morris managed to conceal the narrow smile that was forming on his lips as he returned to the table.

"You're always overreaching, Morris," Barton said. "One day you'll push too far."

Morris was silent.

"Can we leave the paper work to the lawyers?" Barton asked.

"No. I want a short memorandum of understanding signed by the two of us before I leave."

Fifteen minutes later they signed the memorandum of understanding. Barton was still scowling. The angry look on his face confirmed that he had been taken by Morris. Morris had a dour, humorless, deadpan expression—his normal dress for business negotiations.

Morris extended his hand to Barton. The older man refused to take it.

Barton straightened up and stood at attention, glaring at Morris. They were no more than a foot apart. The hatred in Barton's eyes was evident.

"You'll find that Washington is a different world," Barton said. "You won't be able to run a government agency like you've run this little empire."

Morris started walking slowly to the door. Barton pursued him, his face red with anger. It was more than the $40 million. As the Director of Energy, Morris could hurt Barton's investments in Saudi Arabia.

"You'll fall one day," Barton shouted at Morris. "When you do, I hope to hell you fall hard—good and hard."

Two hours later a black Fleetwood limousine rolled into the sprawling Los Angeles airport. Seated alone in the back of the car, Morris was now cleanly shaven and impeccably dressed. His gray silk suit was custom made at Brooks Brothers. He was wearing Gucci loafers, his cuff links were eighteen-carat gold with an American flag in the center—formed from tiny diamonds and rubies.

Morris thought about the data on recent oil price increases that he had seen yesterday. There was something strange happening. He couldn't quite put his finger on what it was. He was convinced that prices were well above the levels that the free market would establish. And increases were sudden and unrelated to any traceable event. Someone was pushing those prices up. Morris would find out who it was.

Anne Walton was waiting for him at Butler Aviation. She stood in the center of a crowd of people, in front of the television cameras, her long blond hair flowing down the sides of her face and kissing her shoulders. Large round sunglasses were protecting her eyes. Her silk blouse was deliberately open at the neck to expose the thin cleavage between her well rounded breasts—just enough to stimulate the fantasies of evening television watchers.

Anne was fielding the questions gracefully, her eyes sparkling.

"No, I don't have any doubts about giving up my television series. I've played 'Undercover Woman' for three years. It was time for a change."

A reporter for *Variety* started speaking. His voice was drowned out by the roar of airplane engines. But Anne had the essence of the question.

"Washington will accept the fact that I'm living with George Morris, even though we're not married. The capital is only six hours away. It's not in the last century."

Morris looked at Anne with pride. He had captured her with a dogged persistence after Philip Jordan introduced them about six months ago—two months after his divorce from Marjorie. Even though there were no children, it had been a bitter divorce provoked by Morris when the reason for his union with Marjorie had passed. He no longer needed those interest-free loans that her father's bank had given him. Nor did he want to be beholden to Marjorie.

Marjorie wasn't prepared to let him go. She had seen through his tough veneer and loved the lonely man trying so hard to prove himself. Recognizing that Marjorie had seen his weaknesses and resenting it as pity, George found it even more imperative to leave.

He didn't feel particularly guilty about ditching Marjorie. He had paid dearly for those loans. Ten years spent in the company of swell old San Francisco families—"friends of my family," Marjorie had called them. He never felt comfortable with them. They refused to accept him. He knew that. He was always the poor son-in-law—an Okie from down south. Now they could all read about the sale of his stock tomorrow morning in the business section of their *Chronicle*. Forty million dollars wasn't bad for a poor son-in-law. Mr. Von Gilder could turn to his wife and say, "Do you remember that poor Okie whom Marjorie married . . ." Well, that article in tomorrow's *Chronicle* would just be the beginning. They would be reading about him every morning. The butler would have to bring a lot more sugar to sweeten their coffee.

Once he met Anne Walton, America's latest sex symbol, Morris made up his mind that she would belong to him. And so he pursued her just as he had pursued money, objects of art, rare silver coins, and race horses. And when she had capitulated and agreed to move in, they threw a gigantic party, inviting scores of movie and television personalities. The *Los Angeles Times* had called it "Beverly Hills's Biggest Bash of the Year."

Morris watched with admiration as Anne bantered with the press—enjoying every minute of it. "Long on looks and short on brains," Jordan described the sexy actress who had spent one semester at UCLA—long enough to be elected Homecoming Queen. But with Anne's other assets she didn't have to be a philosopher, Morris thought. She was his finest acquisition—a face and body worth ten or fifteen million dollars in the current entertainment market—a symbol of his success and virility.

As soon as the reporters saw Morris, they shoved microphones in front of his face. There was a sudden burst of flash from a camera.

"I'm sorry, gentlemen. No questions."

When they entered the large DC-8, Morris settled into one of the comfortable thick velvet lounge chairs, opened his large briefcase, and pulled out a stack of background papers on the production and pricing of oil.

Anne walked over to him, lifted the sunglasses onto her hair, and kissed him gently with her sensuous mouth. He remained seated, impassive, as she sank gracefully into the thick velvet cushion of the chair next to him. She crossed her legs slowly, permitting the white silk skirt to lift well above her knees.

"You're ready to conquer Washington, no doubt," Anne said.

"Completely. The deal with Barton went according to plans. I just have a lot of reading to do before tomorrow morning."

As the plane took off, Morris turned back to his papers.

Anne pulled the sunglasses from her head and placed them carefully in her bag. Then she removed a small mirror, studied her face carefully, and put the mirror away. She picked up a copy of *Vogue* and started turning the pages.

Anne thought about her agent's words, "You're crazy to give up the show and go to Washington with Morris."

But she was twenty-eight with ten nonstop years in the entertainment business. The show had started to slip in the ratings. Next year it would slip even more. Anne had noticed two small lines in her face. Next year there would be two more.

"Always sell high," Anne had once heard Morris say. So this daughter of a Hollywood cameraman decided to cash in. She wanted Morris to marry her. She had raised the subject once, but he had brushed it aside. She let it drop, knowing that he could not be pushed.

"What time do we get to Washington?" Anne asked.

"Four-thirty into Dulles," he replied without looking up.

"I booked us into the Watergate Hotel. The house in Georgetown won't be ready until Saturday."

Morris never even heard her words. His eyes were riveted on a graph that showed the sharply rising price of oil during the last year. There has to be some rational explanation, Morris thought. Prices just don't rise that much.

While the DC-8 flew eastward, another plane—this one with the United States Air Force insignia—lowered its landing gear at Andrews Air Force Base near Washington. General Alvin Thomas, the Chairman of the Joint Chiefs of Staff of the United States Armed Services, walked slowly off the plane and headed toward a waiting car.

He was a tall, imposing figure with a full head of black hair and a thin mustache. His shoulders were broad and his chest large, thrusting forward his four gold stars and his numerous decorations.

The General looked like a professional football player. He was very strong. He would outlast anyone over a long distance.

He wasn't smiling. He had a sullen and morose expression on his face.

A solitary figure was standing at attention next to the car —Major Malcolm Cox—the General's personal aide.

As the car headed toward the Pentagon, Thomas turned to Cox.

"Major, did anyone try to locate me in the three days I was gone?"

"Not to my knowledge, sir."

"Then you are the only person in the office of the Joint Chiefs who knows that I was in Saudi Arabia?"

"That is correct, sir."

"And no calls from the President?" Thomas asked in a gloomy tone.

"No, sir," came the reply.

They rode in silence for a few minutes. Cox sensed that the General was brooding and upset. The Major felt compelled to initiate some discussion to break the uncomfortable silence.

"I prepared the report that you requested," Cox said, taking a thick blue folder out of his briefcase.

General Thomas glanced at the cover of the document. "Classified and Confidential. For the Eyes of General Thomas Only."

Cox was an ideal subordinate, Thomas thought. He could be trusted to use discretion without being told.

Thomas opened the cover and looked at the title sheet. "This document is a detailed report on George T. Morris. It includes all of the subject's biographical information, his professional experience, his physical and personality characteristics, his habits and mannerisms, and all other information about the subject which could be discovered."

Major Cox does a thorough job, Thomas thought.

"Did you have any difficulty in gathering the information?"

"Some difficulty, sir. Morris is a secretive character. And your instruction that no one should even know that the study was being made limited my options."

Now that Cox had finished the report he was still as mystified as when he had begun. He simply couldn't understand why the old man wanted such a detailed report on the new Director of Energy.

"Is everything in here that I wanted?" the General asked.

"Yes, sir," Cox replied deferentially.

Thomas began leafing through the document. From his quick glance it looked very complete.

"What time will Morris be sworn in tomorrow?" Thomas asked.

"Ten o'clock," Cox said quickly.

"Which of our friends on the Hill have been invited?"

"Senator Wyatt for sure. There may be others."

Thomas muttered something unintelligible to himself.

"Go see Wyatt tomorrow afternoon," Thomas said. "If you show up after five, he'll take you to the Capitol Hill Club for a couple of drinks. I want a full report on that little affair tomorrow morning. I'll be in the office late tomorrow. You can stop back after your meeting with Wyatt."

"Yes, sir," Cox said, sounding very puzzled.

There were no television cameras or reporters waiting at the Presidential landing area at Dulles Airport—only two Secret Service men with walkie-talkies hooked up to their ears. The airport was teeming with people, but they never had a chance to see the new energy chief or America's sex symbol. They rode with the secret service men in a golf cart through underground tunnels to their waiting limousine.

An hour later they were in a suite on the top floor of the hotel. Anne quickly stripped off her clothes and turned on the shower. Morris settled into a large chair in a corner of the bedroom and began reviewing his notes for the speech he planned to make the next day at the White House.

Dripping wet, only a towel draped over her shoulders, Anne returned to the bedroom a few minutes later, sat down at the small vanity table, and began examining her face carefully in the mirror. Morris continued reading while she pursued her task with all of the diligence of a marine drill instructor, stopping periodically to apply some facial cream.

When Anne was finished, she looked at Morris in the mirror, serious and intent.

"If you aren't too busy, George, this might be a good time for making love."

"Not now," Morris replied mechanically and without lifting his eyes. "I want this speech to work."

Anne wasn't surprised by his response. She knew how Morris regarded sex—as a mechanical function, a physical outlet—like the hundred laps he swam each morning.

Anne walked over to the bar, letting the towel drop to the floor. She mixed herself a martini and poured Morris a glass of tomato juice, squeezed a piece of lime, and tossed it in the glass.

Anne looked at Morris for a minute—so absorbed in his papers, his mind operating in high gear. Sometimes he can be so machinelike, Anne thought. But she loved the flair for high living that Morris demonstrated at other times. Anne was excited by the circles of power that Morris traveled in. And she relished the attention his colleagues lavished on her.

She also loved the element of surprise that went with Morris—a man who was constantly taking the unconventional approach. And he refused to compromise. Oh, how he refused to compromise.

"You really think that you can do something about the oil situation?" Anne asked, handing the glass to Morris.

"You're damn right I do, or I wouldn't be here. Somebody has to make personal sacrifices to help the country through a difficult period."

Anne thought about his answer for a moment. Then she started to laugh.

"You might be able to fool yourself with that, but you can't fool me. You're no patriot. You just got tired of your financial and business games. You were looking for a new challenge—some new outlet for your ambition. You'll become intoxicated with the power at your disposal in no time at all. Oh, you'll love it in Washington. You'll fly around the world playing your little power games with prime ministers and kings. I'm just not sure that the country will survive."

There was a long silence.

"Of course I'm interested in the power," Morris said, reaching into his jacket pocket and pulling out a Cuban cigar. "Who isn't?"

As he lit the cigar, Morris recalled with satisfaction how he had engineered his shift from business to politics with carefully concealed and well-placed gifts to President Edwards' party.

He even had a dream in the back of his mind that he might be President one day. It was a dream that Morris had as a boy. It had never left him. But it was only a dream. Morris would be the first to admit that he didn't have the temperament to tolerate all of the bullshit that went with election to office in the American political process.

"It's more than the power," Morris said, thoughtfully.

"What else?" Anne asked.

"This country has to find some way of dealing with its oil problem."

"And if you manage to do that?"

"If I manage to do that," Morris said, blowing smoke into the air, "then I'll become a national hero. For decades every American schoolboy will learn about George T. Morris."

.

# CHAPTER

# 2

"IT'S GOOD TO SEE YOU AGAIN, GEORGE," THE PRESIDENT said as Morris entered the Oval Office.

Morris stepped forward to shake the President's hand. He looked calm and unemotional. That was his veneer. Underneath, he was somewhat nervous and uneasy. Charles Edwards was, after all, the President of the United States. Though Morris had been unimpressed with the man at their one previous meeting, he was prepared to give the office some respect.

As Morris shook hands with the President, he thought that there was nothing distinctive about the man's face. It was ordinary, very American, even his hair was a dull and fading blond, thinning on the top.

Charles Malcolm Edwards was a direct descendant of Malcolm T. Edwards—the Kansas beef baron of the 1890s. He had used his family's money and influence to glide through the politics of his midwestern state along the traditional route—from State legislator to Congressman, and finally to Governor.

During his second term in the State House, he caught the Presidential fever. He had been a compromise at the convention, a narrow victor in the election. Edwards had no strong ideological bent. He was as bland as the wheat of his native state.

Henry Oliver, the President's press secretary, was standing next to Morris, looking anxious to leave. There were already a score of reporters in the Rose Garden. He wanted to brief them before the ceremony.

There was another man in the room—a short man with a closely cropped crewcut and black horn-rimmed glasses. He had a perpetual scowl on his face.

"I want you to meet Fred Stewart, my counselor and my closest adviser," the President said.

Stewart nodded to Morris, but made no effort to come forward and shake his hand. Morris had read about Stewart. He was the President's full-time companion—the man who sat in on meetings and took notes, golfed with him on weekends, and drank with him in the evenings.

If Stewart had been engaged in any other field of human activity, he would have been known as a "lackey." But in politics he was one of the breed of "permanent assistants"— men who latch on to an aspiring politician when he begins his long climb up the ladder.

In Stewart's case, he took his first job with Charles Edwards twenty years ago. After graduation from law school, Stewart landed, with the help of a family friend, a job on the staff of a committee in the State legislature. Charles Edwards happened to be the chairman of that committee. Edwards saw that Stewart was someone who could cut through red tape to get things done. So he lured the young man on to his own staff with a two-thousand-dollar raise. Thus the term of indentured servitude began.

When Edwards went to Washington as a Congressman, Stewart went with him as a legislative assistant. When he returned to be Governor, Stewart returned as a special assistant.

Then when Charles Edwards was elected President, Stewart hoped that he would be given some independent job. Maybe a Cabinet post, or at least General Counsel of a federal agency. He wanted desperately to make some name for himself—not merely to be known as an extension of Charles M. Edwards—like his arms, his legs, and his other members.

But Stewart was bitterly disappointed. "You're too valuable for me to let you get away," Edwards had said when he told Stewart that he would be appointed "Special Assistant to the President," working out of the White House.

Stewart had concealed his disappointment from the President-elect. But it was smoldering during the first twenty-seven months of the Edwards Administration. He attended swearing-in ceremonies of acquaintances and cronies—men who were picked for the jobs that Stewart should have had. He read their pronouncements and press statements in the morning paper. Lately the resentment had been gnawing at his insides. He realized how completely he was trapped, how fully he was being used. He didn't know how much longer he could control the resentment against his master.

"Do you want some coffee?" the President asked Morris, motioning to a pitcher on a side table.

"Yes, thank you," Morris said. Then he belatedly added the words "Mr. President," unsure as to whether they were expected.

Morris was grateful for the offer. A compulsive coffee drinker, Morris found that holding a coffee cup in his hand relaxed him.

As Morris walked over to the side table, he carefully studied the room. The blue floor-to-ceiling curtains with the Presidential seal, which covered the large windows, gave the office a feeling of spaciousness. In reality it was only a little larger than Morris's old office in Los Angeles. Morris gazed at the large portrait of Lincoln on a side wall, looking favorably at him, Morris thought.

"Sit down, Morris," the President said, pointing to a bulky brown leather armchair in front of his desk. Then he noticed

Oliver still standing awkwardly by the door. He dismissed the Press Secretary with a wave of his hand.

Stewart sat down at a conference table in the corner of the office and began examining papers with apparent indifference to Morris.

"Are you settled yet?" the President asked, leaning back in the swivel chair behind his desk and placing the heels of his shoes on the green leather writing surface.

"I haven't had any problems," Morris replied.

Morris disliked small talk, and he hoped that the President was ready to move on to business.

"I'll be very candid with you, Morris," the President said in a serious tone.

Morris winced when he heard those words. They generally meant that the person using them was concealing something.

"I was under a lot of pressure to get rid of Jack Roach as Director of Energy. He managed to alienate the Energy Committees of both Houses of Congress, and Senator Stark was trying to nail him for a while. But it wasn't just that. The polls have shown my popularity dropping lower and lower, and all of the analysts agree that this energy crisis is killing me."

There was a long pause as the President thought about the 18 percent figure that Oliver had shown him last week. "An all-time low," were Oliver's words.

Morris thought that the President had aged perceptibly in the two months since their first meeting. His eyes, which had seemed sharp and alert, now looked dull and weary.

"It's too bad," the President continued. "I had the country in pretty good shape when shortages of oil and gas started wrecking the economy. Now I'm in a helluva bind. Nobody ever thought that we'd end up paying $2.50 or $3.00 for a gallon of gasoline, and we can't even get what we need!"

Suddenly the intercom began buzzing. The President picked up the telephone and listened carefully for several minutes. "Of course you didn't get anywhere in the negotiations," the President said. "I knew that the Russians would never accept that position. We have to be ready to compromise if we want an agreement."

Morris looked up when he heard the word "compromise." He studied the face of the President, listening so intently.

Then he looked at the wall behind the President's desk. It was covered with articles that proved the President's pedigree—diplomas from Andover and Princeton, membership plaques in a host of snooty clubs, even his picture as a young man with the Duke of Wales on a sailing boat in the English Channel.

Morris stared contemptuously at that wall—barely concealing his resentment. He had never before given much thought to Edwards' personal background. He had simply thought of Edwards as "the President." Suddenly he saw the President in a different light. The descendants of beef barons were American aristocrats. Charles Edwards had been born with every advantage that Morris had been lacking. He was like all those other shits from Skull and Bones. Morris felt a little uncomfortable. He would have to prove himself all over again. Forty million dollars in a Zurich bank, and he was still proving that he was good enough to play in the big leagues.

The President was too absorbed in his conversation to notice Morris. When the President put down the receiver, he walked over to the side table and slowly poured a cup of coffee, still thinking about his telephone conversation. With long strides he crossed the room to the windows that faced the south lawn. He stood there for a moment sipping the coffee. Then he started talking again.

"There are two immediate problems that I want you to focus on, Morris. First of all I need to know the actual cause of the shortages in oil and the enormous increases in retail prices that have occurred in the last six months. I'm getting conflicting reports. The oil companies are blaming OPEC, and OPEC is blaming the oil companies. Frankly, I can't separate fact from fiction, and I have to know who is really at fault before I can decide what action to take."

That should be easy enough to determine, Morris thought.

"And the second problem?" Morris asked.

"Second, I want you to prepare a comprehensive energy program for the next five years. Something that realistically assesses what we will have and how we can live with it."

"You must have a dozen of those sitting around," Morris replied, sipping his coffee.

"And none of them worth a shit."

"When do you want something on these two problems?" Morris asked.

"Get back to me by the first of June. That gives you six weeks."

As he walked to the Rose Garden with the President, Morris was coming to one conclusion fast. He didn't like being relegated to the role of a subordinate—even with the President of the United States.

Outside the Marine Band struck up "Hail to the Chief." The sun was shining brightly, reflecting from the metal instruments of the band. A small crowd of Senators and Congressmen with a sprinkling of reporters and other government officials were assembled in the center of the garden. Anne Walton was standing next to the podium, jammed with microphones—the position generally reserved for the wife of a man being sworn in.

Three television cameras with their ABC, CBS, and NBC decals started to whir as the President began speaking in a somber monotone.

"This morning's appointment of the new Director of Energy, or Energy Czar as you press people call him, may be the most important in this entire government. You are all aware that shortages of oil and natural gas have forced the closing of industrial plants this past winter with layoffs for millions of our workers. There has been great suffering in the country during this past winter. There have even been deaths due to cold and overexposure when communities ran out of heating oil."

The President paused for a moment to observe the confirming nods from those in attendance.

"Gasoline stations are frequently without gas. And if you are fortunate enough to find a station that has gas, you end up waiting hours for the privilege of paying $2.50 or $3.00 a gallon. The price of oil has produced a galloping inflation that has placed Italy and England in a situation of virtual bankruptcy and is seriously eroding our own financial stability. In short we simply have to come to grips with our energy crisis. Our very survival is at stake."

The roar of an airplane making its approach into National Airport could be heard. The President paused for a minute, letting it pass. Then he continued, "I have looked long and hard for the man who could perform this difficult job, and I believe that I have found that man in George Morris. He has earned his reputation and his fortune by bold and innovative financial management. This is precisely what this country needs to survive its energy crisis. We wish him all luck in this difficult endeavor."

Morris then took the oath, speaking clearly and with self-assurance. His eyes looked straight ahead, sparkling in the sunlight, showing a firm determination, a sense of mission. He made a short statement, words that he had practiced carefully. He wanted to sound honest and sincere, like a man who could be trusted, a man who would lead other men. But he didn't want the President to feel he was being upstaged.

When Morris finished speaking, he noticed that the President was smiling. His statement had been successful. As Morris stood between the President and Anne posing for pictures, a woman holding a stenographic pad was staring at him, with a combination of curiosity and desire in her eyes.

"You could be arrested for what you're thinking, Francine," Bill Marks from *The New York Times* whispered to the woman with the stenographic pad.

"I'm interested in Morris," she replied.

"I could see that."

"No, really, Bill, I've been digging around to see what I could find out about Morris. He's a real comer, definitely worth watching. He started out with twenty thousand dollars, and built it into a financial empire. He's also a bit of an egomaniac."

"Then he should fit in real well around here."

"You're becoming cynical in your old age, Bill," Francine said. "You were supposed to be the last of the idealists in the Washington press corps."

"I was, but I've been working with you too long," Marks replied, walking away.

The crowd gradually drifted to the large magnolia tree at the far side of the garden where there were two tables filled with small sandwiches and pastries from the White House kitchen. Morris winked at Anne as she walked away with two stately matrons who were asking her what it was like to do a television show. Suddenly Morris felt a strong tugging on his arm. A giant of a man with broad shoulders and a toupee that was streaked with gray was holding Morris tightly. His eyes were glazed as he struggled to recover from a hangover in the morning sunlight.

"I'm William Elliott, the Secretary of Defense," the man said.

"I recognized you from your picture," Morris replied.

Morris had seen that face often in the newspapers. Before being appointed Secretary of Defense, Elliott had been a six-term Congressman from Illinois, who rose to be Party Whip in the House. He was the acknowledged master of political infighting for choice committee assignments.

"Well, I just wanted you to know that you're replacing a helluva good man in Roach. Some of these bastards you'll meet here wanted Roach out, and the President didn't have the spine to stand up to them. But Roach is still a good man," Elliott said loudly. "He's done more for our party than the President ever will."

Having spoken his piece, Elliott then walked away with a scowl on his face.

Morris was thinking about what Elliott said when he heard the deep bass voice of Senator Stark.

"It's good to see you again," Stark said. "I trust that you found your confirmation hearing an educational experience."

"I guess it was a necessary process, Senator Stark," Morris replied. "But I sure as hell thought it was a waste of time."

The Senator's face became flushed.

"Don't jump to conclusions too fast," Stark said. "The Congress has its own job to do in this energy area, and we're not about to give it up to the White House."

A waiter clad in a tuxedo jacket approached with a tray containing coffee and fruit punch. Morris lifted a cup of coffee from the tray. Behind him he could hear a white-haired man mutter, in a southern accent, "I don't want any of that piss water to drink. In the old days, when LBJ was here, a gentleman could get a drink at the White House."

The man came up and shook Morris's hand. "I'm Wilbur Wyatt from Alabama," he said. Then he added, "Chairman of the Senate Armed Services Committee," carefully emphasizing each word to give his full title the dignity that he thought it deserved.

Wyatt stood next to Morris, keeping silent while Stark droned on about the deficiencies and errors of Morris's predecessor. Morris listened quietly, thinking to himself, How could such a roaring asshole achieve a position of power in the United States Senate?

When Stark finally got tired of hearing himself talk and drifted away, Wyatt and Morris were standing alone.

"I'm no expert on this energy business," Wyatt said, "but I'll tell you what I think."

Without waiting for Morris to answer, Wyatt continued talking.

"I think that the President has been as soft on this issue

as a woman's tit after a warm milk bath. He should have been tougher with those Arabs long ago. Now this country is in bad shape. I hope to hell you've got the backbone to straighten them out. They're trying to bleed this country. You better believe that."

"Well, I'm starting with an open mind, Senator," Morris replied.

Wyatt's words made Morris recall what the President had said in his telephone conversation in the Oval Office. "We have to be ready to compromise."

A bee flew around Morris's head and finally settled on the edge of his coffee cup.

"I'll give you some advice, young man," Wyatt said. "Go talk to General Thomas, the Chairman of the Joint Chiefs. Thomas is a great American, and he's spent a lot of time in Saudi Arabia. Thomas says that the Saudis already have more money than they can handle."

Suddenly a loud clanging noise drowned the sound of voices in the Rose Garden. Henry Oliver announced that the House would be voting on the Defense Budget in thirty minutes. Limousines were waiting for all those who wanted to return to the Hill.

"You follow my advice, young man," Wyatt said to Morris as he walked away. The Senator's reminder was unnecessary. His words had made an impression on Morris.

By noon Morris managed to pull himself away from the President, Anne, and lesser luminaries. A limousine deposited him at the Agency's headquarters—an eight-story gray stone box that occupied a full city block on Independence Avenue.

When Morris entered the door marked "Office of the Director," Helen Forrest sprang to attention next to her typewriter.

She was a tall, heavy-set woman, with brown hair tied neatly in a bun. She looked organized and methodical—the type of woman who becomes the private secretary for a top executive.

Miss Forrest introduced herself and offered to lead a tour of the huge penthouse suite.

"I'm too busy for office tours," Morris said curtly. "Get Green down here."

She just stood there looking at Morris. In almost thirty years as a government secretary, no one had ever been so rude to her.

"Walter Green, the Assistant Director," Morris said when she failed to move.

Then he disappeared behind the heavy wooden door that led to the Director's working office.

A few minutes later Green appeared. The two men greeted each other coolly. They had met only briefly during Morris's confirmation hearing. But each one had investigated the background of the other. Now they stood face to face eyeing each other with mutual suspicion and hostility.

The Assistant Director was a lawyer from New York and that made him immediately suspect in Morris's mind. To make matters worse, Green had come to Washington at the time of the civil rights movement. He had gotten involved in the antiwar effort and then joined the fight on pollution. He was, in short, a classic knee-jerk liberal, and Morris had little use for them. They were simply not practical in their approach to problems.

Morris was also appalled that Green could be content spending his whole career as a number two man. What's wrong with the man? Morris thought. Why doesn't he want to be boss—the ultimate authority in some fiefdom?

Finally, Morris knew that Green's wife was a well-known psychiatrist in Washington—comforting the anxieties of the powerful and the socially prominent. Morris had an absolute loathing for the profession of psychiatry. To Morris, those who sought its balms needed a good swift kick in the ass.

Green, on the other hand, saw Morris as the personification of the Harvard Business School in the computer economy— a man devoid of emotion and dedicated to the god of business efficiency. To Green, Morris's sole objective in life was money and power, and those tarnished his character.

"Sit down, Green," Morris said, pointing to an upholstered purple velvet chair that had a low back and looked as if it belonged in a bedroom. Green settled his tall frame awkwardly in the chair.

Morris then explained to Green the two priority problems that the President had given him.

"I'll need all the reports, studies, or other data that might be relevant to those problems," Morris said. "I'm particularly interested in information about OPEC and any recent OPEC actions. I'll need the information as soon as possible. I intend to feed it into my computer."

Green started to smile. "What the hell's so funny?" Morris asked.

"We don't have the information like that."

"What do you mean?"

"I mean that we don't have central files. Each of the 235 professionals in the Agency keeps his own files in his own specialized area. The kinds of problems that you are raising involve practically every one of the Agency's people. You'd have to get material from all of their files."

"Jesus Christ," Morris said, whistling to himself. "It's no wonder that nobody in Washington knows what's going on. This place is in even worse shape than I thought."

Green sat silent, waiting for Morris to continue.

"Then do this," Morris said. "Make me a list of every professional in this Agency with his field of expertise. Include office room numbers and telephone numbers—home and office. And have it on my desk by the time I get here at seven-thirty tomorrow morning. Is that clear?"

"Very clear," Green said, as he walked slowly out of the office, shaking his head. If Morris is to be the national saviour, he thought, I may prefer the energy crisis.

General Thomas was sitting at his desk watching the last

rays of sunlight disappear into the western sky. His hands played with the letter from the Boston psychiatric hospital. He read the last line again: "We continue to bə hopeful that your wife's condition will improve in the future."

How was he to know that this daughter of New Orleans aristocracy would crack when he was gone for long periods of time? What had she expected? He was a military man.

Thomas wondered why he even ended up being married to Rose at all. Then he thought about the words of his old friend Mordechai Zal, the retired Israeli general, "The history of the world is the story of lost opportunities."

Enough sentiment, he thought, tucking the letter under the blotter on his desk.

Thomas took a key ring out of his pocket and walked over to the side chest, unlocked it carefully, and removed a thick blue folder—the report on Morris.

He stopped to straighten the diploma from the Air Force Academy over the chest. Then he carefully examined each of the model airplanes scattered throughout his office to make certain that none of them was dusty. General Thomas was proud of those airplanes. He had rebuilt the country's air force in the post-Vietnam era when "military preparedness" was a term with sinister connotations.

Then Thomas thought about the airplanes that he had seen on his visit to Saudi Arabia this week. He recalled precisely where they were stationed.

General Thomas leafed through the report on Morris that Cox had prepared. His initial reading had been careful. He simply wanted to make certain that he remembered all of the details.

He paused at the final paragraph of the conclusion. He had underlined it late last evening. "Morris is not fearful of adopting an unconventional approach to a difficult problem. His formula for business success was driving ambition, detailed financial analysis, and the courage to speculate. He is prepared to take risks that others consider unreasonable. He is precise and methodical in his execution as well as his planning. He refuses to compromise."

Morris may be the right man, Thomas thought to himself with a slight smile on his face. Let's see what approach he takes. Then he closed the folder and locked it in the chest.

A few minutes later Major Cox arrived.

"I'm sorry to be so late, sir," Cox said. "That Wyatt drinks like a fish."

"Well, what did you find out?" Thomas asked, anxious to hear the report.

"Not very much from Wyatt himself, I'm afraid. He told me how he'd given Morris a lecture about what a great American you were."

"That's certainly helpful," Thomas said sarcastically.

"He offered to call Stewart to get some information on what went on privately in the discussion between Morris and the President."

Thomas was startled by the Major's words. He had heard that Stewart was unhappy because he hadn't been given a Cabinet post by Edwards. But Thomas hadn't imagined that Stewart was sufficiently embittered to leak information from the White House. Loyalty was a powerful motivating force, Thomas thought. And disloyalty, even more so. It could be exploited. He would open up his own line of communication with Stewart.

"And what happened when he called Stewart?" Thomas asked in a matter-of-fact tone.

Cox paused for a minute. He wasn't used to three large scotches. He made a great effort to recall precisely what Wyatt had said. Suddenly Cox's mind cleared. He remembered the conversation.

Cox repeated it all, talking very quickly, hoping to complete the report before his mind stopped working again. He told Thomas about the two assignments that the President had given Morris and the June first deadline. When he was finished, Cox took a deep breath and leaned back in the chair, hoping that he would be dismissed soon.

Thomas walked over to the large double window. He studied the outline of the Capitol dome against the darkening Washington sky.

The General gets philosophical sometimes in the evening, Cox thought. I hope to hell this isn't one of those times.

"Don't underestimate the gravity of our energy situation," Thomas said. "Energy is the lifeblood of this country. And if economic disaster strikes this country, political disaster will follow. You can be damn sure of that."

Cox mouthed a mechanical "Yes, sir," waiting for Thomas to continue the lecture.

"This country's inability to deal realistically with its energy problem in the last decade has been tragic, Major. It represents the great failure of American democracy—with jerks like Stark on the Hill and weak-minded imbeciles like Edwards in the White House. They're just not practical. They give the people what they want without providing any leadership. Wouldn't you say so, Major?"

Cox didn't quite know how to respond. He had more respect for General Thomas than any other person in the world. But he also had a strong belief in the American form of government.

"Woudn't I say what, sir?" Cox replied.

"That we've witnessed the failure of American democracy in this energy business."

"Well, it hasn't worked too well, I guess."

There was a long silence. Cox could feel his head throbbing.

"Will there be anything else, sir?" he said hesitantly to Thomas, still standing at the window.

"Just one thing, Major. Between now and June one I want you to keep track of Morris and what's happening at the Department of Energy. Do it quietly and report personally to me on a weekly basis—more frequently if necessary."

"I'll do that, sir," Cox said.

"Thank you, Major. I'll see you in the morning."

With nightfall, the lights were turned on throughout the entire Watergate Apartment complex. But in Apartment D-3205, the only light was provided by the burning tip of Francine's cigarette. She lay in William Elliott's arms, their naked bodies stretched out on the bed.

Jesus. It was never like that with Anita, Elliott said to himself, stroking the inside of Francine's thigh. Even twenty years ago, when Anita was her age, it was never like that.

He watched Francine's large round breasts rising and falling as she puffed on the cigarette. "You must have been a gymnast in college," he said. "You're unbelievable."

Yes, she had been an athlete once, Francine thought. She could still remember how proud she was when she made the tennis team her first year at Highland Park High School in surburban Chicago. She was only fifteen years old, and an honor student too. Francine had had a very respectable upbringing to that point in her life. Her father was a professional on the Chicago staff of the A.M.A. Her mother was an ordinary suburban housewife, a regular for Monday bridge games at the Highland Park Club. They were decent straitlaced conservative Republicans.

That same year—when Francine was still fifteen—her whole world fell apart. Her father was charged with embezzling funds from the A.M.A. There was the trial and all of the dreadful publicity. Then the four months in Allenwood Federal Penitentiary.

Francine, with a stiff upper lip, could handle his whitecollar crime. It was what happened when he came home that she couldn't cope with. The proud man whom she remembered returned completely different. He was utterly destroyed by the experience. The man barely spoke and never smiled.

He didn't even try to work again. He just sat around the house, staring blankly at the television set.

Francine's mother had inherited a goodly sum from her own parents, and the family wasn't lacking for material things. But Francine couldn't accept the change. She needed a father. Saddened, disillusioned, and bitter, she left home six months after he returned, hitting the road for San Francisco. She tried communes for a while and then moved in with a married man in his forties—in the process of getting a divorce, or so he said. She was still searching for a father figure. That relationship lasted exactly three months until he moved back with his wife. At that point, Francine was determined to take control of her life. She passed a high-school equivalency test, worked hard for two years in a junior college, getting a straight A average, and got herself admitted to Stanford. There, her drive and determination made her head of the women's movement and an honors graduate from the School of Journalism.

Francine started off in the Washington office of the *Los Angeles Times.* After two months there, she wrangled an invitation to a party in order to meet Skip Roberts, the editor-in-chief at the *Washington Tribune.* Recognizing all of her assets, Roberts offered her a job as a Washington reporter on the *Tribune.* That was three years ago.

Now she lay in William Elliott's arms smoking her cigarette and thinking. Elliott was the Secretary of Defense—a man very close to the President. For Francine, this could be a valuable relationship.

"What did you think of the White House ceremony this morning?" Francine asked, placing her cigarette in an ashtray.

Elliott was startled by the question. He didn't have the White House on his mind.

"The usual Edwards Rose Garden performance. Dull and uninspiring."

"What about Morris?"

"I don't know anything about Morris," Elliott said, neglecting to add that he started out despising the man because he seemed like some young smart-ass who acted like he knew everything.

She began caressing his stomach with short gentle strokes.

Elliott closed his eyes. He knew that Francine had a reputation of shacking up with anyone who would give her a good story, but he didn't care. Even if others had been here before, the pleasure was well worth it. And as for the stories, he would give her what he wanted, and there was plenty of that. He would give her enough different stories about the President to make him stop reading the *Washington Tribune*.

"Are you sure that you don't know anything about Morris?" Francine asked, dropping her hands lower on his body.

"Why so interested?"

"Oh, just curious."

"Well, you can stop being a reporter."

"Oh, c'mon, Bill," she said, thrusting her body on top of his, "a girl has to earn a living."

"I really don't know anything."

"If you find out something, you'll let me know? . . . Please? . . . It can't hurt anything."

"I'll see what I can get."

"Right now we have to do something about that little thing of yours," Francine said, disappearing under the top sheet.

Elliott began smiling. He was trying to visualize what the *Tribune* story would look like if he had a coronary right here in Francine's apartment. Jesus, he thought, she'd probably write the article herself—under that famous Francine Rush byline.

# CHAPTER

# 3

MORRIS CAREFULLY READ THE WORDS THAT HE HAD WRITTEN in his report to the President.

Responsibility for the enormous increases in the price of oil and the restrictions in supply that have occurred in recent months must be attributed to The Organization of Petroleum Exporting Countries, OPEC, and not to the American oil companies. The OPEC countries instituted increases in the price of oil and reductions in supply that were never announced publicly. In the last six months OPEC secretly raised the price of crude from $15 a barrel to $30 a barrel, and they cut the supply to the United States from fifteen to thirteen million barrels a day. These measures were difficult to trace because the 60 percent of America's oil that was imported was mixed with the crude that was produced domestically. Purchasers have been coerced into silence by the threat of a complete cut-off in supply. There have been repeated rumors about the OPEC price increases, but never any confirmation. This report constitutes such a confirmation.

Morris was confident that his conclusion was correct. But it was only May fifteenth. He didn't intend to deliver the report until June first. He wanted some confirmation.

"Get me Felix Sharp in Houston," Morris said to his secretary. "He's the President of Sharp Oil Company."

A few minutes later she had Sharp on the line.

"Felix," Morris said. "It's your former investment banker, George Morris."

"How could I forget you, George? It was the best deal of my life. Five million for me; five million for you; and five for the People's Republic of Poland. How's the new job?"

"That's why I'm calling you."

There was a long pause. Sharp was afraid to hear what Morris wanted.

"Can you meet me in Houston tomorrow?" Morris asked.

"Take a morning plane. I'll buy you lunch at the Warwick. One o'clock."

"I'll be there," Morris said, putting down the phone.

"Don't you dare quote me," Sharp said nervously. "I'll deny it and call you a liar."

"Relax, Felix, and drink your bourbon. I have no intention of quoting you. I only want confirmation on some preliminary conclusions that I've reached."

"I'll listen to you. But remember if I get cut off on imported oil, I'm dead. I'll lose more than the five million you made for me."

Morris presented a detailed summary of the data that he had analyzed on price increases and reductions in production.

"The bottom line," Morris said, "according to my analysis, is that OPEC is the culprit and you people in the industry would rather take part of the heat than risk a cutoff."

Sharp looked around the Warwick dining room apprehensively. As he thought about it now, this was the wrong place to meet Morris. At least most of the tables were occupied by matrons from the Houston Garden Club. He didn't recognize anyone.

Morris pulled the lime from his glass of tomato juice and began chewing on it, waiting for Sharp to respond.

"Your analysis is precisely correct, George," Sharp said quietly.

Morris took two cigars out of his pocket and handed one to Sharp.

"Do we have any assurance that OPEC won't raise prices still more and cut output further?" Morris asked.

"None at all. Except for what I get by praying every Sunday morning. But if I remember right, you're a damn atheist, George. So you can't even get that comfort." Sharp started to laugh.

"What if OPEC did cut us off altogether? How much oil do you people have in those underground storage cavities?"

"About ten days' worth," Sharp said, confirming the estimate that Morris had seen.

Sharp stopped to light his cigar. "After that ten days," he said, "the American economy comes to a halt. The fact of the matter is that OPEC has this mighty country by the balls."

Morris let Sharp enjoy his lunch without asking any more questions about oil. But when they were sipping coffee, he raised the subject again.

"There's one other question I want to ask you, Felix. Who makes the OPEC decisions?"

"I can give you a legal answer and tell you that theoretically each member of OPEC has one vote. But the practical answer is that Saudi Arabia dominates OPEC. All of the Arab oil producers vote with the Saudis. Iran is the only other major voice. But their market share has declined relative to the Saudis. I'm not sure that Iran could really stop the Saudis from instituting an OPEC policy. So far that hasn't happened. The Shah has gone along with all of the Saudi decisions even if he opposed them."

"One final question. Does the King of Saudi Arabia make his country's oil decisions?"

"Absolutely not. He's signed off and given Yaman Faisel, the Finance Minister, a free hand."

Morris recognized the name immediately. Faisel had been at Harvard Business School when Morris was there. They had known each other, but not well.

When the plane took off, Morris glanced at his watch. It will only be 7:30 P.M. when I get to Dulles, he thought.

Morris was feeling quite satisfied that he had solved the first of the President's two problems. He decided to quit early and go home when the plane arrived.

As Morris's plane flew eastward, Anne sat at Arden's getting her hair done again. Then she wandered through Saks, passing some time there.

"Any calls for me, Louise?" she shouted to the housekeeper when she returned home.

"No, madam."

"Are you sure?"

"Very sure."

A few minutes later, Anne walked out to the pool with only a towel tied around her waist. She carried a pink telephone and a wristwatch. After coating herself with a variety of ointments, she stretched out in a chaise longue. Every few minutes she stared at her watch and then at the telephone.

Anne remembered how that phone rang constantly in her first weeks in Washington. She was invited to luncheons in her honor at La Bagatelle, Jean Pierre, and Tiberio. She appeared on local talk shows and was entertained and interviewed by Washington society columnists. But then the phone had stopped ringing.

At seven o'clock, Anne shook a small silver bell. Within one minute Louise appeared, carrying a tray with a large martini.

As Anne sipped her drink, she thought about her relationship with Morris. What relationship? He was gone in the morning before she got up. He returned at nine o'clock; after dinner he disappeared into his study until well after she turned off the bedroom lights.

At seven-thirty Anne shook the bell again. Louise brought her second martini.

When Morris walked into the house, he spotted Anne from

the window lying on her stomach, the towel under her face rolled up like a pillow. He walked out to the pool quietly. She noticed him coming, but she remained motionless.

When he began stroking her soft warm buttocks, she was still silent. After a few minutes, he began reaching between her legs.

"Not now, George," she said tersely. "I'm not in the mood."

"That's a helluva greeting when I come home early," Morris said, sounding surprised. She had never before turned him down.

"I'm sorry," she said sarcastically. "I haven't seen you before nine o'clock since we got to Washington. I don't know how to act."

Morris sat down in a chair next to the chaise longue.

"You knew that this would be an important new job for me when you decided to come."

"That's fine for you, but I'm just bored stiff. I'm going out of my mind. There's not a God damn thing to do."

"Go to a museum."

"I've been to all of them."

"Then go read a book," he said, sounding irritated. "You learned how to read."

"Go fuck yourself!"

Morris got up and walked into the house. He conceded to himself that he had been pretty busy in Washington, but it was a problem of national importance. Dammit, she should be more understanding, he thought.

"I have a good idea for you," Morris said two hours later over dinner. "Why don't you give some parties here on Saturday evenings—something spectacular like we gave in Beverly Hills. Get the best catering firm. You could probably attract celebrities from the arts, movies, and television. You could get people in town from the Kennedy Center, and you could even get some of your friends from Los Angeles and New York."

Morris was relieved when Anne liked the idea. He had

originally suggested it as a way to occupy Anne and keep her out of his hair. But as he explained it to her, he began to see advantages for himself.

Morris was sitting at his desk the next morning thinking about a comprehensive five-year program when Green walked in the office.

"You know I don't like to be disturbed between nine and twelve," Morris said sharply. "What do you want?"

"I'm sorry to disturb you, but I received a call from Senator Stark. He wants you to appear before his committee next Tuesday at ten o'clock."

"Tell him I'm not going. I'm not making any public statements until I've delivered my reports to the President on June first."

"Stark's a powerful person in this area."

"Screw him," Morris said dispassionately.

"Now wait a minute, George. You kept me on in this job. So I'm going to give you some advice. You can't disregard this request. When you do come up with a program, it's going to need Congressional approval and that means Stark. You'll have to cater to him whether you like it or not," Green said, raising his voice.

Morris was surprised by Green's tone. He wasn't used to having a subordinate disagree with him.

"Call him back and tell him I need two more weeks—anytime after June fifth. You're obviously on good terms with Stark. He must owe you something. Use one of those IOU's to buy me two weeks."

"I'll do what I can," Green said, shaking his head and looking perplexed.

A few minutes later Green returned.

"Stark will wait until June fifth, but he said what the hell's taking Morris so long."

"I'll tell you what's taking me so long, Walter. You and

your colleagues who have run the country's energy program for the last ten years have screwed the whole thing up so badly."

Morris walked over to the humidor on his desk, took out a large Cuban cigar, and lit it slowly, blowing large puffs into the air.

Green looked down at the carpet. He didn't like Morris's accusatorial tone. He and his colleagues had done a reasonable job under the circumstances. He wanted to explain that to Morris, but he stopped himself. Maybe Morris was right.

"Before you leave, Walter, there's something I want to ask you," Morris said. "Have you ever heard of a company called American Fusion Corporation?"

"Vaguely. They developed a new process to use hydrogen fusion for unlimited cheap energy a couple of years ago. They even had an R and D contract with the Air Force for a while."

"What happened to the contract?"

Green was silent for a minute, trying hard to recall the details.

"At some point the Air Force cut off their funds. I remember that. General Thomas, the Chairman of the Joint Chiefs, made the decision personally, but I can't remember why."

"You have no idea?"

"None at all."

Then Green decided that his lack of information was not flattering, and he feebly added, "But I wasn't involved in that area."

Morris got up from his desk and walked over to the window. He felt vaguely uneasy about General Thomas's decision to terminate the hydrogen fusion research program. He wasn't quite sure why. Then he recalled his conversation with Senator Wyatt in the White House Rose Garden and the Senator's comments about General Thomas's active interest in Saudi Arabia.

"Do some checking," Morris said to Green. "There's something here that doesn't make sense."

Morris spent most of the next two weeks with Janet Koch in the computer center. They took the data about energy availability and consumption and fed it to the computer, testing various hypotheses.

On May 29 Morris sat at his desk reading the finished product—a forty-two-page document which contained a five-year program for energy utilization. On the first page it stated:

> If this program is followed, the United States will achieve independence from OPEC oil at the end of a five-year period. This program is based on the price of oil and the level of production that is currently in effect. It assumes reasonable increases in prices and further modest decreases in production.

Morris turned to the Executive Summary of the program:

> This program calls for drastic action. It imposes severe gasoline rationing. Each owner of a car would be permitted ten gallons of gasoline a week and an extra allotment of fifty gallons twice a year to permit the taking of intercity trips. Exceptions would be made for commercial drivers of taxicabs, trucks, and the like. But not for commuters. It requires the conversion of homes and apartment buildings from oil and natural gas to electrical heat within the next five years. And it requires public utilities to shift to coal, nuclear power, or water power to generate electricity.

Later in the day Morris described the program to a skeptical Green, who began shaking his head.

"It will end up in the wastebasket," Green said. "The Congress will never buy it."

"What do you mean?" Morris asked, sounding startled.

"They'll say it's too stringent. They'll turn you down. That's the way democracy works."

"This is different."

"Why?"

"Our back is against the wall now. We've run out of time. People are scared."

"It doesn't matter. You can't tramp on free enterprise."

"Don't talk to me about free enterprise," Morris said, raising his voice and rising in his chair. "I made $50 million in ten years in free enterprise."

"That's what they'll say."

"What?"

"He's made his. He wants to stop anyone else from doing the same. Hell, you may never even persuade the President to send this program to the Hill."

"He gave me a free hand."

"Wait and see."

Green stared at Morris sitting quietly in his chair evaluating what had been said. Green had developed a grudging respect for the new Director of Energy. He was so thorough and methodical in his work. In all of Green's years in the government he had never met anyone like Morris. The trouble with him, Green thought, is that he just can't get it through his head that the government doesn't work with the efficiency that he demands.

"I appreciate what you're telling me," Morris said. "But I'm prepared to defend the program. It's the only way to break the stranglehold that OPEC has over this country."

Green was silent. He had done his job.

"I intend to call the President tomorrow," Morris continued, "to set up a meeting."

Morris picked up a cup of tepid coffee sitting on his desk. He sipped it slowly.

"There is only one troublesome fact about all of this," Morris said. "My whole program is based on the price of oil and level of production that OPEC is now using."

Morris sounded cold and unemotional, like a surgeon describing an operation for a critically ill patient. His words made Green feel very uncomfortable.

That evening Anne was waiting for Morris at the door when he arrived. Her hair was perfectly done, and she was dressed in a new Chloe.

"Good news, George," she shouted. "I've been offered a part in a new Broadway Show. It's called *Mafia Woman*. If it works, I would have the lead. I direct one of the big mafia organizations—proving that the last sex barrier has been broken. I have a team of hit men working for me. It's not a bad idea."

As Anne spoke, Morris listened with half an ear. He wasn't tuning her out deliberately. His mind was still focused on breaking the OPEC stranglehold.

"Let's celebrate and eat out this evening," she said.

"I don't know, Anne. I want to read my report over again."

"Oh, once won't kill you. Besides, starting tomorrow I'll be in New York Monday through Thursday evening. I won't be here to bother you."

"Okay," he said reluctantly.

"Good. I'll call Jacques at La Bagatelle and get a table."

As they ate oysters Rockefeller, Anne continued to rattle on about the great possibilities she saw for *Mafia Woman*. When she finished the last oyster, she said, "I know that you're not listening to a word I'm saying, George. But I'm so happy. I don't even care."

Later, when she sipped her coffee, Anne began to realize that she knew even less about Morris's energy program than he knew about *Mafia Woman*.

"Do you think that your energy program will succeed?" she asked, feebly trying to appear interested.

Morris just smiled. It was late, and he had no intention of getting into a serious discussion with Anne about energy.

"I'm the typical American consumer," Anne said, trying again. "I have confidence that you and your colleagues will pull us out of this mess. We'll have plenty of energy. You'll take care of it."

"And if we don't?"

"You will. If not, La Bagatelle will switch to candlelight," she said, smiling.

As Morris and Anne were dining at the restaurant, Ahmad Zadak, the Iranian Ambassador, was riding in the elevator that went directly to Yaman Faisel's penthouse suite at the Waldorf. He was tightly clasping a thin black briefcase in his hand.

When the doors opened, Ahmad was stopped by a burly man with an Arab headdress and a long curved sword at his side.

"I am Abdul, His Excellency's Chief of Security," the man said.

Ahmad had never heard subordinates refer to Faisel as "His Excellency" before. He must have promoted himself, Ahmad thought.

"I would like to see Mr. Faisel. Tell him that it is Ahmad Zadak."

"You had no appointment, and he is occupied just now," Abdul said, looking embarrassed. "Perhaps he can see you in the morning."

One look at Abdul's face told Ahmad that Faisel was undoubtedly engaged in debauchery with one or more women somewhere in his massive suite. That was just as well, Ahmad thought. He had no need or desire to talk to Faisel.

Ahmad opened the briefcase and removed a brown business-size envelope. He handed it carefully to Abdul, pointing to the neatly typed words on the front of the envelope. "To Be Opened Only By Yaman Faisel."

"There is no need for Faisel to call," Ahmad said. "The message speaks for itself."

Then he rode down in the elevator, feeling very much like a man who had just planted a bomb.

# CHAPTER

# 4

YAMAN FAISEL WOKE UP WITH A GIANT HANGOVER IN HIS suite at the Waldorf. The Saudi Finance Minister tried to lift his heavy body out of bed, but it refused to budge. With his eyes still partially closed, he groped toward the night table on one side of the bed searching for his watch. Instead he encountered the warm, soft flesh of a sleeping woman's back.

Faisel then rolled his bulky frame toward the other side and picked up the telephone.

"What time is it?" he asked in Arabic.

"Seven-thirty in the morning. Tuesday, May thirtieth, Your Excellency, and the temperature is 50°," the operator replied, also in Arabic.

Faisel looked down at the wad of fat hanging over his middle, resembling an inner tube. He pushed on the bed with both hands and brought himself to a sitting position. From there he dropped to the floor and put on his pajamas.

Faisel then pressed a small red button twice very firmly. Abdul quickly entered.

"Give the tramp five hundred dollars and get rid of her," Faisel said, pointing to the girl still asleep on the bed.

"Yes, Your Excellency."

Faisel began walking slowly toward the bathroom. Suddenly he stopped and wheeled around.

"Any calls for me during the night?" he asked.

"The Iranian Ambassador in Washington arrived here at eleven o'clock. He left you this envelope," Abdul said, handing a brown business-size envelope to Faisel.

Faisel quickly read the words on the envelope. Then he tore it open. Inside there was another envelope. This one was white and only slightly smaller than the first. It contained the words: "Read the message inside and destroy at once."

Faisel opened the second envelope carefully. He slowly pulled out a sheet of white paper and read: "His Royal Majesty, the Shah of Iran, reluctantly approves the July fourth program." The word reluctantly was underlined.

Faisel smiled to himself. What a strange man, the Shah, he thought. He gives the illusion of power on the outside, but faced with a chance for bold action he becomes insecure and timid.

But what difference does it make what his state of mind is, Faisel thought. He has given his approval. That's what counts.

"I want to call a press conference for 10:00 A.M. this morning in the Empire Room," Faisel said to Abdul. "See that the American and foreign media are notified. Tell them I have an announcement of great importance."

"Yes, Your Excellency."

"Then direct the chef to cook my breakfast. Figs, raw fish, scrambled eggs, and three lamb chops."

The woman on the bed began to stir. She turned over on her back, exposing a full head of black hair that covered her face and a torso that identified her as a belly dancer. Faisel gave her one final look of lust and headed toward the bathroom.

Faisel waited until ten-thirty before marching confidently into the Empire Room. He always enjoyed keeping the media waiting, especially in the United States.

He stood silently at the podium for several minutes, his eyes studying the large crowd to pick out familiar faces. Faisel had been looking forward to this day.

Armed guards with automatic weapons covered the perimeter of the room. Two guards at the doorway frisked a reporter who was just arriving. Another guard closed the large double doors that lead into the Empire Room from the hotel lobby.

"I have called this press conference as the spokesman for the OPEC nations," Faisel said, speaking English slowly and carefully. He wanted the reporters, busily scribbling on their shorthand pads, to capture each word.

"The OPEC nations," Faisel continued, "have decided to implement a new program calling for drastic increases in the price of oil and reductions in output. The United States will be permitted to purchase one million barrels of oil a day instead of the fifteen million that it purchased last year. The price of that oil will be $75 a barrel."

A huge gasp went up from the crowd. Cries of "Oh, no!" could be heard. The Saudi guards gripped their automatic weapons tightly.

Faisel waited for the cries to die down.

"We have also decided," he said in a sadistic tone, "that the new program will take effect on July fourth, in honor of America's Independence Day."

A reporter rose to his feet in the middle of the crowd and shouted.

"Why? Why are you doing this to us? Tell us why?"

"My dear friends," Faisel said, "we bear no ill will toward the American people. Ten years ago the Royal Government of Saudi Arabia and its OPEC partners began to realize that we should have enormous wealth and power in the world because of our oil. We have repeatedly sought at every international conference some realignment in the world's economic and political order that would give us the position that we are entitled to. We were given promises by Henry Kissinger and then by Jimmy Carter. We waited patiently; but nothing ever happened. Our oil will not last forever. We simply cannot continue to receive worthless paper money in return for our depletable natural resource. It is more valuable to us in the ground. I hope that you will understand."

With that Faisel marched quickly from the platform. A security blanket of armed guards moved in to cover the departing Finance Minister from every conceivable direction.

Absolute chaos broke out at the Waldorf. Reporters fought with each other to use the telephone. One woman, shouting "You dirty bastard," took off her shoe and tried to throw it at Faisel. She was quickly seized by two armed Saudi guards.

At ten-fifty WCBS interrupted its morning program to announce, "OPEC has declared economic war on the United States." Fifteen minutes later the same newscaster said, "The New York and American stock exchanges will be closed for the remainder of the day in view of the OPEC announcement."

The news first reached the Department of Energy on the wire service machine in the basement of the building. Roger Norton, Director of Telecommunications, spotted the announcement as it was being typed. He quickly tore the thin yellow sheet from the machine. Norton frantically pressed the elevator button. When nothing happened, he raced up nine flights of stairs. He pushed past Green's secretary and threw the sheet on Green's desk.

The Assistant Director's face turned white when he read the announcement. He seemed paralyzed for a moment. Then he shouted, "No! It can't be," and raced down to Morris's office.

Green barged into Morris's office without knocking and handed the yellow sheet to Morris, shoving it into his hand. Morris read it in disbelief. Then he read it again, letting each word sink in.

"Jesus Christ!" Morris shouted. "Those bastards are trying to destroy this country."

"What about the comprehensive energy program you developed?" Green asked. "Maybe you can revise your program. Tighten it up a little more."

"Not possible. I had trouble formulating the program with twenty-three million barrels a day. With eleven, it's hopeless."

Morris walked over to his desk and picked up two copies of the report that he had intended to deliver to the President. With a casual flip of the wrist he tossed them across the room. They landed in a black leather wastebasket.

"It's not a question of economics anymore," Morris said. "It's a question of national survival. For the last ten years we've had our head in the sand. Well, we finally got kicked in the ass."

Green sat silent, looking very glum.

"You know, they thought you wouldn't let it happen," Morris said.

"Who did?"

"The people out there in the country. They thought that you clowns here in Washington knew what you were doing. They thought that you wouldn't let it happen."

Suddenly there was a sharp piercing noise from the intercom.

"Mr. Morris, the White House is on the phone," Helen said.

As Morris picked up the telephone, he heard a very somber voice.

"This is William Black, the President's Assistant for International Affairs. Have you heard about Faisel's announcement?"

"Just now," Morris replied.

"President Edwards wants you over here as soon as possible."

This room resembles a mortuary, Morris thought, when he walked into the Oval Office. The President was seated at the head of a large conference table surrounded by Black, Oliver, and Stewart. All four men looked sullen and grim.

Oliver was scribbling something on a yellow pad—maybe a statement for the press, Morris thought. Stewart was biting his fingernails. He was scowling, just as Morris remembered from the earlier meeting in April.

The President pointed to an empty chair and Morris sat down quickly, nodding to the others.

"How bad will it be," the President asked Morris, "if the OPEC program goes into effect?"

"Very bad, Mr. President."

"Don't be too gloomy, Morris."

"I'm trying to give you an honest evaluation, Mr. President. Our economy needs twenty-five million barrels of oil a day. All we will have is eleven—ten from domestic production and one from OPEC."

Morris's tone was calm and unemotional. These were, after all, rational facts that had to be faced. An emotional response wouldn't help in dealing with the facts set in motion by Faisel's announcement.

The President walked over to the side table and poured a cup of coffee. Morris followed him. The others remained seated.

Much of the blame could be placed on earlier Administrations, the President thought. After all, he had only been in office for two and a half years.

"What you're telling me is that we have a real mess on our hands," the President said, sipping his coffee.

"Mr. President," Morris replied, "this is more than a mess. The very survival of this country is at stake. If this OPEC program goes into effect, there will be economic chaos. Unemployment will rise sharply, and the country will move quickly to national bankruptcy."

"What about the five-year program I asked you to prepare?"

"I completed it based upon price and production levels pending before Faisel's announcement. Now it's sitting in the wastebasket. The new OPEC policy makes it impossible to develop any practical five-year program."

"What about conservation? We waste so damn much oil. We all know that."

"It won't come near solving the problem, Mr. President. We can't save fourteen million barrels a day."

For Morris this discussion was confirming a conclusion that he had reached from reviewing documents. He had been persuaded that President Edwards was an honest and decent man, but not too bright. He just didn't know what was happening in the energy area, and he had never tried to learn. He had always viewed that issue as one left for the technical experts while unemployment and inflation were issues that the President could understand. It never occurred to the President to focus his own attention on the cause of the nation's economic ills, which was the dependence of the country on imported oil, rather than the symptoms of unemployment and inflation.

The President rose from the table and started pacing around the room. The others sat in silence. When he made it back to his desk, the intercom on the telephone began ringing. President Edwards depressed the button.

"What is it, Martha?" he asked.

"I'm sorry to interrupt you, sir. But I have General Thomas on the line. He insisted on talking to you. Do you want to take the call?"

The President grumbled something to himself, picked up the telephone, and depressed another button.

"Yes, General, we heard the announcement," Edwards said curtly.

There was a short pause. As the President listened, his facial muscles tightened, the veins on his neck protruding.

"No, General," he said. "We don't need you over here. The situation is under control."

There was a longer pause. Then President Edwards began raising his voice.

"This problem is outside of your jurisdiction, General. I've repeatedly told you that your activities are to be limited strictly to military affairs."

President Edwards put the telephone down and resumed his pacing.

"You know, Bill," the President said a few minutes later, turning to Black, "it's just possible that OPEC has done us a favor. We'll have to switch to other sources of energy— electric cars and solar heat. We'll get along that way. Hell, maybe they've done us a favor—forcing us to get away from that expensive imported oil. What do you think, Bill?"

Black remained silent, hesitating for a moment. He squirmed in his chair. As a former Professor of International Affairs, Black was an expert on American-Soviet relations. Energy wasn't his field. He glanced over at Stewart, who was staring at the carpet. Stewart's eyes contained a strange glint—like cold steel.

"I don't know, Mr. President," Black said. "You'd better ask Morris here. He's the expert."

"Well, Morris, what do you have to say? You seem to have all the answers," the President said sarcastically.

"There's no use talking about alternatives to oil. It's too late for that. That's a long-term solution, and we have an immediate crisis. It takes time to convert to alternative forms of energy, to develop new technology and have it operational on a large scale for 220 million people. It takes years to do it. That's what the experts call lead time. You can't do it in a month, and that's all we have."

Morris paused to observe the glum expression on the President's face as Edwards leaned back in his chair, closing his eyes.

"If we started five years ago," Morris continued in a matter-of-fact tone, "we'd be free of imported oil. But we didn't start then."

Oliver could sense that the temperature of the President was rising sharply as Morris talked. Oliver knew that the

President disliked being told that mistakes had been made during his Administration. Oliver could see that this dialogue between Morris and the President would soon reach an open confrontation. He decided to interject himself.

"People are just going to have to accept the fact that everything will cost a few more dollars. It will be a fact of life," Oliver said.

"It's not a question of paying a few more dollars for oil," Morris replied. "We're going to have economic chaos and national bankruptcy if this OPEC program goes into effect."

"Good God, Morris. You're the gloomiest man I have ever known," the President said. "In addition to all these dire predictions of gloom and doom, do you have any positive ideas of what the hell we can do?"

Before Morris had a chance to respond, a secretary walked into the room and handed a small note to Oliver. The Press Secretary read the note aloud.

"The representative of the three-network television pool is on the phone. He wants to know if you want time this evening to address the country on the OPEC July fourth policy?"

"What do you think, Henry?" the President asked.

"I think you'd better turn it down. There's no point talking to the people until we have something to say."

The President paced around the room twice, thinking about Oliver's words.

"I hate like hell to pass up a chance to get that kind of audience," he said. "But I guess you're right."

Oliver whispered something in the secretary's ear, and she quickly left the room.

"I sure don't need this mess," the President said, sipping his coffee. "Not now. Jesus, I can't afford another beating in the polls. What were we down to last week?"

"Sixteen percent of the people think you are doing a good job," Oliver said.

"That must be another all-time record."

"Well, don't forget, sir, that there were eighteen percent undecided."

Then the President turned to Stewart. "What about fund raising for the reelection campaign? Is that off too?"

"Only slightly," Stewart said.

"Okay," the President said, turning to Morris. "How do we deal with the OPEC announcement?"

Morris sat quietly for a moment. Eight eyes in the room stared at him.

"There's only one thing we can do," Morris replied.

"What's that?"

"Let me set up a meeting with Faisel—one on one in New York. I will try to persuade him that the OPEC program should not be implemented."

Morris spoke these words with a tone of self-confidence. But deep down he was apprehensive. Faisel would be difficult to budge.

"How do you intend to persuade Faisel?" the President asked skeptically.

"I knew him at Harvard Business School. I can appeal to his vanity and persuade him that the new program will have an adverse economic impact for his country in the long run. We're his largest customer."

"But you believe that we'll suffer and not the Saudis in the long run."

"Yes, but he doesn't know that."

"What about Israel, Bill?" the President said, turning to Black. "Can we afford to curtail arms shipments to Israel?"

"I wouldn't offer that," Black said. "Let Faisel raise it."

"Is everybody here agreeable to Morris going to meet with Faisel?" the President asked.

"I think so," Black said cautiously. "It can't hurt."

"Just make sure your meeting in New York is kept secret," Oliver said. "If this doesn't work, and it leaks out, the press will be breathing down my neck."

Stewart remained silent, meditating, absorbed in his own thoughts.

"Okay, Morris," the President said. "Go see Faisel as soon as you can. But Oliver's right. Keep it secret. We'll get you the private plane of one of my Cabinet officers to fly to New York. Let me ask you a question, though. Even if you bring this Saudi around, how do we know he can persuade the rest of the OPEC countries?"

"It doesn't matter," Morris said. "Saudi Arabia is far and away the largest producer in OPEC. The Saudis are sitting on more than 170 billion barrels of oil. They're the key. If they come around, it doesn't matter what the rest of OPEC does."

The President looked astonished as Morris reeled off the figure from memory, his face tense and grim. The man has a good mind, he thought. He's just so damn pessimistic.

"If you can't persuade him," the President said, "then find some way to compromise."

Morris chose to ignore that instruction.

"I have one other problem," Oliver said. "What do I do about Stark and the other people on the Hill? They're going to be calling me soon."

The President thought about Oliver's question. Then he said, "Morris, do you think you can handle that fat-ass Stark and his buddies?"

Morris was startled by the question.

"I think I can," he replied.

"Okay, Henry," the President said. "Give them Morris. Offer to make him available for a public session whenever they want it. He's a big boy. He can stand the fire."

The President scarcely tried to contain the glee in his voice at the prospect of Morris getting fried before the Stark Committee on national television.

"Now, Morris," the President said. "Report back to me after your meeting with that Saudi Minister. And for God's sake, Morris, don't be so negative. We'll find a way out of this. It won't be so bleak. The Good Lord hasn't let us down yet."

As Morris entered his limousine to ride back to his office, he was shaking his head incredulously, thinking about what the President had said. What a crock of shit, Morris thought to himself. He still thinks he's running for President and I'm one of the voters. If he listened to the news instead of his own rhetoric, he couldn't possibly believe what he's saying.

When Morris returned to his office, Helen Forrest was waiting for him.

"You have a visitor," she said. "I put him in your private study."

Morris walked quickly through his working office toward the wood-paneled study. He could hear the loud clicking of billiard balls being hit hard and slammed around the table that Roach had installed in the study. When Morris entered the room, he was surprised to see a man in a heavily decorated military uniform leaning over the table with a cue stick in his hand. There were four gold stars on his shirt. A drink was resting on the edge of the table and an open bottle of bourbon on the credenza. The man's brown eyes sparkled under the bright lights that hung over the table.

"Your secretary told me to make myself at home," the visitor said. "So I did. I'm Alvin Thomas, the Chairman of the Joint Chiefs of Staff."

"The introduction is unnecessary, General."

"Well, I hope I'm not disturbing you by coming here without an appointment," Thomas said stiffly.

"No, not at all."

Thomas has a strange formal manner, Morris thought. He seems awkward and ill at ease. Morris remembered the President's telephone conversation with Thomas earlier in the day. He wondered why Thomas suddenly appeared in his office.

"I spent a lot of time over in Saudi Arabia a couple of

years ago," Thomas said. "I know the place pretty well."

"What was that, military assistance?"

"Yes. We were trying to train their people to fly our Phantoms and F-15's. It was a great failure. They kept dropping them in the Persian Gulf. We finally gave up. There is no way they could ever develop an effective enough military to stop the Soviets. Hell, the Saudis are just a handful of nomads who happened to pitch their tents on the world's most valuable real estate."

"Nobody really thought that the Saudis would be able to use all those arms," Morris replied. "We thought you just wanted to help our balance of payments."

"That's about it. We knew that Saudi Arabia was just an intermediary. Those arms are all in Egypt or Syria. And the Saudis are even reselling some to Latin America."

Morris was still puzzled about why Thomas had come. He had read a great deal about Thomas because the General's background intrigued Morris. He had grown up as an army brat—the oldest son of a career officer who rose to the rank of Major General. After the Air Force Academy, Thomas had gone on to become one of America's most famous Phantom pilots in the Vietnam War. He had been shot down over North Vietnam and escaped from a prison camp by traveling long distances alone on foot. He had been awarded the Medal of Honor by President Johnson, decorated by President Nixon, and redecorated by President Carter.

"I don't want to be rude," Morris said sharply, "but we're both busy people. I assume that you didn't come here to shoot the breeze. So get to the point."

Thomas looked at Morris in silence for a moment, trying to decide whether the man's personal appearance conformed with the written report Major Cox had prepared. They fit very closely, Thomas decided. He liked Morris's brusque, businesslike manner.

"The point is this," General Thomas said. "As I understand it, your job is to recommend some practical program to the President for dealing with the new OPEC policy."

Morris nodded his head in agreement without bothering to ask how Thomas had reached that conclusion.

"When you consider the alternatives," Thomas continued, talking slowly and calmly, "I want you to consider the possibility of recommending to the President that this country launch a military invasion of Saudi Arabia to seize the Saudi oil fields."

Thomas uttered his words carefully, dropping them like bombs from an airplane. When he was finished, he stopped, waiting for Morris to respond. An eerie silence settled over the room.

Morris wasn't quite sure how to respond. He had never been in the military. He had never even remotely considered a military response to the OPEC announcement.

"Why are you telling me this?" Morris asked.

"Because you're in a position of recommending a policy to the President. Because I've studied your background and followed your method of operation. I believe that this approach would appeal to you. It's bold and unorthodox—characteristics that you favor. I'm hopeful that you can persuade the President that he has no other choice."

"Why don't you suggest it to the President yourself? You're the Chairman of the Joint Chiefs."

"If I suggest it, he'll turn it down," Thomas said. Then he stopped talking as Miss Forrest entered the office carrying a silver tray with a pitcher of coffee and two cups. She handed one cup to Morris, glanced disapprovingly at the glass of bourbon in Thomas's hand, and placed the tray on the table. Thomas waited for the secretary to leave before continuing.

"Let's just say that President Edwards and I have had our policy differences over the last two years," Thomas said softly. "My advice is not well received in the Oval Office. I obtained some hints of this new OPEC policy when I was in Saudi Arabia in April, but I didn't even bother to mention those to the President. He knows that I retire in about twelve months. He's willing to tolerate me until then."

Morris finished his cup of coffee and poured another.

"I appreciate your advice, General," Morris said, "but I don't need it. My game plan is to set up a meeting with Faisel in New York. I intend to convince him to cancel the July fourth program."

Thomas gazed at Morris with a look of bewilderment on his face.

"It can't hurt to try," Thomas said. "But you won't succeed."

"Why not?"

"I know the Saudis. They're deeply religious. People like that rarely change any policy."

Morris walked over to the large double window that looked down to the concrete courtyard below. He stared at the statute of Henry Ford in the center of the courtyard that had been erected by a government official with a perverse sense of humor. Suddenly Morris remembered about the hydrogen fusion research program.

"Do you recall an R and D contract that American Fusion Corporation had with the Air Force a couple of years ago?" Morris asked.

"Very clearly."

"Why did you terminate it when the research looked promising?"

The general refilled his glass and sipped slowly.

"I began to realize about seven years ago," Thomas said, "that sooner or later this country would be required to seize the Saudi Arabian oil fields as the solution to its worsening energy situation. I'm a practical man. That fact seemed as inevitable to me as the melting of winter snow with spring. As a result, stopgap measures like the hydrogen fusion program were a useless waste of money. Nothing would be gained by prolonging the inevitable."

"Certainly not past the date of your retirement," Morris said sarcastically.

Thomas ignored the comment. He continued speaking.

"I've gradually initiated training programs in desert warfare in Arizona and New Mexico. They're now a standard part of basic training at bases in those areas. I've even told my subordinates to duplicate Middle-Eastern terrain as much as possible. I've warned them that we'd be fighting there sooner or later."

Morris was listening quietly, amazed at what Thomas was telling him.

"I am always available to consult with you," Thomas said.

Then the general stood in front of Morris for a moment. He was standing at attention, his legs together, his posture as straight as a flagpole. His hands were at his sides. He seemed ready to salute Morris. Then Thomas turned sharply and walked briskly out of the room like a professional soldier during a drill.

When Thomas closed the door firmly behind him, Morris sent for Green. He had no intention of mentioning Thomas's visit to the Assistant Director.

"I asked you to find out about the cutoff of research funds to American Fusion Corporation," Morris said sharply. "What have you learned?"

"Absolutely nothing," Green said apologetically. "I've made a major effort, but I keep running into a stone wall. All I hear is that it was General Thomas's personal order given orally with no explanations."

That was consistent with what the General said, Morris thought to himself.

"Okay, drop it," Morris said. "There's nothing else there."

As Green started to leave the office, Morris stopped him.

"What do you know about General Thomas's relations with the President?"

Green was embarrassed by the question. Mrs. Thomas had been a patient of his wife before the General sent her to Boston Psychiatric. Green knew more about the General than professional ethics permitted.

"Nothing definitive," Green replied with a strange tremor in his voice. "Only Washington gossip."

Morris could tell that Green was lying. But he wasn't interested in the source of Green's information.

"What's the gossip?" Morris asked.

"Strong disagreements between the two men at the beginning of the Administration."

"Over personality or policy?"

"Mostly policy. Thomas isn't an anti-Communist crusader. But he sees American foreign policy suffering badly from what he calls the post-Vietnam syndrome. According to Thomas, since the fall of Saigon, this country has been unwilling to use military force as a part of foreign policy. Every astute politician in the world knows that. As a result, Thomas claims that our foreign policy has no credibility because there's no force behind it. The President outright rejected Thomas's view. Told him it's a lot of horseshit. Told him to stick to military affairs and keep his nose out of foreign policy."

As Morris thought about Green's words, the Assistant Director started talking again.

"My own personal opinion is that the President is absolutely right," Green said.

"I didn't ask for your opinion," Morris said curtly, looking annoyed.

As he opened the door, Green felt sorry that he had been so expansive on Thomas's relations with the President. Felicia would be very unhappy if she found out.

Morris watched Green leave the office. Then he walked over to the window and stood there for several minutes, looking perplexed and replaying in his mind his conversation with General Thomas. Finally Morris decided simply to forget about his whole conversation with Thomas—to chalk it up as an academic exercise.

Morris spent the next couple of hours trying to locate the Saudi Finance Minister to arrange a meeting. That bastard

Faisel is trying to avoid me, Morris thought. Trying to make me believe that he's not interested in talking. It's a negotiating ploy.

Morris left messages at the Waldorf, the U.N., "21," and half a dozen other expensive restaurants in midtown Manhattan that Faisel was known to frequent.

At two-thirty Faisel returned Morris's call. He was talking from a phone plugged to his table at La Grenouille.

"Oh, George Morris from the United States Department of Energy," Faisel said, trying to sound surprised.

"You may remember me from Harvard Business School."

"Yes, of course, I remember you from that school," Faisel said scornfully.

"I want to meet with you on the OPEC announcement," Morris said, "today in New York."

"Today is out of the question. I have a speech at the U.N. and other pressing commitments."

"But the situation is urgent."

"Urgent for you, but not for me," Faisel said.

"What about tomorrow?"

"Tomorrow evening is the earliest. Eight o'clock at the Waldorf."

"I'll be there."

"Come alone," Faisel said. "Don't bring General Thomas or any of his stooges."

Morris was surprised by Faisel's comment. General Thomas must have made his views known in Saudi Arabia, Morris thought.

"I was planning to come alone," Morris said, as he put down the receiver.

Morris spent the rest of the day assembling facts for his meeting with Faisel. As he left the office at ten o'clock, he picked up a copy of the *Evening Star*. The front page was filled with a parade of horribles generated by the OPEC announcement. Morris turned on the light in the back of his limousine and quickly read some of them: the stock markets were expected to plunge to twenty-year lows when the exchanges reopened tomorrow; a spokesman for the National Industrial Association predicted that if the OPEC oil program became effective on July fourth, six thousand American businesses would have to shut down—many permanently; an airline industry spokesman announced that unless the airline industry received priority fuel, their schedules would be severely cut; and the Association of Public Utilities warned that electricity would simply not be available after July fifteenth in many heavily populated areas.

When he arrived home, Morris went straight to his second-floor study. He removed some papers from his briefcase—notes that he had made about his meeting at the White House. He placed them in the center desk drawer and carefully locked it.

Then Morris turned off his mind to forget about Faisel for a while. The house was quiet with Anne in New York. He swam one hundred laps in the pool under the evening stars. Then he sat alone on the patio enjoying a charcoal steak, which Louise had cooked, with a bottle of Château Margaux.

Only after dinner, when he sat in the still evening air, puffing gently on his cigar, did Morris start thinking about the oil crisis again. The adrenalin started moving. He was looking forward to his meeting with Faisel.

Francine held the telephone close to her mouth. She was talking softly. Elliott was outside on the patio. She didn't want him to hear.

"You're sure that you're flying Morris up to New York in Bill's plane tomorrow?" she said to the pilot.

"Absolutely. Estimated time of arrival is seven P.M. Butler Terminal, at La Guardia."

"And from there?"

"He goes by limo to the Waldorf. We wait at La Guardia for return tomorrow evening."

"You're beautiful," Francine said. "I owe you a big one."

She made a small kissing noise into the mouthpiece and set down the telephone.

Well, well, Francine said to herself, I'll be waiting for you, George T.

Francine wasn't the only one who was thinking about George T. Morris that evening. Ahmad Zadak, the Iranian Ambassador, sat in his suite in The Pierre, reviewing the instructions he had received from Tehran, direct from His Royal Highness the Shah: "It is imperative that you establish personal contact with Morris well in advance of July fourth. Do it informally and socially. You may select the approach."

The instructions could have included one more sentence: "Failure will not be tolerated." But that would have been superfluous. Ahmad knew very well that the Shah never tolerated failure.

# CHAPTER

# 5

MORRIS LOOKED OUT OF THE WINDOW OF THE BOEING 727 racing to New York. He always liked flying alone in private airplanes because it gave him a feeling of wealth and power. This plane, which was normally used by William Elliott, the Secretary of Defense, was as lavishly furnished as any corporate jet that Morris had flown in.

When Morris entered the Waldorf lobby, he was stopped by Abdul, who introduced himself as Faisel's Chief of Security. Three Saudi guards dressed in Arab headdress and carrying automatic weapons quickly descended on Morris, pressing him into the center of an equilateral triangle.

"His Excellency is expecting you," Abdul said to Morris. "Please follow me."

Abdul marched rapidly through the lobby with Morris two paces behind. The three guards stuck with Morris, remaining equidistant from him and making it a curious procession. Each of the guards had his finger pressed tightly on the trigger of his weapon.

They marched past Peacock Alley. Morris saw four Arab shieks sitting and drinking Turkish coffee. He could hear the roll of the backgammon dice. The pungent smell of heavy Turkish tobacco filled Morris's nostrils.

When they reached Faisel's private elevator, Abdul came to a sudden halt. He gave one of the three guards an order in Arabic. The man dropped his weapon and began searching Morris very thoroughly.

"This is no way for Faisel to treat an old classmate," Morris said.

"Following yesterday's announcement, it has become routine for anyone who wishes to have an interview with his Excellency," Abdul said in heavily accented English.

In the penthouse Morris and Faisel immediately recognized each other though they hadn't been together for twelve years. They shook hands coolly and stood three feet apart—each man studying the other carefully.

The two men were dressed practically the same. Each had a blue pinstriped suit with a vest, and each had a golden chain stretched across his vest. Their shirts were white, their ties drab conservative banker's silk. But there the similarity ended. The Saudi's appearance bore testimony to twelve years of gluttony and indulgence—whoring around in the finest castles of the world. The American's suggested the restraint and discipline of a man whose drive for money and power overcame all else.

"Would you like a drink?" Faisel asked.

"No, thank you."

"Coffee, then?"

"Please."

"One scotch and one coffee," Faisel said to one of his servants who stood at the door.

Morris was not surprised by the order. He knew that the Islamic ban on alcohol had been disregarded by Faisel when he was still at Harvard. Morris had heard stories of orgies at Faisel's Beacon Hill house, but he had never been invited.

After the drinks arrived, Faisel dismissed all of his guards and servants, setting up the one-on-one meeting that Morris had hoped for. The two men sat down in plush velvet chairs next to a large brass coffee table.

"You may begin, Morris," Faisel said. "You wanted this meeting."

"It's hardly a secret as to why I am here," Morris said, talking slowly and dispassionately. His opening words had been carefully rehearsed. "I was startled by the OPEC announcement. It will of course pose some inconvenience for the United States, but we will survive. What surprised me is that the action is so contrary to the long-term economic interests of your own country. This is why I have come—to suggest to you that OPEC cancel its July fourth program and leave prices and production at their current levels for the next five years."

Faisel listened to Morris with a slight smile permanently fixed on his face.

"Why do you say it's contrary to our own economic interests?" Faisel asked, sounding amused.

"Because we are your largest customer. Our purchases permit you to continually increase the deposits of dollars, marks, and pounds that you have in banks around the world."

"But our deposits are worthless. We are paid in dollars. You and I both know that the value of these dollars shrink each day with inflation and devaluation. One day we will wake up and find that we are holding billions of dollars in worthless paper and all of our oil will be gone. Where will we be then?"

Morris was listening carefully to Faisel. The Saudi was raising precisely those arguments that Morris would have raised in the same position.

"I realize that what I am asking you to do," Morris said, "takes a great deal of courage. It is always difficult to change one's direction. But if you cancel the July fourth program, I believe that history will regard you as a true statesman."

Faisel laughed. "History depends on who is the historian."

Faisel ordered another drink for himself and more coffee for Morris. For the next hour they went around and around the same ground, covering the same arguments—with Morris trying to persuade Faisel that the July fourth program was contrary to Saudi Arabia's own economic interest and would reflect unfavorably on Faisel. Morris was facing an absolutely stone wall. Faisel refused to budge.

"Perhaps we can undertake some type of a joint American-Saudi economic partnership," Morris said, trying to change his approach.

"A new version of the old Kissinger promise," Faisel replied, grunting to himself. "We were taken in once—not again."

"What about Israel?" Morris said, recalling the discussion between the President and Black. "Perhaps you want us to extract some concessions from Israel—to reduce their supply of arms?"

Faisel started to laugh. "You Americans always think that you can pacify us with some concessions from Israel. You deceived yourselves into believing that long ago. It's an insult to our intelligence, but we let you go on believing it. It lulled you into a false sense of security. You thought you could always buy us off by extracting some concessions from Israel. That theory is dead wrong. We hate the Jews. Yes. But we are playing this game for bigger stakes than Israel."

"You really believe that you will gain from the economic chaos that results from the OPEC program?"

"Absolutely. In the short run we will acquire real estate and industrial property in the United States from bankrupt firms. In the long run we will create a new economic order. Our oil is worth more in the ground. It has taken us a long time to realize that. But we are finally there."

As Faisel spoke, Morris realized that the man was not only serious, but that his plan had been carefully conceived.

"You see, my dear Morris," Faisel said, "we must act now while we still have our oil. Once that oil is gone, we become nomads again."

"Then why are you selling us even one million barrels a day? Why not cut us off altogether?"

"That's a sop for the Shah, who apparently feels indebted to you for your military assistance. Also some of the smaller members of OPEC want to maintain the flow of petro dollars."

By now Morris could tell that his negotiation was in trouble.

"Give us time," he said. "Cut us down gradually over the next five years."

"While you achieve independence from OPEC oil?" Faisel laughed. "I'm no fool," the Saudi said. "I sat in the same economics classes at Harvard Business School as you did."

Morris didn't need an economics lecture from Faisel. He knew very well that classic capitalistic economics was being applied. They could use this as a textbook example of monopolistic behavior—if anyone ever wrote textbooks again.

"Anyhow, don't talk to me about time," Faisel said. "You had plenty of time. We gave you a warning with the 1973 embargo. You refused to listen. Instead of moving toward independence from OPEC oil, you became more dependent on it. You've had your five years—already twice."

"We can bring pressure to bear," Morris said, trying to sound confident.

"That's a bluff, and you know it. You have no bargaining chips left."

As Faisel uttered those last words, an arrogant smile appeared on his face. Then Faisel called to one of his servants.

"Walk Morris to the elevator. His interview is concluded."

When the Director of Energy walked out of the elevator, he had a very grim look on his face. He was not accustomed to emerging empty-handed from any negotiating session. He was livid with anger. Morris clenched his fists, the blood rushing to his face.

Morris vowed that he would find some way of dealing with the OPEC policy. Faisel had won this round, but there would be others.

Morris walked down the thickly carpeted steps toward the Park Avenue entrance of the hotel. The limousine was waiting four blocks away at 53rd between Park and Lexington to take him to the airport. This pickup point had been arranged to avoid detection by the press. As far as he knew, the media were not aware of his meeting with the Saudi Finance Minister.

As Morris started through the revolving doors into the humid evening air of Manhattan, he had the feeling he was being followed. It was a feeling that Morris had known before. He had been followed twice in Iran by the Secret Police and once in Russia by the KGB when he was negotiating foreign transactions.

He turned right, walking north on Park Avenue, slowly, looking straight ahead, trying to avoid any signal that he knew he was being followed. He wanted to find out who it was.

Morris listened carefully. He heard the clicking of a woman's heels. When he slowed down, the clicking slowed down. When he walked faster, the clicking increased.

He crossed Park Avenue listening for the clicking. A taxicab slammed on its brakes, narrowly missing Morris. The driver honked furiously. "What the hell's wrong with you, mister?"

Morris paused to look in the window of a jewelry store. Then he recrossed Park Avenue to the east side. The clicking followed him.

The sticky evening air of Manhattan made Morris perspire. He wiped his face with his handkerchief as he walked north on Park Avenue.

When Morris reached 53rd Street, he turned right quickly, hid behind a corner of the building, and looked back toward the Waldorf. He could see a woman standing quite alone in the middle of the sidewalk—a woman with large round breasts and a funny wide-brimmed white straw hat. She raced into the coffee shop on the corner.

Morris wondered who she was and why she was following him. She was probably working for Faisel, he thought. The

Saudi was anxious to know what Morris would do after their meeting.

It was nine-thirty when the limousine dropped Morris at La Guardia at the Butler Aviation Terminal for private planes. Morris saw the pilot and copilot, dressed in their military uniforms, playing backgammon in the waiting lounge. When the pilot saw Morris, he slammed the board closed. Both men rose to their feet and saluted.

"That's enough," Morris said. "We're trying to keep a low profile on this trip. How soon do we leave?"

"Give us ten minutes to warm up the engines."

"I'll meet you on the plane."

Morris walked briskly over to the newsstand, bought a *New York Post,* and then walked toward the gate, reading the paper as he walked. He was anxious to see if there was any news about his trip to New York. He saw nothing on page one. Then he started turning the pages. His eyes were riveted on the paper.

Suddenly Morris felt a gentle tugging on his arm.

"Say, aren't you George Morris?" a woman asked.

Startled, Morris looked up. Standing in front of him was the woman with the large round breasts and the wide-brimmed white straw hat. She was wearing a red T-shirt with Givenchy written on the sleeve and a brown khaki wrap skirt. She had a broad smile on her face.

"Say, aren't you George Morris?" she asked again.

Morris was absolutely incredulous. There was no point lying.

"Yes, I'm George Morris. Who the hell are you?"

"I'm Francine Rush, a reporter from the *Washington Tribune.* We never formally met, but I was at your swearing in."

She pulled a press badge from her white straw purse and showed it to Morris.

"Oh, for Christ's sake," Morris said, sounding disgusted that the secrecy of his mission had been blown.

Francine understood why Morris was disgusted, but she chose to ignore it.

"I have a little problem, Mr. Morris," she said quite innocently. "I managed to miss the last commercial flight back to Washington. I wonder if you could give me a ride?"

Morris stared at her. What a little bitch, he thought. She's no more than twenty-five years old. She thinks that she's another Woodward or Bernstein. For two cents he'd tell her to shove off with this cock-and-bull story.

On the other hand she was with the *Tribune,* which was an important paper. And she was no dummy. She had managed to find out about his trip to New York and to follow him around the city. He would be smart to try to accommodate her.

Morris stood looking at Francine, trying to make up his mind.

"If you give me a ride home, Mr. Morris, I promise not to conduct any interviews on the plane. I won't ask you what you were doing in New York, and I won't even take any notes."

"You probably have a hidden tape recorder."

"No hidden tape recorders. I promise."

Morris hesitated.

"You can search me," she said, smiling and lifting her arms.

One thing was clear to Morris. She wasn't hiding a tape recorder in her bra. She wasn't wearing one.

"Oh, come on, Miss Rush," he said. "I'll take you."

Morris and Francine were seated in large reclining chairs next to each other when the plane took off. Once they were airborne, she walked over to the bar, demonstrating an obvious familiarity with the plane.

"Do you want a drink, George?" she said, deciding to drop the Mr. Morris.

"No, thanks. I don't drink."

"Do you want some coffee, teetotaler?" she asked, while pouring herself a solid measure of scotch.

"Yes, coffee, please."

"I'm not used to being a stewardess," she said, handing him the coffee.

He sipped the coffee slowly. The best way to handle her is to try to avoid any conversation, Morris thought.

It wasn't that easy. Two minutes later Francine started again with a broad smile on her face.

"If you don't drink, why do you and Anne Walton give those lavish parties every Saturday evening? They say the booze flows like water."

"I like to watch other people drink."

"I'd sure like to come to one of those parties, George."

"Maybe you'll get an invitation one day."

She continued smiling.

"What are you trying to prove with those parties?"

"Now, now, Francine. Remember, you told me that there would be no interviews," Morris said calmly.

He looked out of the window. There were bright lights on the ground sparkling in the darkness of the night.

Two minutes later she started again.

"I looked at some of our old editorials in the morgue at the *Tribune* this morning," Francine said. "Do you know that we actually warned that this could happen six years ago when the United States became so dependent on OPEC oil?"

Morris remained silent.

"I'm frightened by the whole thing," she said. "Do you really think that the situation is as bleak as some of the commentators have said?"

"We're working on a solution."

"What kind of a solution?"

"A solution that will permit you and your friends to keep on living in the style that you are accustomed to," Morris said sarcastically.

"I mean what restrictions on oil will you impose?" she asked in a tone that sounded like a lawyer during cross-examination.

"You're starting to come on me like a reporter again, Francine. Remember, you said 'No interviews.' "

Francine sipped her drink slowly, looking at Morris through the corner of her eye. He was leaning back in the seat; his eyes were closed.

She reached over and slowly placed her hand on top of his. She began gently caressing the back of his hand. Morris quickly pulled his hand away. Without saying a word to her, he opened his briefcase, pulled out the *New York Post* and began reading it with apparent indifference to Francine.

She got up and walked to the bar. After fixing herself another drink, she stood there for several minutes watching Morris read his paper.

Okay, you cold son of a bitch, she thought to herself. I'll manage to get beneath that tough outer shell. There's got to be a soft spot somewhere. And I'll sure as hell find it.

Francine returned to her seat next to Morris. The two of them rode silently back to Washington.

When the plane started its descent to Andrews Air Force Base, Francine said, "I'm really sorry, George, that our relationship got off to a bad start. It's my fault. I know it. I'll do better the next time. I promise."

Morris smiled weakly at her. He hoped that there would never be a next time. But he knew how unlikely that was. There would be more encounters with Francine Rush. Morris was certain of that.

As Morris's plane landed in Washington, Anne was being greeted by the maitre d'hôtel at Sardi's in New York. The after-theatre crowd of diners stopped to stare as Anne was ushered to a private room upstairs. The occasion was a party given by Lionel Holt, the President of Western American Corporation—the financial backer of *Mafia Woman*. Holt had invited a score of people connected with the show and one man who wasn't. That man was Holt's creditor. He asked

Holt to arrange the party and to invite him. That man was Ahmad Zadak, the Iranian Ambassador.

Anne immediately noticed Ahmad during the cocktail hour. The tall and thin Iranian looked to Anne like a continental prince from somewhere in the Mediterranean. He was a man who paid attention to every detail of his appearance. He moved easily among the guests, gracefully holding his champagne glass.

When Holt introduced Anne to Ahmad, the Iranian took her hand and kissed it gently. He told her that he had recorded every one of her shows from "Undercover Woman" on a video casette recorder. He frequently played them in Tehran to liven an otherwise dull evening.

"Why my show?" Anne asked innocently.

"Because, my dear, you are the most beautiful actress on any screen."

As Ahmad flattered her, Anne blushed. She was pleased. It had been a long time since a man had talked to her like that. That wasn't Morris's style. And it gave her a big boost after twelve tough hours in the dingy Broadway theatre and her cubicle of a dressing room.

As the guests later moved toward the dinner table, Anne was pleasantly surprised to find that her name card was placed between Ahmad and the boorish old man who handled sets. As for the Iranian, he was hardly surprised. He had arranged the seating.

By the time the cannelloni appetizers were eaten, Anne and Ahmad had drifted off into their own private conversation—impervious to the others present. Anne was charmed by the Iranian with the warm smile and the thin face. He spoke at length of the foreign countries he had traveled in and the strange and wonderful sights he had seen. And Anne, who had never left the United States, except for one trip to Europe with Morris, was captivated. Ahmad told her about the glistening beauty of Tehran in the second coming of the

Persian Empire. She sipped champagne and closed her eyes, listening to the soft sound of Ahmad's voice.

Anne thought about how bored she had been those last days in Washington before she came to New York, sitting around waiting for the phone to ring, sitting around waiting for Morris to come home. Her hopes of marriage to Morris were fading fast. She was a healthy young woman with normal drives that weren't being satisfied. She was involved in a relationship that was, to put it mildly, in a rut. Now here was this suave Iranian. He could be a very pleasant diversion.

She and Ahmad were still talking and sipping champagne an hour later when the other guests had gone. An impatient waiter, anxious to leave, hurried them along. Ahmad offered to have his limousine take her to her hotel.

When they arrived at the Park Lane, Anne was still wide awake and intrigued by Ahmad.

"Can I offer you a nightcap in my suite?" she asked.

"Oh, my dear. I would love to. But it's really quite late. You work tomorrow."

"I insist."

"Then how can I refuse?"

As they walked into the suite, Anne was surprised to see a dozen long-stem red roses and two ounces of Joy sitting on the marble table in the entrance hall. Anne read the card that Ahmad had sent with the gift and smiled. He comes on a bit much, she thought. But so what? She didn't care. She was flattered that he made the effort.

A half an hour later they were sitting on a couch in the suite sipping champagne.

"What's your friend George Morris like?" Ahmad asked.

The Iranian's tone was casual, matter of fact. It gave the appearance of harmless curiosity. But beneath the Iranian's smile, there was a deadly serious motivation. He remembered well his instruction to establish personal contact with Morris. Being permitted to select his own approach, and being a man who preferred to mix pleasure with business, Ahmad had selected Anne as his vehicle. He was enjoying every minute with her. But he never lost sight of his objective.

"Please don't ask me about Morris," Anne replied. "Don't spoil a beautiful evening."

The Iranian quickly changed the subject. There was still a lot of time until July fourth. He would try again after he solidified his relationship with Anne.

A few minutes later Ahmad gently placed his arm around Anne's waist. She leaned toward him, pressing her breasts against his chest. He kissed her, holding her tightly in his arms.

"I've spent my whole life in search of true beauty," the Ambassador said.

Why not, Anne thought. He's probably a skillful lover too. It goes with the rest of his personality.

"Then follow me," Anne replied, as she began walking toward the bedroom, unbuttoning her blouse.

# CHAPTER

# 6

THE *Washington Tribune* WAS WAITING IN FRONT OF MORRIS'S front door when he left the house the following morning. He snatched the rolled-up paper from the "Welcome" mat and tucked it under his arm as he bounded down the steps to the waiting limousine. In the car Morris turned on the reading light and spread out the paper on the portable table.

As the car drove through the still silent streets of George-town, Morris cast his eyes over the Tribune. He quickly saw his picture in the center of the front page. Next to the picture was an article under the Francine Rush byline. Morris read the opening paragraph carefully.

George Morris, the Director of Energy, was seen leaving the Waldorf Astoria in New York last evening at nine o'clock. There is speculation that he met with Yaman Faisel, the Saudi Finance Minister, but there has been no official confirmation of such a meeting.

About an hour later the President read the Francine Rush article while he was having breakfast with Mrs. Edwards. When he saw the article, he started choking on a piece of bacon.

"Oh, God damn it!" the President shouted. "I wanted

secrecy for that meeting in New York. Now we'll look like we're negotiating out of desperation."

Mrs. Edwards was used to her husband's outbursts when he read the Tribune at the breakfast table. She continued eating her eggs in silence, ignoring his tirade.

President Edwards picked up the phone that was sitting in the middle of the table.

"Get me Oliver!" he shouted.

There was a pause.

Then the President started talking again.

"Did you see the Francine Rush article, Henry?"

"Yes, Chief. I did," Oliver replied feebly.

"That burns my ass. I told Morris that I wanted secrecy."

"Well, Francine can be a tough reporter."

"She's got too damn much moxie for her own good if you ask me. Somebody will break her in two one day."

"I'd like to meet that man," Oliver said.

"Well, there's no use crying over it now. Get Morris over here at nine o'clock for a report on his meeting."

"I'll have him here, Chief."

Oliver carried out his commitment. At precisely five minutes to nine, Morris's limousine pulled into the driveway of the west wing of the White House. Oliver was waiting for Morris on the steps. When Morris shook Oliver's hand, he was struck by how large and white the Press Secretary's teeth actually were.

"He's sore as hell about that Francine Rush story," Oliver said. "We wanted secrecy on that meeting. Otherwise it shows weakness."

Morris nearly laughed. They're worried about not showing weakness, he thought. They're like little boys trying to stop the flood by putting their fingers in the dike.

"I wonder how Francine got her story?" Oliver said.

Morris remained silent.

"If you're ever with her, be careful, George. She'll sleep with anyone who will give her a good story. Right now she has an ongoing affair with Bill Elliott, but that won't stop her from jumping into the sack with somebody else. You had Elliott's plane yesterday. Maybe she's screwing his pilot, and that's where she got her information."

Morris looked down at the ground.

When Morris and Oliver entered the Oval Office, Black and Stewart were already with the President. The four men listened carefully when Morris gave a lengthy report of his meeting with Faisel.

Morris had complete recall of every detail of the meeting. He presented all of the facts in an unemotional machinelike monotone. It was like hearing a cassette recorder that had been turned on in the suite at the Waldorf.

When Morris was finished, the President picked up a pencil and started tapping it on his desk.

"Do you think that Faisel is serious?" the President asked.

"Yes. I do. He's absolutely serious."

"You don't think that he's bluffing? That he'll back down right after the fourth?"

"The probability of that is less than .001."

"Talk English to me," the President said, sounding annoyed.

"Less than one in a thousand. Virtually no chance."

"You don't see any possible compromise?"

"None at all, Mr. President."

The President walked over to a credenza and poured hot coffee from a china pitcher into a cup.

"Do you fellows want some coffee?" he asked.

The other three men rose in unison, walked over to the credenza, and poured coffee.

"I guess I'm not surprised that you didn't succeed in your meeting with Faisel," the President said. "It was a long shot anyhow. You were the only one who thought it would work."

Morris resented that comment, but he kept quiet, grabbing the bottom of the conference table to restrain himself.

The President rose from the table and wandered over to the window. He stood for a moment looking at the yellow and orange marigolds that dotted the south lawn of the White House.

Stewart stared at the President standing motionless at the window. The President's Special Assistant was doing all he could to restrain his glee at the fact that Morris had failed and Edwards was now in one helluva difficult position. He had visions of Edwards being impaled in public view.

Suddenly President Edwards wheeled around and looked at Morris.

"Well, Morris," he said, "this is your show. What do you propose to do now?"

"I haven't decided yet, Mr. President," Morris said. "I want a few days to think about it."

"I can give you six days. No more. Let's reconvene this same group next Wednesday, June seventh, at nine o'clock in the morning. By the time of that meeting, Morris, I want you to come up with an emergency energy program that will keep this country running smoothly after July fourth when the new OPEC policy goes into effect."

"That may not be possible."

"Everything's possible. Don't be so damned pessimistic. If you can't do it, I'll find somebody who will."

Morris walked out of the White House shaking his head. There's simply no sense of reality in this building, he thought.

When Morris returned to his own office, Green was waiting next to Helen Forrest's desk.

"Is this more good news?" Morris said to Green as the Assistant followed him into his office.

"I'm afraid not," Green said blandly. "Senator Stark called. With the OPEC announcement, he won't wait until the fifth to get you before his committee. He wants you tomorrow. And he won't take no for an answer."

Morris recalled the President's nickname for Stark—"fat-ass Stark."

"Call Stark back," Morris said to Green. "Tell him I'll be there. But do one other thing. Go see him privately today.

Tell him in confidence about my meeting in New York yesterday and establish one ground rule for the hearing. No questions about the meeting in New York. I don't want to destroy our negotiating position—if we still have one."

"He may not buy it."

"Tell him national security is at stake."

"He still may not buy it."

"Then I'll lie about it. I'll say I didn't go."

"He'll put you under oath and prosecute you for perjury."

"I thought we were all on the same side."

"We are, but since Watergate the Congress hasn't been the same."

"Well, go try anyhow."

When Green left the office, Morris pressed the intercom.

"Miss Forrest, get Janet Koch up here."

As soon as she received the call, Janet raced across the hall, carrying a booklet of computer printouts. She was trying to catch her breath as she entered Morris's office. She saw Morris standing in front of the window, looking out. He was still thinking about the President's words: "Well, Morris, this is your show."

"This may be the most difficult assignment I've ever given you," Morris said to Janet.

Morris then explained the results of his meeting with Faisel. He described the new task that the President had assigned.

She listened carefully when he spoke, each word permanently filed in her computer mind.

"The bottom line is this," Morris said. "You should assume that the OPEC program goes into effect on July fourth. Have the computer determine what we can do to keep this country financially sound for the next five years until we develop the alternatives to OPEC oil."

Janet had some doubts as to whether any answer could be provided to the problem that Morris had raised. But she gave no hint of those doubts.

"When do you want the results of the computer analysis?"

"Deliver the printouts to my house late on Saturday. I'll study them Sunday when I go out to the country with Anne."

"I'll have them for you, Mr. Morris."

Morris worked all afternoon and well into the evening preparing his statement for the Stark committee. By ten o'clock he was mentally and physically exhausted. The whole building was quiet except for the computer center where Janet was still feeding information to the Morris 6000.

As the evening wore on, Janet had taken frequent glances down the hall toward Morris's office. When she saw the lights go out in his office, she promptly cut the power to the computer, grabbed her handbag, and walked quickly toward the elevator. She arrived just as the doors were opening.

"Any progress?" Morris asked as they entered the elevator.

"A good start," Janet replied. "I want to get some dinner and begin fresh in the morning."

She was holding her breath, hoping that he would ask her to join him for a late dinner. But nothing. Only silence. And finally: "I'll see you in the morning, Janet," Morris said as he walked to the limousine.

Unlike George, Anne Walton was not prepared to let the final hours of the evening pass quietly. She and Ahmad Zadak were dining late at La Côte Basque. The Iranian had been waiting for her when she left the theatre.

When they sat down in the restaurant, he handed her a small box. It was a magnificent brooch with diamonds and emeralds in the shape of a rare Iranian bird.

"Will you introduce me to your friend George Morris?" he asked over coffee.

"He's not much fun. You wouldn't like him."

"I understand that he's very bold and aggressive."

"But only in business matters. You wouldn't like him."

Anne was intrigued by Ahmad's interest in George. At first she was annoyed by his questions, but now she was faintly amused. She freely talked about Morris with Ahmad, describing how he had built his financial empire in such a short period of time and how he was determined to have every American schoolboy learn about George T. Morris.

"Once George has decided to do something," Anne said, "he will do it. He's the most determined man that the Good Lord ever made."

Ahmad didn't ask any more questions about Morris.

Later when they were lying in bed together, when Anne was sleeping softly, filled with contentment, the Iranian thought about Anne's words: "He's the most determined man that the Good Lord ever made."

Ahmad got up quietly from the bed. He walked into the living room of the suite and picked up the telephone.

"I want to send a Telex message to Iran," he said softly to the operator.

When Morris arrived at the office on Friday morning, Green was waiting for him.

"What happened with Stark?" Morris asked.

"He promised not to ask you about the meeting with Faisel, but he won't try to stop other committee members."

"That's certainly helpful," Morris said sarcastically.

"You can't blame him. You have to understand his point of view."

"Oh, bullshit. I didn't get where I am by seeing things from other people's point of view. I hate talk like that."

"What are you going to tell Stark's committee?" Green asked.

"I'm going to throw out some of the proposals in my old program—the one the computer developed before the OPEC announcement."

"But that's all outdated now."

"I know that, and you know that. But the committee won't."

"I think you'd do better to be straight with the committee," Green said.

"And do what? Tell them that this country has been royally

screwed by the King of Saudia Arabia, that we face absolute disaster in thirty-four days, and that we don't even have any suggestions of how to alleviate the suffering and damage that will occur. Do you really want me to say that?"

"Well, not in those words."

"Hell, those clowns on the Hill would never believe that kind of statement anyhow. Everybody in this town thinks the country is invincible."

"What do you hope to accomplish by giving them the outlines of your old plan?"

"Oh, it has a lot of controversial items like gas rationing and increased use of coal and nuclear energy. It will set off a whole series of fights in the Congress—North against the South; environmentalists against business interests; California against the rest of the country, and some others."

"What good will that do?"

"Well, it will tie the Congress up until July fourth, and get them off my back. That will give me time to come up with something."

When Morris approached the main entrance to the Dirksen Senate Office Building, he thought he was in the middle of a circus. Pickets marched along the sidewalk with signs that read "Lower Gasoline Prices Now" and "We Want Our Jobs Back." Vendors sold balloons and snow cones, television cameras were set up in the doorway to the building, and a few hookers were soliciting business. When the reporters saw Morris approaching, they shoved microphones into his face. Morris pushed through the screaming mob, thinking to himself, That Senator Stark has really gotten out all the stops for this one.

The Energy Committee Hearing Room was ablaze with the glow of lights from television cameras. The press table was crowded. There were all of the Washington regulars like Francine Rush and Bill Marks, and a host of out-of-town correspondents as well. Francine winked at Morris, but he pretended that he didn't see her.

Morris's prepared statement went without interruption. But the fireworks began during the question-and-answer session.

Senator Price asked Morris what he intended to do about the severe costs that would be imposed on consumers by his proposals?

"I can't do anything," Morris replied dispassionately. "I'm sorry, but there are no free lunches in the real world. Everything costs something. For ten years you people in the Congress have been playing havoc with the country by telling the people that we could handle our energy situation without radically changing our standard of living. That has helped Congressmen get reelected, but it sure hasn't helped the country. If you ask me . . ."

Senator Stark interrupted Morris. Stark's face was bright red, and he rose to his feet shouting at Morris.

"Don't you try to put the blame for this on the Congress, young man. The only mistake we ever made was looking to the executive branch of the government for leadership."

It was clear that Morris had struck a raw nerve. It was "C.Y.A. time," as they say in Washington. Time to "cover your ass."

Senator Bell from New York jumped in.

"Mr. Morris," he said, "there was a report in the *Washington Tribune* that you went to New York Wednesday and that you met with Yaman Faisel, the Saudia Finance Minister. Would you please comment on that report?"

"There is absolutely no substance to that report," Morris said, looking straight into Bell's eyes.

Then Morris held his breath waiting to see if Senator Stark or Francine Rush would jump to their feet to call him a liar. Both remained silent. Stark had obviously been convinced by Green that disclosure of the facts about the meeting would prejudice the national security. And as for Francine, well, she had something else in mind. She had just earned herself an invitation to one of Morris's Saturday evening parties.

Then Senator Bell started talking again.

"How much longer do you think the OPEC countries will continue to reduce output and increase prices?" he asked.

"I don't know," Morris replied.

"Well, don't you have any idea?" Bell asked with his tone of voice rising carefully for the television microphones.

"I'm not the Energy Minister of Saudia Arabia," Morris shot back, starting to lose his composure.

"Well, you are the Energy Director of this country," Bell said sarcastically. "Do you really think that the program you unveiled today without prior consultation with Congress will solve this energy situation?"

"Well, Senator, let's see how much these steps help before we decide whether anything else has to be done."

Bell began screaming, "We don't have time, boy. Time is running out. Before this latest OPEC announcement the economic indicators showed that our rate of unemployment was twenty percent because of the price of oil. The rate of inflation was thirty-five percent. Now the OPEC countries have announced massive new output restrictions and price increases which are effective in four weeks. We need cheap energy, and we need it now."

"That's not my fault," Morris replied. "I didn't create the problem. I just got here. You people have been sitting around talking for the last ten years."

General Thomas used the prerogatives of his office to obtain a videotape of Morris's appearance before the Stark Committee from one of the three television networks. That evening when he arrived home, he played the tape, projecting the image on the large screen that occupied a wall in his wood-paneled downstairs study.

Thomas listened carefully to each word, looking at Morris with admiration. Thomas enjoyed every minute of it. Good for Morris, Thomas thought. It's about time we had somebody who refused to take any crap from a Senate committee.

Thomas bitterly recalled his own appearances before hostile Congressional committees. In contrast to Morris, he ended up putting his foot in his mouth.

Suddenly the telephone rang. Thomas turned off the tape.

"It's Fred Stewart here," the voice at the other end said. "I'm sorry to be so late, General, but I've been with the President all day."

'That's quite all right," Thomas replied. "I was just sitting here watching Morris before Stark's Committee on the video-tape. He did a helluva good job."

"As far as the Chief is concerned, he did too good a job. He wanted to see Morris get knocked down a peg."

"What report do you have for me?" Thomas asked anxiously.

Stewart described yesterday's meeting with Morris at the White House.

"Then he struck out completely with Faisel," Thomas said, sounding relieved. Morris had almost persuaded Thomas that he might succeed with Faisel.

"Completely," Stewart said. "And the ball's now in his court to come back to the President with a recommendation."

When Thomas set down the telephone, he thought for a moment about paying a second call on Morris—before Morris reported back to the President on the seventh. No, better to let it alone. He decided that Morris had received his message loud and clear.

He'll come around, the General said to himself. He doesn't really have a choice.

Thomas walked downstairs to the kitchen. He scrambled a large pan of eggs, doused them with ketchup, and opened a can of Michelob. Then he turned on the television set. I shouldn't be fixing my own dinner at this point in my life, Thomas thought to himself.

# CHAPTER

# 7

ANNE AND MORRIS SAT IN GLOOMY SILENCE IN THE BACK OF
the limousine as it sped westward in Virginia along Route 50.
They passed through the towns of Middleburg, Upperville,
and Paris as they started climbing into the mountains near the
West Virginia border. Periodically they heard the ringing of
church bells, calling the faithful to the myriad of churches
that dotted the countryside.

Morris looked at the three large briefcases that were resting on the floor of the car next to the jump seats. Each one
was stuffed with papers—analyses, charts, and computer printouts. Today was a critical day for Morris. His goal was to
develop a definitive program for dealing with the oil crisis
in the quiet and serenity of a country estate that he and Anne
had rented for Sunday escape during the summer.

Anne was leaning back in the car with her eyes closed,
rubbing her forehead.

"Do you think that this *Mafia Woman* show is really dead?"
Morris asked.

"Absolutely," Anne said tersely. "Somebody just woke up
to the fact that the script never was worth a shit."

That means I'm unemployed again, Anne thought. I get to

sit around all day and wait for the privilege of an hour with George T. Morris—if I'm lucky.

The car stopped for a red light in a small town.

"Do you know the Iranian Ambassador in Washington—Ahmad Zadak?" Anne asked, trying to sound matter of fact.

"I've heard of him, but I don't know him."

"He wants to meet you."

They started moving again. Morris was puzzled.

"How do you know him?" Morris asked, sounding like a prosecutor during an interrogation.

"You don't have to cross-examine me. I'm just trying to be helpful. I met him at a party that Holt, the money man from the show, gave at Sardi's last week. He said he wants to meet you. Don't ask me why."

Morris was intrigued by Anne's words. He wondered why the Iranian wanted to meet with him. He rolled the thought around in his mind for a minute. Better not to seem too anxious, Morris decided.

"Put him on the guest list for one of our Saturday night parties," Morris said. "Not this week. Next week."

He'll be in the house well before then, Anne thought to herself as the car raced through the countryside.

When they arrived at the house, they played two sets of tennis. Each set followed their familiar script. Anne roared off to an early lead. She had grace and form. Her strokes were smooth and deep, moving Morris from corner to corner. He responded with jerky staccato strokes that produced no consistency.

But then midway through the set and trailing badly, some strange force took hold of Morris. A look of grim determination came on his face. Suddenly he was returning practically every ball that Anne hit. He was all over the court, running from side to side, going to the net and racing to the baseline, lobbing and slamming. He was perspiring heavily and breathing furiously, but he never slowed up. In the end he won 7 to 5 and 6 to 4.

Later in the morning Morris settled down at a large desk on the screened porch with a pot of coffee. He began busily studying the computer printouts that Janet Koch had delivered to his house late on Saturday.

Anne was lying on a red rubber raft at the edge of the pool. She was stretched out on her back, her nude body facing the sun. Her large brown nipples were erect and pointing to the sky. In the background the mountains of Virginia also faced skyward.

They remained in these positions for the next two hours, each one silently absorbed in his own world.

Then Anne walked over to the house and returned a few minutes later with a gin and tonic. Morris never even saw her leave or return. After taking a few sips of the drink she lay back on the raft, her face looking toward the sun. She rested the drink on her navel. The bottom of the cold glass felt good against the warmth of her skin.

Suddenly Anne sat up on the raft, picked up the gin and tonic, and called to Morris.

"Hey, George, forget about those papers for a while. Let's make love."

"Not now, Anne, I'm busy," he said without lifting his eyes from the printouts.

"That's what you always say."

"Give me about an hour."

"What are my choices? The stable boy isn't here on Sundays."

Morris was too absorbed in the computer printouts to hear her last comment. He kept turning the same pages again and again, reading and rereading the same words and symbols, and thinking to himself. Two words appeared over and over again on the printouts: "Acquire oil."

Morris thought back to his conversation with Faisel. The

Saudis were just doing what any good monopolist would do
to maximize profits. There was no use kidding about it. The
Saudis would gain economically from this cruel game. They
would end up with property and real estate in the United
States. They would be able to reorder international economic
affairs after the chaos died down. And they would be able to
prolong the length of time that their oil would last—and hence
their power—for many, many years.

Yes, the Saudi oil would last for a very long time. They
had much more than any other country. They were sitting
on 170 billion barrels.

Then Morris thought about the strange visit he had had
from General Thomas on Tuesday. He could see the General
leaning over the billiard table, the cue stick in his hand, the
four gold stars sparkling on his shirt. A very odd discussion,
he thought.

Suddenly the picture became clearer and clearer to Morris.
At once Morris understood what the computer was trying to
tell him with the words "Acquire oil." General Thomas was
right. There simply was no other way to avoid a terrible national disaster. The United States had to seize control of the
Saudi Arabian oil fields by military force. There was enough
oil in those fields to satisfy United States demands for a long
time.

The longer Morris thought of the idea the more he liked
it. It was precisely the type of bold, imaginative action that
had become his trademark in business.

It would be a throwback to the old days in American history
—expansion by military conquest. There was some precedent.
Our oil fields in Texas had belonged to the Mexican government before a group of Americans settled there and seized
the land by force. Now that Texas was drying up why not a
new military conquest to replace those old Texas fields?

Morris looked over the figures on United States consumption once again. It looked to him as if the Saudi takeover
would completely solve the problem. There would still have

to be a gradual shift away from the use of oil for energy and heating over the next five years in order to preserve this valuable natural resource for a longer period of time, but it could be done. The important point was that the Saudi seizure would completely solve the present threat to America's survival.

As Morris thought over the events of the past week it seemed strange to him that no one at the White House, no one in the Congress, and no one in the press had even suggested the possibility of a military takeover of the Saudi Arabian oil fields. Indeed, precisely the same thing had happened at the time of the 1973 embargo.

Morris tried to search his mind for an explanation. The United States had apparently abandoned the use of military force as a part of foreign policy even where its vital economic interests were at stake. But why? Why was the use of military force a no-no? Was it still the aftermath of Vietnam or what?

Morris could recall the arrogant smile that came on Faisel's face when he had told Morris that the United States had no bargaining chips left. Yes, Faisel was assuming that the United States would never employ military force to seize the oil fields and avert the July fourth oil program. He was wagering 170 billion barrels of oil that he was right.

Morris was excited. He had the answer. His blood began rushing through his body as it did whenever he launched a new business venture.

Then Morris took off all of his clothes. He gave a warlike shout, "Wake up, Anne, I'm coming!"

He raced over to the pool with a broad smile on his face. He slapped Anne playfully on her bare buttocks with the palm of his hand and dove into the sparkling blue water.

She screamed loudly and dove in after him, pursuing with long, smooth strokes. She caught him around the waist in the shallow end of the pool, and they embraced. He was still smiling broadly.

"What do you look so happy about?" she asked.

"It must be your body," he said.

They both laughed, knowing that he had discovered something in those computer printouts that he did not intend to share with her. This didn't disturb Anne. She was used to Morris being secretive in his business affairs. And anyhow she wasn't really interested in the little financial games that he played. Those could be his own private world.

Morris held her in his arms and stroked her breasts. Then they made love primitively in the shallow water of the pool. Morris was more passionate than he had been in months.

Even as he made love to Anne, Morris kept thinking about the flow of oil, all of that Saudi Arabian oil, 170 billion barrels of oil. He could visualize the Saudi Arabian desert crowded with oil wells, each one with an American flag on its top. They would gush forth inexpensive American oil for a very, very long time.

# CHAPTER

# 8

WHEN JANET KOCH ENTERED MORRIS'S OFFICE ON MONDAY morning, she found the Energy Czar even more intense and serious than usual. There were no morning greetings.

Morris explained to Janet the conclusion that he had reached on Sunday in short, terse sentences that were spoken in rapid succession like an automatic weapon. She listened quietly and impassively . . . not interrupting Morris and not questioning him.

"I want you to do a double-check verification on my conclusion," Morris said.

"Following the usual system?"

"Yes. Evaluate all other conceivable alternatives. I think you will conclude that the seizure of the Saudi oil fields is the only way to avoid national bankruptcy."

Morris paused for a moment. The words "national bankruptcy" stuck in his throat. For some, those words meant loss of jobs, loss of income and shelter, even starvation and death. But Morris came from the world of finance. For him they conjured up a different parade of horribles—the United States government unable to pay interest on Treasury bills, bonds, and notes; no social security checks going out into the mail; and no more salary checks for government employees. Those unique green checks in lunchbag-brown envelopes that the United States government puts into the mail in massive quantities at the beginning of each month would cease.

Then Morris continued. "I just want to be sure of my conclusion."

"When do you want it?"

"By one o'clock. Bring your results and join me here for lunch."

"You'll have it then, Mr. Morris."

When Janet departed, Morris went over to the intercom and pushed three times.

"Yes, Mr. Morris," Helen said.

"Has the coffeepot broken this morning?"

"I'm sorry, sir. I forgot. I'll bring you a cup right now."

This was just an example of the inefficiency of government, Morris thought. It's just impossible to train career government people to follow efficient, orderly work habits. Maybe the military succeeded, but the civilian branches were a dismal failure. Private businesses would all fold if they operated with the government's efficiency.

Morris spent the remainder of the morning reading books about the seizure of the Suez Canal by England and France in 1956. The plans for the Saudi takeover would have to be left to the military people, he knew. But still he wanted more background before his meeting with the President. It was important to be thoroughly prepared.

Morris had been in the Middle East twice—both times in Iran. His only two dealings with the Saudis had involved financings that his investment banking firm had handled. He had reached two conclusions about doing business with the Saudis. It was necessary to bribe every member of the royal family in sight; and there couldn't be any Jews involved in the transaction.

At precisely one o'clock, Janet returned to Morris's office. Her arms were loaded with computer printouts. They sat down to the usual Spartan lunch that Morris ate at his conference table—a scoop of cottage cheese over lettuce, three Rye Krisps, a half a grapefruit, and a cup of black coffee. As one of the secretaries placed the coffee on the table and closed the door, Janet got a sudden craving for a good cheeseburger, some french fries, and a chocolate milkshake. But she had never been consulted about her order. When you had lunch with Morris, you ate what he ate.

For the next hour Morris interrogated Janet about each of the computer analyses she had run. He would have been a great trial lawyer, Janet thought. He's analytical and thorough. No possibility was left open. Each alternative was examined with dogged persistence. He considered an immediate conversion to solar energy. They talked about electric cars constructed with government financing. They even talked about a temporary move of millions of Americans from the northeast to Arizona.

They went into the study and spread the computer printouts out on the billiard table. They talked a strange, foreign language—the language of the computer with symbols and terms. When one spoke, the other listened carefully, waiting until he was done before speaking. They were like two parts of a machine, finely honed and functioning in harmony.

At precisely two o'clock, Morris said to Janet, "I'm satisfied. There is no alternative to the takeover of the Saudi oil fields."

She gathered up her papers. There would be no words of praise. No thank you. Only the satisfaction of knowing that she had survived the grueling mental test.

When Janet left the office, she decided to walk to L'Enfant Plaza. She wanted that cheeseburger with the french fries and the chocolate milkshake. She needed a break.

But not Morris.

"Get Green in here!" he shouted to Miss Forrest.

When the Assistant Director walked into the office, he found Morris looking sharp and alert.

"I'm going to tell you my conclusion," Morris said, "because I don't want you undermining me at the White House and on the Hill. If you have some objections, raise them to my face."

As Morris explained his proposal for the takeover of the Saudi oil fields, he knew very well what Green's initial reaction would be. He was right.

"It's the most ludicrous idea I've ever heard," Green said.

"Don't give me conclusions. Give me reasons," Morris demanded.

"The President will never approve it."

"That's my problem. I'll take on that responsibility. That's not a reason."

"Because the United States doesn't throw around its military muscle with small nations anymore. Those days are gone."

"That's right. We just let them push us around economically."

"If we ever did anything like this again, every Third World country would despise us for decades. It's brutal colonialism all over again," Green said, raising his voice.

Morris was enjoying this discussion. He had anticipated the objections that Green would raise. He could have written a script for the conversation.

"Oh, bullshit," Morris said. "Every African, Asian, and Latin American country is stuck in hopeless poverty. Why? Because of the price of oil."

"What difference will it make to those countries if we take over the oil. They'll still get screwed."

"Wrong. We'll roll back the prices to cost—to $2.50 a barrel. We don't need the profits. We gain from the overall stimulation in world trade."

"At $2.50 a barrel, that oil will be gone in twenty years."

"Wrong. We're far and away the biggest consumers. We can get away from imported oil in five years. That was established by the comprehensive energy plan that the computer prepared before Faisel's announcement."

They continued their debate into the afternoon. Green had his instincts and his firmly held beliefs. But Morris had complete possession of the facts and the statistics. Morris knew that he would break Green sooner or later, and he was prepared to continue until he did. After all, Green was a man whose liberal philosophy was built on the base of logic and reason.

"What about the casualties that would occur in this type of operation?" Green asked. "What about the men who would die?"

"I don't think in those terms."

"No, you don't. You manipulate people to serve yourself."

"All leaders are that way," Morris said cynically. "Some are just better at it than others."

"I still don't think it's right. It's not moral," Green insisted.

"What's right? What's moral? Are riots in Italy right? Is it moral for Africans to starve because they can't afford fertilizer made from petroleum at $75 a barrel? Is it right that a shipload of art from the Louvre and the Uffizi go to pay for heating oil? Is it right that millions of Americans will be out of work, destitute, and maybe even freezing to death while some monarch executes his plan to take over our real estate?"

Finally, Green started to weaken. He slowly began to reevaluate the Morris proposal. Maybe it wasn't merely brutal colonialism rearing its head again. If the Saudi oil were distributed fairly and cheaply by the United States, it could be humane. It would be possible to alleviate suffering.

Green had learned his politics in the Kennedy era. Men had the ability to improve the world if they used imagination. Sometimes radical solutions were needed for radical problems. If the invasion were done quickly and efficiently, perhaps there would be no casualties.

"Why Saudi Arabia?" Green asked. "Why not Iran?"

"We tried it both ways on the computer. Saudi Arabia is better for three reasons. First, the oil reserves are significantly larger. Second, the Shah's defenses and military capabilities are much greater. Third, if we seize Saudi Arabian oil, the

Shah might behave rationally and cooperate in a new oil distribution program. If we do it the other way, God only knows what the Saudis will do. There's no rationality in Riyadh."

When Morris finished talking, Green looked at him with a strange mixture of admiration and disgust. Green admired Morris's thoroughness, his mastery of facts. But Morris was manipulating Green, and Green knew it. Morris was pushing him reluctantly toward a conclusion that Green disliked intensely. Yet Green was powerless to resist the arguments that Morris advanced.

In the end Green's instincts crumbled. His clear notions of morality became clouded. The computer had scored a victory.

"Okay. I've had enough," Green said reluctantly. "You can try to persuade the President. I won't oppose you. If you win him over, I'll go along. But I don't think you'll do it. He has internal political considerations to worry about."

"We'll see about that," Morris said confidently.

Green started to walk slowly from the room.

"There is one other thing," Morris said. "As a part of this operation we will have to evaluate how much damage the Saudis could do to their oil fields if they decided to blow them up before the invasion is completed. Also we need to know how long it would take to make repairs afterwards and who has the experience to do that work. I want you to prepare a study on these questions."

"Shouldn't I wait until you get the President's approval?"

Morris shot a furious look at Green.

"Get started now," Morris barked. "Time is of the essence. I'll get that approval. You don't have to worry about that."

Green left the office, walking slowly, looking gloomy and sullen.

"You look like you've been through a wringer," Helen Forrest said to Green as he walked past the secretary who guarded the approach to Morris's inner sanctum.

Meanwhile, the adrenaline was rushing fast in Morris's

body. He was anxious to move on to the next step.

"Call Walter Matthews for an appointment with the President," Morris barked to Miss Forrest on the intercom. "Tell him I want to see the President late this afternoon or this evening."

A moment later Helen was on the intercom. "I have Mr. Matthews on the line. He says your appointment is Wednesday at nine o'clock in the morning."

"Tell him it's important. I can't wait until Wednesday."

A few seconds later it was Helen again. "Mr. Matthews says it's quite impossible. The President's schedule is full. You can meet with Mr. Black if you want to."

"Oh, for Christ sake," Morris shouted. "I'll talk to Mr. Matthews myself."

"I'll connect you."

It's the old game of access to the king, Morris thought. They get their power from controlling access to his power.

"Mr. Matthews," Morris said, "this really is quite an important matter. I can't wait until Wednesday."

"Well, I'm sorry, Mr. Morris," Matthews said. "But his schedule is all committed. Late this afternoon he has a meeting on natural resources with the governors of five western states. Tonight there is the reception for the President of Peru. Tomorrow he flies to Utah to dedicate the Teton Dam and appear at a party fund raising. At eight-thirty on Wednesday morning he receives an award from the Girl Scouts. Also he has to . . ."

"That's enough," Morris said. "Let me talk to the President directly. I'll work it out with him."

"I'm afraid that's quite impossible now. He's already started his meeting with the western governors. I could connect you with Mr. Black. Maybe you could explain your problem to him."

Morris quickly evaluated his options. He did not want to expose the plan to Black before the President. If Black disapproved, Black might persuade the President before Morris ever had his meeting. On the other hand, if the President's initial reaction was favorable, Black would never raise his voice in opposition.

Morris could probably force an earlier meeting with the President by perseverance and stepping on Matthews. But he would end up alienating the whole White House staff. It was hardly worth it. The short delay didn't mean that much.

"Why don't we forget I called, Mr. Matthews," Morris said with resignation in his voice. "I'll be there at nine o'clock on Wednesday, right after the Girl Scouts. I wouldn't want to interfere with those important commitments."

When Green arrived at home, he found his two sons, Brad and Tommy, ages eight and six, dueling with skewers on the redwood deck of the Green's split-level house in Bethesda.

"Hey. That's enough, fellows. Cut it out!" Green shouted. "Somebody could lose an eye that way."

"He started it," came the cry from Brad.

"I don't care who started it. You stop it. Both of you. Where's your mother?"

"She's still at her office," Brad said.

Green looked at his watch. It was seven-thirty.

"Where's Maria?" he asked.

"She's inside watching television."

"Well, what did you guys have for dinner?"

"Nobody gave us no dinner," Tommy said.

Green walked in the house shouting to the Costa Rican housekeeper. "Maria, what's going on here?"

Maria emerged telling Green in Spanish that dinner for the boys was still cooking.

Green then went into his study muttering to himself. He was still troubled by his discussion with Morris. He put earphones on his head and walked over to the stereo. When he looked at his costly and cherished toy, Green was absolutely horrified. The arm of the turntable was twisted back and out of place. A recording of Beethoven's Sixth Symphony had a deep scratch.

Green shouted through the window: "Brad and Tommy get your little butts in here."

After five minutes of interrogation, Green established that both boys had played with his sacred stereo, which was absolutely forbidden. Red with rage, Green administered a hard spanking to both boys and sent them off to their rooms, screaming and crying.

Fifteen minutes later Felicia walked into the den. Without even greeting her husband, she abruptly turned off the stereo. Green took off the earphones.

"Well, well, my psychiatric wife is finally home," he said sarcastically.

"I want some explanation from you," Felicia said, staring squarely at Green.

"You want an explanation from me?"

"Yes, I do. We have a rule in this house against corporal punishment. It was not arrived at arbitrarily. It was based on my best professional judgment as an expert in this field. And you violated that rule."

"Listen here, Dr. Freud. Let's start with the conclusion that I was just relieving my own anxieties and aggressions. That way we can eliminate a half hour of bullshit and go have dinner."

Felicia stormed out of the room and slammed the door.

An hour later they sat down to dinner. Maria placed burnt Swiss steak on the table, cooked with a spicy Costa Rican sauce. Felicia and Walter sat in stone silence during dinner. Brad looked frightened and helpless. Tommy pulverized his meat by repeatedly smashing the spoon against the plate.

When the family dinner was over, Felicia picked up a book entitled *A Psychiatric Profile of the Stuart Kings* and she sat down to read in the Florida room overlooking the tennis court.

A few minutes later Green appeared in the doorway.

"What happened to the gentle sensitive man that I used to know?" she asked.

"He's still here. I guess."

"You have been an absolutely different person since Morris took over your agency."

"Maybe so," Green said.

He walked over to the bar.

"Do you want a drink?" he asked.

"Campari and soda," Felicia answered.

Green fixed two campari and sodas. He handed one to Felicia and sat down next to her on the sofa.

"Here's to cheap oil," he said sarcastically, raising his glass in a mock toast.

"Did anything special happen to you today? Or is it just the normal domination by Morris that's getting to you?"

"Nothing special," Green said, feeling guilty as he always did when he lied to Felicia. "No, nothing special."

Green was silent. He had stayed in government after all of his friends had gone into private practice. He had still believed that it was possible to improve society. But working with Morris confused him.

"I hate to see you like this," Felicia said. "You take Morris too seriously. You're heading for an ulcer or worse."

There was a long pause. "I'll give you some free professional advice," Felicia continued. "Just do what he asks without thinking about it. Morris won't be here long. Just ride it out."

"Maybe you're right," Green replied. "I'll try not to worry about him."

Felicia's probably right, Green thought to himself. The egomaniac won't be here long. I just hope to hell that he leaves before he destroys us all in a nuclear holocaust.

# CHAPTER

# 9

MORRIS APPEARED CALM AND RESERVED WHEN HE ARRIVED in his limousine at the White House on Wednesday morning. His face was frozen in a gothic look—impassive and unemotional. He was self-confident, certain of success.

He walked along the corridor to the Oval Office in evenly paced, deliberate steps. Other officials could be seen scurrying from room to room, their hair disheveled, their ties loose at the collars. But not Morris. His Hermès tie was firmly knotted, his thick, wavy hair neatly combed. That was Morris on the outside.

Deep down inside there was a great churning. His insides were trembling with excitement. The blood rushed through his body at a furious rate.

Morris was experiencing the vast power of the United States government. He had formulated a daring proposal to solve an apparently insoluble problem, and he was anxious to begin implementation. The President would embrace the idea immediately and even try to take credit for its conception, Morris thought.

People would know that the idea had originated with Morris. When it succeeded, and when American control in Saudi

Arabia was firmly established, Morris would become a national hero. His accomplishment would be memorialized on the covers of *Time* and *Newsweek*, and he would receive a ticker-tape parade in New York. Millions of Americans would hail Morris as the national saviour as they continued to ride in their automobiles and play their color television sets in air-conditioned homes. They would call him the boy wonder of the world.

When Morris arrived at the Oval Office, Henry Oliver greeted him.

"There will be a short delay," Oliver said. "He's still tied up with the Girl Scouts. No more than ten or fifteen minutes."

Morris looked out of the window. He could see the ceremony in the Rose Garden. Three girls in traditional scout garb were presenting a wooden plaque with a gold plate to the President. The sun reflected from the plaque. The girl holding it had a short skirt, terrible knock knees, and heavy table legs. Morris could hear no sounds through the closed windows. But a few minutes later he saw the clapping of hands, and he knew that the ceremony was drawing to an end.

"He'll see you now," Oliver said.

When Morris and Oliver entered the Oval Office, Black and Stewart were already seated at the conference table. Those guys must live here, Morris thought.

The President was in a jovial mood. He was waving around his plaque from the Girl Scouts.

"Morris," the President said, "I'm going to give you this plaque. And do you know what you can do with it?"

Morris remained silent.

"It's not what you think, Morris," the President continued. "You can take off the gold and burn the wood for energy. My Energy Czar."

Morris was still silent.

"You really should try to get a sense of humor," the President said. "You're just too damn serious for a young man."

Morris tried to force a smile. But only the tiniest parting of his lips occurred.

"Okay, Mr. Morris has come here for business," the President said. "Let's get started."

"You asked me to come up with a proposal to respond to the OPEC announcement, and I have one," Morris said.

"Well, before you get started, maybe I better turn on the recorders and tape your proposal. One of the girls can transcribe it later."

"I don't think that's a good idea," Morris said, thinking about the embarrassment that could come from a subsequent disclosure.

"Okay, we'll do it your way. Fred, take some notes," the President said to Stewart.

Morris then summarized the work which he had done since the OPEC announcement. He talked for nearly an hour in quiet measured tones without a single note. He discussed all of the computer analyses he had performed and each of the alternatives he had considered. He disclosed in a dramatic tone his conclusion that the United States should seize the Saudi oil fields by military force. Finally, he described the economic catastrophe which would occur in the United States if this action was not taken.

When Morris was finished, he sat down slowly. All eyes turned to the President. The ball had passed to the man who had the ultimate decision.

"I don't like it, Morris," the President said, shaking his head from side to side. "Not one bit."

"But why not?" Morris asked, with a pained look on his face.

"Because the world isn't what it used to be. We don't have that kind of power anymore. Not since Vietnam."

"What about the British and French capture of the Suez Canal in 1956?" Morris said. "They would still be in control if Dulles and Eisenhower hadn't self-righteously kicked them out."

"That was almost thirty years ago. Good God, man, the world has changed. Where did you ever get the illusion that we have that kind of power? Hell, the Russians would never tolerate it."

Then the President turned intensely serious.

"I'll tell you one thing, Morris," he said. "I'm not leading this country into any nuclear war. That's for damn sure. I've got my obligations to the people who elected me."

"I'm not worried about the Russians," Morris replied. "They're becoming larger importers of oil. We should be able to persuade them to accept our military takeover in return for oil at low prices in the future."

"Well, you may not be worried about the Russians, but I sure as hell am."

Then the President turned to Black.

"What do you think, Bill?"

"I agree with you, sir," Black said. "We sure don't want to end up in a war with the Russians over some oil."

By now Morris was starting to lose some of his patience.

"We're not talking about some oil," he said. "The survival of this country is at stake. Didn't anybody here understand what I was saying?"

"We understood okay," the President said. "You're just naïve in foreign policy. You don't know that we abandoned the use of war as a part of foreign policy after Vietnam. It's just not a feasible option."

Morris continued to argue with the President for the next half hour, but he got nowhere.

"It's simply out of the question," the President kept repeating over and over again.

"What do you think, Henry?" the President asked Oliver.

"I agree with you completely," Oliver said. "It's just too risky."

"What about you, Fred?" the President said, turning to Stewart.

Stewart hesitated for a moment.

The President shouted at him, "Good God, man, speak up."

"Well, I'm not sure that Morris's idea is that bad," Stewart said. "It just burns my ass thinking about the Saudis sitting on the biggest cash box in the history of the world."

"You're not telling me that I'm wrong, are you?" the President asked scornfully. "You're not telling me that I should accept this proposal of Morris's, are you?"

The President's tone was disdainful and derogatory. Stewart had heard it before. The President didn't like to be questioned by subordinates about decisions he had made. Once he made up his mind on something, he insisted on complete support from his staff.

Stewart had worked with Edwards a long time. He knew well that if you questioned the President's judgment, your own judgment and your motives were immediately suspect.

Stewart realized that there was no use picking up the banner for Morris. The President's mind was made up. He would only dig in stubbornly. Stewart's loyalty would be tarnished. He would be fired within a week. It had happened to other members of the White House staff. There was nothing to gain by that approach. He was miserable in his present position. But he didn't see any better alternatives—not yet, at least. Stewart yielded gracefully.

"No, I mean it is fine as a theoretical idea, but I agree that it's not practical."

"You had me worried for a minute, Fred," the President said. "I thought you were going over to Morris's side."

Then the President turned to Morris.

"There is just no way that I will accept your proposal," he said in an intensely serious tone. "And that is final."

Morris realized that he was facing a lost cause. He looked into the President's eyes. "Then, what do you think we should do, Mr. President?"

"Institute some measures to conserve oil," the President

replied. "Let's have some real conservation this time."

"With all due respect, sir, it's too late for that," Morris shouted angrily.

"Oh, I don't know about that. We'll somehow find a way to muddle through after July fourth. You have to believe in the American people, Morris. We have a lot of inner resources."

"I'm telling you one last time. Unless you accept my proposal, you will have an economic disaster on your hands on July fifth. We won't muddle through. And historians will end up calling Herbert Hoover a great president compared with Charles Edwards."

"Don't push me too far," the President said angrily. "Don't forget the respect that goes with this office."

Morris sat frustrated, silent and gloomy at the end of the table.

"You're just going to have to come up with something else," the President said. "I want you back here by the fourth with a new comprehensive energy program based on the oil that we'll have."

Morris walked out of the Oval Office sullen, dejected, and frustrated. He was dealing with an immovable object, and he knew it. Neither reason nor logic would prevail. His great plan to save the country would never get off the ground.

Morris despised failure more than anything in the world. Failure left Morris with a vaguely nauseous taste in his mouth. That taste was there now.

When Morris left the Oval Office, the President sat shaking his head as Black, Stewart, and Oliver gathered up their papers.

"That guy Morris surprised the hell out of me with his proposal," the President said. "What a half-assed idea. He just doesn't have any feel for the practicalities we operate under."

"Well, we wanted a high-powered businessman," Black

said. "Somebody who would manage our energy program like a business. That's what we got. Morris puts all the data in the computer and out comes the answer: go to war. So that's what he tells us."

The President started to laugh. "Yeh, that's what we got," he said. "The computer man."

"Let's face it," Oliver said, "Morris just doesn't have any experience in Washington. He's wet behind the ears."

"I hope that's all it is," the President said, looking very serious.

"What do you mean?" Oliver asked.

"I hope to hell he's not being influenced by our distinguished chairman of the Joint Chiefs—General Thomas. A lot of that nonsense that Morris was spouting today sounded very similar to arguments that General Thomas presented to me right here in this room after I took office. He scared the hell out of me until I realized that I was the Commander-in-Chief and Thomas was working for me."

Stewart was listening carefully to the President, absorbing each word. Oliver and Black were busily shuffling papers.

"I'm worried about Morris," the President said. "I need to know if Thomas is influencing him."

Then he turned to Stewart.

"Why don't you do a little quiet checking, Fred," he said. "If you find out that Thomas has appointed himself as a special consultant to the Director of Energy, let me know."

"I'll be happy to."

Then the President turned to Oliver.

"That poll you showed me this morning didn't make me too happy."

"I didn't think it would," Oliver replied.

"I better start making more public appearances. Get out in front of the people. That'll give them confidence. What's going on in town tonight?"

"I don't know," Oliver said.

"Go get a newspaper."

Oliver left the office and returned two minutes later carrying the morning *Tribune*.

"The Kennedy Center has the Philadelphia Philharmonic and the New York City Opera. There's an O'Neill at the National, and Arena has a revival of *The Great White Hope*," Oliver said.

"What about baseball?"

"Well, the Nationals are playing the Yankees at RFK."

"Let's do that, Henry. You and I will go out there."

As the President uttered these words, Oliver's face was completely deadpan, but his insides were boiling. Oh, Christ, he thought, Clarissa will just kill me. She has four couples coming to dinner. Two of them are her old colleagues from Radcliffe. She's been marinating that damn lamb for two days. I promised her it wouldn't happen again. Oh, shit! But what were his choices? This was the President of the United States.

"I'll notify the Secret Service, Mr. President," Oliver said. "I'll tell them we'll be going to the game this evening."

As soon as Stewart returned to his office, he checked the list of telephone numbers in his personal directory. He quickly found the number he was looking for: the private phone in General Thomas's office.

The call came as Thomas was talking with Miss Crosby, a slight lady with gray, thinning hair and a bony face. Miss Crosby was the oldest secretary in the office of the Joint Chiefs—dating back to the days of General Marshall, some said.

Thomas picked up the telephone, and put Stewart on hold while he finished his discussion with Miss Crosby.

"You're certain that such a plan was actually prepared in 1973?" Thomas said.

"Absolutely, General Thomas. I even found the file number. It's 73-42."

Thomas quickly jotted the number on a pad.

"Thank you very much for coming to see me," the General said. "It's people like you that keep this government running. I plan to recommend you for a special citation for thirty-five years of distinguished service."

Miss Crosby was flattered. She started to blush as she walked quickly to the door. Before she had a chance to open it, Thomas said, "I don't have to tell you how important it is to keep our discussion confidential."

"Oh, no, sir," she replied. "All of my office business is always treated confidential."

Then Thomas depressed the hold button, activating his call with Stewart.

"I'll give you a complete summary of the meeting at the White House," Stewart said as he began glancing over his notes.

As Stewart talked, Thomas remained silent, listening carefully, nodding his head periodically. He broke into a smile when he heard that Stewart had been given the task of investigating his involvement with Morris.

When Thomas set down the telephone, he walked out of his office carrying a brown leather briefcase. He rode down in the elevator to the basement of the building. Then he walked quickly toward a second elevator—marked with the sign "Restricted to approved personnel only."

Thomas took a key from his pocket to operate the second elevator. Then he descended still further into the bowels of the earth.

When the heavy metal doors opened, he walked down a long silent corridor, dimly lit with round lightbulbs hanging from the ceiling. His shiny black shoes tapped smartly on the gray stone floor.

General Thomas entered the file room adjacent to the war strategy theatre and glanced around—searching for the officer on duty. The room looked empty. As he looked down the long rows of metal shelves filled with red files, he spotted a

Second Lieutenant lounging in a chair, reading a book. James Bond, he thought.

"Are you supposed to be on duty, Lieutenant?" General Thomas shouted.

The Lieutenant took one terrified look at General Thomas. He quickly dropped the book and jumped to attention, saluting as he rose.

The Lieutenant stood at attention, his face bright red with embarrassment. I'll probably lose my rank, he thought. But how the hell was I supposed to know that General Thomas would be here himself? He's never been in this room before. He always sends Major Cox.

Thomas remained silent for several minutes, prolonging the Lieutenant's agony. He would be easier to deal with that way. Finally Thomas was satisfied.

"You realize, of course, that your orders require you to be alert and on duty at this desk at all times," Thomas bellowed.

"Yes, sir," the Lieutenant said weakly, waiting for the axe to fall.

Then Thomas suddenly changed to a sympathetic tone of voice.

"I'm prepared to overlook this breach of orders this one time, Lieutenant. I realize that very few people ever enter this room and that the duty becomes monotonous."

"Thank you, sir," the Lieutenant replied, sounding surprised.

"I want a file," Thomas said, handing the Lieutenant a slip of paper with the number 73-42.

As the Lieutenant searched for the file, General Thomas looked at the gray notebook sitting on the desk. The files in this room fell into two categories. There were those that could be taken from the room and the party taking them was required to sign the gray book indicating that he had the file. Then there were those top-secret files which were never to be taken from the room. Their use was restricted to the file room. General Thomas wasn't certain how File No. 73-42 was classified, but he had a good idea.

As the Lieutenant handed Thomas a red file folder, the General's eyes immediately saw the white sticker on top: "War contingency file No. 73-42. Top Secret. Do not take from Pentagon war strategy file room."

"I'm taking this file upstairs to my office," Thomas said emphatically. He waited to hear if the Lieutenant dared to mention the violation of orders that this involved.

The Lieutenant, still intimidated, only managed a weak "Yes, sir."

"And it is imperative that my visit to this room not be disclosed. Is that clear?"

"Yes, sir."

Thomas placed the folder in his briefcase and returned to his office.

"Any calls for me?" he anxiously asked the secretary as he passed through the reception area.

"No, General Thomas."

He walked into his office and locked the door. As Thomas sat down at his desk, he looked at the beige telephone. It would ring before long, Thomas was certain of that.

With great care, he pulled the discolored papers from the red file folder that was stamped 73-42. This file contained the contingency military plans for an invasion of Saudi Arabia which had been prepared in 1973 at the time of the oil embargo. The Pentagon regularly prepares military contingency plans for a whole host of possible military actions. But very few people knew about the existence of File No. 73-42.

After the 1973 embargo ended, no one in the Pentagon gave any further thought to an invasion of Saudi Arabia, and the plans had never been updated. Thomas had been stationed in Frankfurt in 1973. He only learned about the existence of File No. 73–42 that morning when Miss Crosby called it to his attention.

Thomas spread out the large maps and diagrams on the desk. The plans were precise and fully developed. They called for an invasion by sea and by air from the Persian Gulf. The diagrams even identified the ships which would be involved in the invasion and their average travel time to Ras Tannurah, the key oil port in Saudi Arabia. The plans could have been implemented on twelve hours' notice. How close had the United States come to that action, Thomas wondered. Had Kissinger killed the idea or Nixon?

The plans didn't show any Saudi Arabian ground-to-air missile systems. That was consistent with 1973 realities. In the ten years since, the Saudis had installed extensive batteries of Hawks and other American ground-to-air missiles—all pointing eastward toward the Persian Gulf. Those would have to be taken into account, Thomas thought. American technology had so thoroughly perfected these missile systems that they were automatically activated, armed, and fired. No human participation was involved. General Thomas smiled to himself. Even the Saudis could operate these missiles.

Thomas finished a careful review of the file, making notes on a yellow legal pad in a shorthand with strange symbols resembling planes and ships. Then he put the papers back into the folder, just as carefully as he had taken them out.

When Morris returned to his office from the meeting at the White House, he was silent and pensive. He walked over to the window and looked out at Independence Avenue below. Across the street there was an eight-story square building occupied by the Department of the Army, which had outgrown its space in the Pentagon. The building was known as Pentagon Annex A. Armed guards marched along the sidewalk in front of the somber gray building. The guards were neat and trim, the rifles on their shoulders glistened in the morning sun. They marched back and forth suggesting a military presence in an area of town so strongly dominated by civilians.

Morris walked back to his desk. He sat there alone for

the next twenty minutes—thinking and sipping coffee.

Suddenly Morris pressed the intercom.

"Miss Forrest, get me Green. Right away."

When Green entered the office, he found Morris sitting at his desk with a cold gaze lacking any human emotion.

"Well, you were right," Morris said to Green. "The President turned down my idea of a military seizure of the Saudi oil fields."

Thank God for that, Green thought.

"I'm sorry for you," Green said to Morris. "What do we do now?"

"Oh, in the words of our leader, we'll muddle through somehow."

"Is there anything that I can do to help?"

"Yes, there is one thing," Morris said, sounding dejected. "I want you to complete that study evaluating the damage that the Saudis could do if they blew up their own oil fields and the work that would be involved in repairing the damage."

"I'll be happy to complete it," Green said. "But with all due respect, sir, I don't see the point of it in view of the President's decision. It would just be a useless report."

"That's not my decision. President Edwards wants the study made. He feels that the OPEC announcement has converted the whole Middle East into a fairly volatile political situation. There's a chance that the Soviets might initiate some type of military action involving Saudi Arabia. If that happened and the Saudis blew up their own oil fields, you know who would be given the job of cleaning up the mess."

Green looked puzzled. He didn't expect such thorough planning by Edwards.

Morris immediately sensed Green's doubts.

"It wasn't Edwards' idea," Morris said, still sounding dejected. "It was Black, the great Soviet expert, who claims that we better have this base covered."

Green started to smile. He wasn't surprised that Black had suggested that idea. He knew that Black viewed the Soviets as always poised and prepared to move into any political vacuum that developed in the world.

Morris could tell that Green bought his story. He decided to push one step further.

"That Black certainly believes in his pet theories," Morris continued. "It wouldn't surprise me if we put some American military units on alert just as a precaution in the event of Soviet military action."

Helen Forrest entered carrying two cups of coffee. She placed one in front of Morris and the other in front of Green.

When she left, Green asked Morris, "When do you want this report on the blowup of the Saudi oil fields?"

"Well, it's not a priority item. Finish it in about ten days. Bring it out to my house a week from Saturday in the morning. We'll have a seven o'clock breakfast meeting. That's about all that this project deserves."

"I agree with that," Green said.

As Green started to leave the office, Morris stopped him.

"There is one other question I wanted to ask you. What do you know about Frederick Stewart?"

"The President's counselor?"

"Yes."

Green hesitated.

"A lot of people thought he would have a Cabinet post when Edwards was elected. He's been with the President a long time. I don't know any more than that."

"Okay, Green, that's all I need now," Morris said, dismissing his assistant.

Morris sat alone sipping coffee and thinking. He took a pad of paper from his desk and doodled some numbers. After a few minutes he crumpled the paper into a ball and threw it into the wastebasket.

Then Morris began looking in the government telephone directory. He picked up his telephone and dialed, 545-6700, the number of the staff of the Joint Chiefs at the Pentagon.

"General Alvin Thomas, please," Morris said decisively to the switchboard operator.

After passing through two secretaries, Morris finally heard a voice say, "General Thomas, here."

"General Thomas, this is George Morris, over at the Department of Energy."

Thomas wasn't at all surprised. This was the call he had been waiting for.

"What can I do for you, Morris?" General Thomas asked.

"It's something we had better discuss in person. Can you meet me tomorrow morning?"

"Yes, of course," Thomas said. "What time?"

"Let's meet in the dining room at the Metropolitan Club at six-thirty. It should be deserted then."

"That's okay with me," Thomas said, realizing that his morning squash match had just been preempted.

"There is just one other thing," Morris said. "I would appreciate it if you kept our meeting confidential."

"Certainly," Thomas replied. "I'll see you then."

Thomas placed the receiver down gently. He walked over to the large bay windows in his office. He watched two small navy craft cutting a path in the still waters of the Tidal Basin. Morris was moving precisely as Thomas thought he would. The General saw everything falling into place.

# CHAPTER

# 10

THE RAIN FELL HEAVILY WEDNESDAY EVENING. IT WASN'T A normal spring shower. It was a torrential storm accompanied by high winds that uprooted the trees in Rock Creek Park and sent them swirling furiously toward the Potomac. Behind the rains came a heavy mist that blanketed the Washington area. By daybreak Georgetown resembled London—the London of Sherlock Holmes.

Morris rode quietly in the back of his limousine as the car smoothly cut a path through the fog. When he arrived at the Metropolitan Club, it was precisely six-thirty. A black Lincoln Continental limousine was already parked on H Street in front of the building. The license plate was "DOD-JC."

Morris paused for a moment on the steps of the Club. He could detect only the faintest traces of Lafayette Park on his left. Normally, Morris would have a clear view of the White House behind the park, but this morning it was not visible, having completely disappeared in the morning fog.

As Morris climbed the wide wooden staircase in the center hall, he could feel the sense of history bearing down. This four-story red brick structure with the large wide windows had probably heard more conversations of significance to American politics than any other building in Washington except perhaps the White House and Capitol.

This morning it was deserted except for a solitary figure in a military uniform who stood at the window peering into the fog. As Morris approached the figure from the rear, he could tell that it was General Thomas.

The two men exchanged a short greeting. Then Morris pointed to a table in the corner which had a pot of coffee on a burner, two cups, and a plate of croissants—just as Morris had ordered. Morris poured two cups of coffee, placing one in front of General Thomas.

"I want you to know, General, that I reached the same conclusion as you. I, too, concluded that our only practical alternative is a military seizure of the Saudi oil fields. I recommended that approach to the President yesterday. In the strongest possible terms. It was rejected—completely and out of hand."

"Will you make another effort to convince the President?" Thomas asked, without acknowledging that he knew about the results of the White House meeting.

"There's no point to that. He's made up his mind. He won't change."

Thomas waited patiently. He wanted Morris to open the subject.

"At any rate I didn't call you down here to rehash the futility of yesterday's exercise," Morris said, slowly sipping hot coffee.

"Why then?"

"Are you listening carefully?"

"As carefully as I can at this hour of the morning."

There was a long pause. Outside the window the curtain of fog was lifting slowly. A waiter replaced some silverware at the other end of the dining room.

"Very well," Morris said, hesitating for a moment. "I want to proceed with the plan to seize the Saudi oil fields by military force. I am prepared to do it without the President. I will organize it with your assistance."

Morris was looking at Thomas. His cobalt blue eyes were staring into Thomas's eyes. He sat that way for a moment like a professional in a poker game, trying to look into the General's mind through his eyes.

"I want to know whether you'll join me in this operation," Morris said slowly.

Thomas never even hesitated.

"I'll join you," Thomas said emphatically.

He desperately wanted that one final chance to operate his big war machine.

Morris was relieved.

"There is one ground rule," Morris said. "You will be the General directing military activity in the field, but I will be in charge of the overall operation. I will be the Commander-in-Chief. Is that acceptable to you?"

Thomas sat quietly for a moment thinking about the question.

"That is acceptable to me. I would treat you with the same authority as I have every President that I have served under until Edwards took over the White House."

Morris was pleased with that answer.

"What do you intend to do about the President?" General Thomas asked.

"I am not proposing a coup d'etat," Morris said, "only a small military operation. We will not assassinate the President or anything like that. We will simply keep all of the information about the attack concealed from the President until it's over. We will organize and execute it without him ever finding out."

Thomas looked a little disappointed. He would have preferred to dispose of Edwards once and for all.

"But he will find out once the invasion takes place," Thomas said, sounding puzzled.

"Of course. But my assumption is that if we pull it off efficiently and quickly, by the time the President finds out, the American military will be in control of the Saudi oil fields. What can he do then? The country will be euphoric with the successful military action. You and I will be national heroes. He'll have to accept the fait accompli. He'll even try to take full credit."

Morris paused for a moment. Then he continued.

"Anyhow, I don't think that President Edwards would ever admit publicly that he didn't know this operation was being planned. Remember, I'm not suggesting a revolution—only a small military operation."

As Morris finished speaking, Thomas thought about his words. The more General Thomas thought about the idea, the better he liked it. It offered considerable advantages over the classic Latin American coup that Thomas had envisioned. Yes, the idea was very clever, even ingenious, he conceded.

"Let's turn to the operational questions," Morris said, anxious to move along. "Are you in a position to tell me if it's feasible from a military standpoint to seize the Saudi oil fields within a short period of time—a matter of hours or one day at most?"

"That's a difficult question," Thomas replied. He hadn't been thinking about such a short time period. "You should know that the Pentagon prepared plans for a military takeover of the Saudi oil fields in 1973."

Morris interrupted, "Are you serious?"

"Absolutely. The Pentagon is always preparing contingency plans for different types of operations. We may even have been pretty close to moving on this one. I don't know if Kissinger or Nixon killed it. But the point is that I'm not satisfied with those plans. They don't take into account recent Saudi missile installations."

"You told me in our earlier meeting that the Saudis couldn't operate the hardware."

"We were talking about planes. We've developed these missiles so that they operate themselves by computer."

"The RX-1500?"

"Yes."

"I tried to get the contract to develop that computer when I was still in business," Morris grumbled. "But Global American got it."

Morris thought about Mr. Barton with his white hair, shaking his finger when they settled on forty million dollars in cash. Morris remembered that Global American had extensive economic investments in Saudi Arabia.

"I want to make a thorough investigation of the feasibility of the operation from a military standpoint," Thomas continued, "including estimates of casualties before I answer your question definitely. I want to make that study myself. I don't want to be responsible for another Bay of Pigs. I also want to make an evaluation of the strength that the Soviets have in the area—nuclear and conventional. We have to consider very carefully what response the Soviets are likely to make. We also have to consider how the Shah might react. We've managed to arm him to the teeth."

"My analyses tell me that the Soviets will be oil importers in the near future," Morris said. "They might not be unhappy with an American takcover if we promise reasonable prices."

"I have also seen reports from Anderson at the CIA that the Soviets will soon be oil importers," Thomas said, "but I don't think that you can quickly jump to the conclusion that they wouldn't intervene. That question has to be carefully considered. And regardless of what we think they will do, with the Soviets you always have to be prepared for the unlikely. So in any event we will need back-up forces to offset Soviet strength in the area."

"How long will you need to complete your feasibility study?" Morris asked.

"It's the eighth today. I need about ten days. A little

more to be safe. Let's say I'll be done by June twenty-first. If you absolutely need it sooner, I can have it. But it won't be as thorough."

"No, take the time. A precise, efficient operation is essential. It must be substantially completed before the President finds out. The twenty-first is okay. The OPEC policy doesn't become effective until July fourth. My most recent estimates show a complete ten-day supply of oil reserves at present rates of consumption. That gives us until the fourteenth."

Morris stood up to stretch his legs. He looked out of the window. The fog was lifting. The sun was struggling mightily to break through the clouds. When he sat down, he started talking again.

"There is one other thing," Morris said. "We have to evaluate how much damage the Saudis could do to their oil fields if they decided to blow them up before the invasion was completed. We also need to know how long it would take to make the repairs. I'm having these issues evaluated by my assistant at the Department of Energy."

Thomas looked concerned.

"I've heard of your assistant, Green. He's close with Stark. Isn't there a possibility of a leak?"

"Don't worry about Green," Morris said. "I've already given him a cover story. He has no idea that we're going ahead with the operation."

Morris then explained to Thomas what he had told Green about the President's concern with a possible Soviet action.

Thomas smiled. That's pretty good, he thought. He might even be able to use that story himself.

"Also have him find out which people have the expertise to make prompt repairs," Thomas said. "If they're in Texas, as I suspect, I can have military aircraft standing by to fly them to the area once the attack is launched."

"That's already being done," Morris said, nodding his head.

Thomas was impressed with Morris's thoroughness.

"Now we come to the key question," Morris said. "How

do we keep any information about the operation from getting to the President until after the invasion has taken place?"

A waiter walked toward the table carrying a pitcher of hot coffee. Morris picked up his hand, motioning to Thomas to halt the discussion until the waiter was gone.

Thomas was thinking about Morris's question.

"To do that," Thomas said slowly, "we need two other people with us, Stewart at the White House and Bill Elliott, the Secretary of Defense."

Morris grunted when he heard Elliott's name.

"Why those two?" he asked.

"Elliott and I provide the President with all of his information about military developments and activities of the Pentagon. Unless there's something in the newspapers or on television, he only gets what we tell him. I'm sure of that. No one else from the military has access to the President, and he never makes inquiries on his own. Stewart is critical because he's with the President during every waking hour of Edwards' life except when he's screwing his wife—and maybe even then. Stewart could head off anything that looked suspicious. It would be like putting a blanket around the President."

"Will the military people follow your orders without receiving confirmation from the President?" Morris asked.

"Absolutely. I normally give all the orders for troop and equipment movement. That's my job as chairman of the Joint Chiefs. Everybody under me will just assume that I am following the President's orders."

Morris drained his cup and refilled it from the pot. The sun was starting to shine through the large glass window next to the table. Morris pulled the curtain.

"What about Anderson at the CIA?" Morris asked.

"We might have to bring Anderson into this at some future point. But I don't want to do it unless it's absolutely necessary. My theory was that we keep it to as few as possible."

"I agree with that," Morris added quickly.

"Also," Thomas continued, "Anderson is a hard one to figure. He may decide that he owes all of his loyalty to the President. We have to leave him out of it if we can. In the meantime, I intend to pick Anderson's brain about the Iranian military strength. I can do that unobtrusively.

"How do we get Stewart and Elliott on board?" Morris asked.

"I think we can get Stewart. He's bitter and resentful toward the President. He served Edwards like a slave for the last twenty years. He expected something big when Edwards was elected. Not another Special Assistant job. Something on his own. He would enjoy being disloyal. The greater the act of disloyalty, the more he would enjoy it."

Morris looked skeptical.

"Are you sure of that?"

"Absolutely," Thomas replied self-confidently. "I'm already getting reports on meetings that take place in the Oval Office."

"What about Elliott?" Morris asked. "How do we get him on board?"

"Let's talk to Stewart first. He may have some idea as to how we can get Elliott. They're both good party men."

"Then arrange a meeting with Stewart. The three of us. Right here, tomorrow morning at six-thirty."

Thomas nodded in agreement. He would arrange the meeting.

"You really think that we need Elliott?" Morris asked as they started to walk away from the table.

Morris was thinking about his conversation with Oliver after his trip to New York. As long as Elliott was sleeping with Francine Rush, Morris didn't like the idea of getting into a deal with the Secretary of Defense. The whole thing might end up in the *Tribune*.

"The answer is yes," Thomas said. "We need Elliott. He's in the middle—the one vital position that links the White House with the Pentagon. He receives information on everything the military is doing in the Pentagon's standard system of reporting, and he reports daily to the President. A few years ago we could have done it without the Secretary of Defense. But Edwards has established civilian control at the Pentagon."

"Then you're telling me that we have no choice. We have to include Elliott."

"I'm afraid that's true."

Morris continued to worry about Elliott after he and Thomas had left the Metropolitan Club.

Ahmad Zadak was walking slowly as he entered Faisel's suite at the Waldorf.

"You look nervous and worried, my friend," Faisel said, smiling slightly.

"I have come here at the Shah's personal instruction. The government of Iran is formally requesting that you as the chairman of OPEC convene a special meeting as promptly as possible."

"And the purpose of the meeting?"

"To reconsider OPEC's new price and production policy which is scheduled to take place on July fourth."

Faisel took a package of cigarettes from his pocket. He offered one to the Iranian, who declined. Faisel slowly lit a cigarette, considering his response.

"You are well aware," Faisel said, "that a written request signed by six members is required to convene a special meeting. Unless you can produce such a document, you will be required to wait for the next regular meeting which is scheduled for August first in Geneva."

Ahmad grimaced when he heard Faisel's response. Both men knew that Iran could not find five other members to join in the request.

"Are you certain that you wish to take that approach?" Ahmad asked.

"Absolutely," Faisel replied, ignoring the threatening tone that he had detected in the Iranian's voice.

# CHAPTER

# 11

STEWART ARRIVED AT THE METROPOLITAN CLUB WITH
Thomas. It was clear to Morris that Thomas had not briefed
Stewart on the purpose of the meeting. Morris poured three
cups of coffee and waited for Stewart to sit down.

"How would you like to do something on your own?"
Morris asked Stewart in a bland and unemotional tone.
"Something big? Of national importance. Something without
Edwards?"

Stewart was startled by Morris's words—but only for a
minute.

"I would like that very much," he replied. "Yes, indeed.
I would like that."

Morris then described the plan in detail, emphasizing that
a final decision would not be made until after General
Thomas completed his feasibility study.

"We need two things from you," Morris said. "First of
all, we need you to find some way to bring Elliott into this
operation."

"And the second?"

"If the operation goes forward, we need you to develop
and to execute a plan for isolating the President during the
critical hours at the beginning of the attack. It is essential to

prevent the President from obtaining any information until the invasion is substantially completed."

Small beads of perspiration formed on Stewart's forehead. He had struggled with his conscience during the past weeks when he started leaking information from the White House —first to Senator Wyatt and then to General Thomas. But he was getting such pleasure, actually orgiastic pleasure, that he couldn't stop himself. Or, more precisely, he didn't want to. It was his way of evening the score with Edwards. Since Edwards didn't let the genie out of the bottle, the genie would break the bottle. It was as simple as that.

But Morris was asking him for disloyalty of a different type. Something much more significant. . . . Still, Morris was also offering him a chance, a chance to do something on his own. He could become a national hero for something he did. He could get out from under the stifling hands of Charles Edwards. It was a difficult question. He just wasn't sure.

Morris drained his cup of coffee, watching Stewart wipe the perspiration from his forehead.

Besides all of that, Stewart thought, he would be acting in the national interest. Or would he be? Wasn't that just a rationalization? Wasn't that the ultimate bugaboo that was used to justify everything from interning Americans of Japanese descent during World War II to tear-gassing demonstrators during the war in Vietnam?

"This is serious business," Stewart said, nervously. "You're asking me to help you seize control of the military apparatus of the United States Government. You're asking me to engage in a criminal conspiracy."

Stewart suddenly started to smile. Morris was surprised. He had never seen Stewart smile before. But he wasn't smiling from joy. It was the smile of tension. The smile that appears on the faces of students in the middle of a long exam, on witnesses during a grueling cross-examination, and on war-weary soldiers as they enter battle for one more time. Sure Stewart wanted to join Morris. He was being strangled by

Edwards. Morris was offering him a chance to strike out on his own. And in doing so, to deal a mighty blow to Edwards. But he was also worried about the risks involved.

"I want to be damn sure before I do something that could put me in Allenwood."

"But you can't end up in prison," Morris said. "When the invasion succeeds, we'll all be national heroes."

"And if it doesn't succeed?"

"I never consider the possibility of failure," Morris said.

Stewart sat there for a moment, weighing the risks and benefits in his mind.

"Okay. You can count me in," Stewart said somberly. "It's too good to refuse."

Morris breathed a big sigh of relief.

"Let's talk about your two assignments," Morris said. "On the isolation of the President, I want you to develop a plan before June twenty-first. By that time General Thomas will have completed his feasibility study. We're going to meet on that date. I will call each of you the night before with the exact time and place. Is that clear?"

"Very clear," Stewart said.

"Now, about Elliott," Morris said, taking off his jacket and placing it over a nearby chair. "How can we bring Elliott into our little operation?"

Stewart thought about the question for a minute, tapping his finger on the table.

"There is a way," Stewart said. "He'll do it because he hates the President's guts. Ever since the convention. Edwards promised Elliott the Vice-Presidency. I was there. It was at the Drake Hotel in Chicago. They were drinking heavy, but the President was still sober. I'm sure of it. He knew that Elliott wanted the Vice-Presidency bad. Hell, Elliott had been hinting at it for weeks. Suddenly the President went over and put his arm around Elliott and said, 'Bill, if you can deliver Illinois, I'll give you the Vice-Presidency.' Jesus, when Elliott heard those words, he nearly went crazy. I thought he was going to pull the President's pants down and start licking his dick. He was so happy."

"Well, what happened?"

"Elliott delivered Illinois okay. Then right after the President got the nomination, he leaked Elliott's name as a trial balloon to see what reaction he'd get. Early the next morning the governors of six southern states showed up at his suite. 'Unless you take a southerner,' they told him, 'you're dead in November.' Well, the truth is he had never really made up his mind on Elliott anyhow. So he picked Clayton. There was a bloody scene when he told Elliott. He promised him any other job, and Elliott took Defense. But, in the last year, Elliott's started drinking more. He's paranoid. Thinks the President is trying to ease him out altogether."

"Four men and four different motivations," Thomas said.

Morris ignored Thomas's comment. It was the opening for a philosophical discussion, and Morris wasn't interested in that. Besides, Morris was still worried about Elliott. Nothing that Stewart had said alleviated his anxieties.

"I want to make it clear to you both," Morris said, "I'm only including Elliott because I have to. I'm scared to death of having him in."

"Why are you so worried about big Bill?" Stewart asked.

"Well, for one thing, he's sleeping with a reporter."

"Franny with the hot pants."

"You know about her?"

"Everybody knows about her. Besides being a great lay, she's one helluva good reporter. And a very intelligent girl."

"That's what worries me. I'm afraid she'll find out what's going on from Elliott."

"You don't have to worry about that," Stewart said. "Like I told you, he hates the President with a vengeance. It's his mission in life to 'get the bastard,' as he once said. He'll know that if we pull this off, it will make the President look like a fool. If he tells Francine, the *Tribune* publishes it, and the deal is off."

Morris still looked concerned.

"Okay. Set up a meeting with Elliott. We'll do it here Monday morning at six-thirty. Right here."

"Listen, George," Stewart said. "I'll grant you that Elliott is a lush; and right now he's going through a period when he's chasing his cock. But you can depend on him. Believe me. You can depend on him."

Friday was also an important day for William Elliott. The Secretary of Defense made up his mind after three martinis at lunch that he would accept Francine's invitation and move into her Watergate apartment. After twenty-seven years of marriage, he was ready to leave Anita. He was still a vibrant, active man. He needed someone young like Francine. Anita had dried up long ago. Hell, he was only going this way once.

Elliott waited until four o'clock when he knew that Anita would be playing golf at the Club. Then he drove to his Bethesda house and quickly packed two suitcases. It was better that way. He could avoid a scene.

Elliott left Anita a short note: "I moved out." No further explanation was required. After all, she was an intelligent woman. She must have known about his affair with Francine.

Then Elliott drove to the Watergate apartment to wait for Francine to return from Chicago.

He was sitting on the patio, sipping a martini and watching the sun set over the Potomac when she opened the door.

"I've decided to take you up on your invitation," Elliott said.

"What's that?"

"I've decided to move in."

Francine was startled for a minute. She had underestimated Elliott.

"You're a good man, Bill," Francine said, regaining her composure. "I'll open the champagne."

Francine was delighted. With Elliott in her apartment she

would be closer to the White House than any other reporter in Washington.

As they sipped champagne, Elliott said, "Let's celebrate and go to the Madison tomorrow evening."

She hesitated for a moment, thinking about what she had planned.

"I'm sorry, Bill. I can't do it tomorrow. I'm working."

"It's a Saturday evening."

"Potentially a big story. I would have never taken it if I had known you were moving in tonight."

"Okay. I'll go out to the Club myself tomorrow evening. We'll have our celebration on Sunday."

"It's a deal."

Francine suddenly remembered the card resting on her bedroom desk.

"Wait here, Bill," she said. "I'm going to slip into something comfortable."

She closed the bedroom door and looked at the card: "Anne Walton and George Morris request the pleasure of your company for cocktails and buffet on Saturday evening, June 10, at 9:30 P.M. at their home. Black tie required."

She carefully folded the card and placed it in the desk drawer. No, Francine wouldn't pass up this party for the world.

# CHAPTER

# 12

ELLIOTT FINISHED KNOTTING HIS TIE AND WALKED OVER TO the door of the apartment. Francine was standing there with one hand on the knob, waiting patiently for the signal to open the door. She was wearing a loose fitting white T-shirt and Levi's that she must have been poured into.

He put his arms around Francine, pressing the soft, round flab of his stomach against her body and rubbing the back of her leg. Those doctors are not such experts, Elliott thought. I'm in the prime of my life.

"I could still call the Congressman and tell him that I can't make dinner at the Club," Elliott said.

"They're looking forward to having you," Francine said, opening the door.

He kissed her once firmly on the lips and walked out of the apartment, glancing back as he walked down the long curved corridor to the elevator.

When he was out of sight, she closed the door quickly. Thank God he's finally gone, she thought.

Francine then took a long, long bath. She struggled with her hair at length, combing and brushing it one way and then another. She dressed slowly and carefully, wanting to look her very best. She had heard that there were always celebrities from New York and Los Angeles at the Morris parties.

She selected a striking bare-shoulder Givenchy original that Senator Walters had purchased for her on a trip they had taken to Paris two years earlier. She liked the dress because it accentuated each line in her body. Nothing was left to the imagination.

She tried it first without any underwear, looking at herself carefully in the mirror. This won't do, she thought. I want to look provocative, but not cheap. She compromised with a pair of tight-fitting Dior pantyhose. Much better, Francine thought.

When the cab arrived in front of Morris's large house on R Street, a doorman in tails and high gray hat opened the door for Francine. She walked slowly up the steps, passing through the open front door into a pink marble-floored entrance hall with a large hanging chandelier. Anne came forward to greet her, wearing a long Pucci dress.

"I'm so glad you could come, Miss Rush," she said. "I do hope you will enjoy yourself."

Francine cast her eyes around carefully with the discerning gaze of a journalist. Immediately in front of her was a grand winding staircase. On the right she saw a large formal sitting room with a thick Oriental carpet in the center. Small clusters of people were engaged in serious conversation—each one carefully balancing a champagne glass. She recognized Robert Redford talking intently to Morris.

On the left there was a large formal dining room with a table that seated twenty. As she began wandering through the dining room, a tuxedoed waiter carrying a tray which held a sterling silver champagne bucket approached.

"Champagne, ma'am?" he said. "Or would you like something else?"

"Champagne, please," she replied.

The waiter placed the tray on a side table and carefully removed the wine from the bucket. As he poured, Francine strained her neck to read the label. Dom Pérignon, of course, she noted. Undoubtedly a vintage year.

Francine wandered around the dining room table nearly breathless. There was a fish section with Iranian caviar, cold Maine lobster, and crabs rémoulade. A waiter in a white jacket stood shucking oysters. At the other end of the table another waiter was serving Beef Wellington. In the center were fresh fruits and vegetables that Francine had never seen in Washington markets.

She could hear the music from *West Side Story* coming from the back, and she followed the sound. In the center of the yard was a large kidney-shaped pool bathed in floodlights; to the right of the pool was another gigantic buffet table identical to the one inside.

To the left of the pool a group of eight musicians surrounding a Steinway baby grand piano played while some of the guests danced and others watched the man playing the piano. Elizabeth Taylor and John Warner were engrossed in conversation with Roger Eaton, the Democratic National Chairman. Francine recognized Charles Anderson, the head of the CIA, and Philip Hamm, the Chairman of the FTC.

For the next hour Francine wandered among the guests doing what she did well—eavesdropping. She moved frequently from group to group. Talking seldom, but listening carefully, she made notes in her mind that she would easily recall when she sat down at a typewriter later that evening. She heard Saul Bellow talk about the true state of morality in America, and Charles Anderson about the catastrophic consequences the OPEC oil policy would have for the United States.

She tried vainly to find Morris but he always seemed to elude her. She finally trapped him near the diving board.

"Why, Francine Rush," he said. "I hope you are finding enough stimulation here tonight."

"Indeed I am, George. Thank you for the invitation. I am curious, though, to know how you arrive at your guest list."

As he pondered her question, a waiter approached.

"There's a telephone call from Tokyo, Mr. Morris."

"You'll have to excuse me, Francine."

When Morris failed to return in five minutes, Francine headed toward the dining room. On her way she noticed a narrow wooden staircase that extended from the kitchen to the second floor. She removed her shoes and walked up the stairs softly.

Francine could hear Morris's voice on the telephone in his study on the R Street side of the house. There were no other sounds on the second floor. She glanced toward the back of the house. Francine saw a large room that looked like the master bedroom.

She tiptoed quietly toward that bedroom. When she was safely inside, she closed the door quietly and began looking around.

There were two closets. One was jammed with Anne's clothes. The other closet had at least twenty men's suits in various shades of dark blue and gray. She checked the labels —part Brooks Brothers and part Anderson & Sheppard in London.

In one corner Francine saw a large vanity table with at least two dozen jars of skin creams and lotions on top. She uses one helluva lot of crap on that million-dollar face, Francine thought.

Francine spotted a leather-top English antique desk in another corner of the room. She began opening the side drawers quickly. It was obviously Morris's desk. The papers in the drawers were his—letters, bank statements, stock certificates. She tried to open the center drawer but it was locked. Jesus, she thought. That must be where he keeps the goodies.

As Francine was wondering what to do about the locked drawer, she could hear Morris's voice from the other end of the hall. He was talking louder than normal, as people sometimes do on overseas calls.

"No, I don't know why the Saudi Arabian government is

applying economic pressure to the international interests of Morris Investment Company," Morris said.

There was a long pause. Then he said, "Listen, Armstrong, I've told you before I don't want you calling me in Washington with business questions. When I took this job, I severed completely with the company. Go talk to Barton. Global American is the parent now."

Francine removed a paper clip from one of the bonds in the side drawer. Then she twisted the clip into a small piece of wire. Leaning over the desk and thrusting her large round buttocks toward the door, she inserted one end of the paper clip into the lock on the desk drawer. She twisted and twisted. Suddenly the lock snapped, and Francine pulled out the drawer carefully.

Just as she was about to survey the promised land, she heard Morris's voice in the doorway to the bedroom.

"Why you little bitch," he said calmly, "I should call the police. I could have you locked up for this."

At first Francine looked embarrassed. But she quickly recovered."

"What can I say?" Francine replied. "The people want to know what you're planning to do about the new OPEC policy."

"What did you take?"

"Nothing, I swear it. You can search me."

"Don't play games with me, Francine," Morris said abruptly.

He walked across the room and leaned over the desk drawer, trying to determine if anything was missing. Francine moved away from the desk. She was seated on the bed behind Morris.

"Do you believe in horoscopes?" Francine asked, chattering as if nothing had happened.

Morris ignored her question.

"I'm a Cancer," she said. "My horoscope said that I should be nice to a gentleman from the West. A long and happy relationship is promised."

Morris continued to ignore her.

She sat quietly for a couple of minutes, gazing at the back of this man who was so intent on preserving his secrets. What was he hiding, she wondered. Then she moved up behind him, quickly and silently, clasping her arms firmly around his waist and thrusting her breasts into his back.

Morris rose sharply, pulling away from her.

"I'm not interested, Francine," he said in a matter-of-fact tone. "You just don't turn me on."

"Why don't you give it a try?"

"You've got five seconds to get the hell out of this house, or I'll call the police."

"You wouldn't dare. You wouldn't want to read about us in the *Tribune* tomorrow morning. I can see the headline now: 'Energy Czar attacks female reporter and then calls police when she refuses to submit.' "

Morris was silent.

"No, lover boy," she said. "You're not calling any police. I'm going down to enjoy the rest of your party."

Then she walked quietly from the room. As she left, she said, "Oh, you don't have to worry about locking your bedroom door. I won't be back up here. There's nothing here for me."

Francine didn't mean that. She was still determined to find some way of reaching Morris. He was a tough nut to crack; but that only whetted her appetite.

When she left, Morris continued his inventory of the desk. All of the computer printouts that said "acquire oil" were still intact. He also found the notes that he had made after his meetings with General Thomas.

Morris locked the desk drawer. She might come back, he thought. He would have armed guards stationed at the house twenty-four hours a day.

# CHAPTER

# 13.

WHEN ELLIOTT ARRIVED AT THE METROPOLITAN CLUB ON Monday morning Stewart was waiting at the top of the circular center staircase. They shook hands, and Stewart led the way through the deserted lounge to the dining room. Elliott was startled to see Morris sitting at a table, his cold, stone face staring straight ahead.

"What's he doing here?" Elliott asked Stewart. "You didn't tell me that Morris was coming."

"You two know each other, I see," Stewart said.

"We've been to a number of receptions together," Elliott said coolly.

Morris poured three cups of coffee, handing one to Elliott.

"I usually like a Bloody Mary with breakfast," Elliott said.

Morris ignored his comment. But Elliott continued, "My granddaddy used to say, 'You can't trust a man who doesn't drink.' "

Stewart decided to take control of the discussion.

"Listen, Bill," Stewart said, "for the last two years you've been yelling into my ear that one day you're going to get that bastard in the White House for what he did to you at the convention."

"You bet your ass," Elliott said. "I'm just waiting for the right chance."

"Well, the right chance is here now. George Morris and I are thinking about a little governmental operation, and we need your help. George is going to explain it to you, and I want you to listen carefully."

Morris then described the plan in detail, carefully and precisely. At first he had been concerned about the disclosure to Elliott. What if Elliott didn't go along with the plan and then leaked their discussion? Morris quickly swept aside those thoughts. They hadn't taken any affirmative action. If Elliott didn't go along, that would be the end of the plan. If Elliott disclosed the conversation, Morris, Stewart, and Thomas would deny what Elliott said. The three of them had greater credibility than Elliott.

"Holy shit," Elliott said when Morris was finished. "That is some idea. If it worked, we would make the President look like a horse's ass. Sooner or later people on the inside in this town would know privately that we took the government away from him. And if he ever gave me any trouble again, I could threaten to go public. That's beautiful."

"Then you'll go along with us?" Stewart asked.

Elliott was hesitating. Perhaps his initial reaction was too fast.

"What if it doesn't succeed?"

"It will succeed," Stewart said. "Our buddy Morris here doesn't fail. That's why the President brought him to Washington to handle the energy program."

"What if I don't go along?"

"Then there's no plan," Morris said.

"I don't know," Elliott said slowly. "I just don't know. I'm no fool. I know damn well that if this doesn't work, we all end up in the pokey for criminal conspiracy. Look at the whole Nixon crowd."

"It will work," Morris said firmly.

Elliott just sat there staring into his cup. He was stunned

by the proposal. This whole idea was so different from anything he had ever done. He despised Edwards more than any other man alive. But he still respected the Constitution and that bastard Edwards happened to be the President.

Oh, sure, Elliott had bent the rules a little now and then, but he had never thrown out the whole damn book before. Besides all that, he was a loyal American. And Morris was asking him to commit treason. The whole idea seemed so bizarre.

Suddenly Stewart, sensing Elliott's doubts, interrupted his thoughts.

"I'll tell you one thing, Bill, if you want to get the President, you better not turn us down. This is probably your last chance. I'm hearing a lot of noise in the Oval Office these days that sounds like the Chief intends to sack you pretty damn soon. He calls it self-preservation. 'I'll run Elliott out of Washington,' he says, 'before old Bill does me any damage.' "

"Are you bullshitting me?" Elliott asked. He had never heard those reports before.

"I wish I were, old buddy. But he's made up his mind to boot you out. And I don't think he's going to wait too long."

As Stewart talked, Elliott's eyes started to sparkle. A fiery hatred burned deeply inside the man. He was like a torch. Stewart had control of the fuel. He was fanning the flames. Morris was watching with admiration.

"Okay, Fred, I get the picture," Elliott said. "I just need some time to think about it."

"I can give you the rest of the day," Morris said. "No more. Call me at home this evening. If the answer is yes, then just sit tight until the twenty-first. We'll meet again that day. I'll call you the night before with the time and place. If the answer is no, then we'll all forget about this meeting, and your friend Edwards will stay in control."

Morris rose from the table and started to leave. Suddenly he said to Elliott, "There is one other thing, Bill. I will be

very frank with you. If we go ahead, we need absolute
secrecy. It's well known that you're having an affair with a
reporter. That's your business. But some people tell me that
she vacuums your brain each night and publishes the results
in the *Tribune*."

Stewart started to smile.

"Just wait a minute, Morris," Elliott said. "The only thing
she gets from me is what I decide to give her. And I only
give her tips that will hurt the President. That's all. Anyhow,
I'm no fool. I know that if Francine found out, she would
publish it in the *Tribune*, and that would kill the plan and
ruin us as well. It would be a great victory for the man in
the White House. There's no way I would give her this information."

"Are you sure that you can handle her?" Morris asked.

"You're damn right. What do you know about Miss Rush?"

"Nothing. Nothing at all."

Elliott didn't believe Morris, but he didn't want to hear
one more story about Francine's promiscuous behavior.

When Morris left the room, he could hear Elliott calling
to the waiter. "I need a Bloody Mary, Pat. God, how I need a
Bloody Mary."

On Monday afternoon Anne lay back in bed watching
Ahmad gently stroke her body. She was amazed that he was
revived and active again. The man's sexual appetites were
nearly insatiable. After two hours with him this afternoon,
Anne was exhausted.

"When will I get to meet your friend, Morris?" Ahmad
asked.

"Call him at the office. He'll see you," Anne said glibly,
joking with Ahmad.

The Iranian didn't like that idea. He didn't want to request
a formal conference. His instructions were to meet Morris
informally, socially.

"That's too formal. I mean socially," Ahmad said, sounding just a little anxious. The days were moving along. He didn't have that much time left. He had to establish his contact with Morris, to complete the first phase. The Shah needed time to take over from there.

Anne leaned up and gently kissed Ahmad on the ear.

"We're having a party Saturday evening, the seventeenth. You're invited. You can bring that opera singer friend of yours, Maria something or other—the one with the big tits."

Anne laughed quietly to herself. She didn't care what other affairs Ahmad had. He was purely a source of amusement. She had no attachment to him at all.

By the time Ahmad left the house, it was already six-thirty. A half hour later Anne was stretched out at the pool, trying to regain her energy when Morris suddenly appeared. He didn't want to miss Elliott's call.

Anne gave Morris a puzzled look when he asked Louise to fix him a martini. He even seemed slightly nervous, she thought, for the first time since she had known him.

About nine o'clock the telephone rang in the living room. "I'll take it in my study," Morris announced. Then he raced upstairs before Anne could respond.

She looked for a moment at the white telephone sitting in the living room. She was tempted to pick it up and listen quietly. George would never find out. But she rejected that temptation. She just didn't want to know.

Morris, in the meantime, picked up the phone upstairs. "Morris here."

"George, it's Bill Elliott. The answer is yes. Count me in."

"Very good," Morris said, sounding relieved. "You won't be sorry."

# CHAPTER

# 14

FOR FORTY-EIGHT HOURS GENERAL THOMAS ASSEMBLED AND reviewed every bit of information that the Pentagon had about present Saudi Arabian military defenses. The longer he looked, the less he liked what he saw. The United States had installed a wall of missile batteries along the east coast of Saudi Arabia. These missiles pointed east toward the Persian Gulf and Iran.

The world's richest oil field, the Ghawar Oil Field, lay just to the west of those missile batteries. The oil centers of Dhahran and Ras Tannurah were in the heart of this electronic Maginot Line. Thomas found himself wondering why the United States hadn't erected a defensive barrier on its own east coast equivalent to that erected on the east coast of Saudi Arabia.

It would be suicidal to try to penetrate that barrier from the Persian Gulf with conventional planes and ships, Thomas thought. Newer American weapons could neutralize the missiles, but it would take time and some missiles would get through. There would be heavy casualties.

There had to be a better way, Thomas decided. But what was it? The General worked late into the evening, alone in the Pentagon war room moving metal models of planes and ships around a magnetic map of the world like chessmen. But the answer eluded him.

By Thursday morning Thomas was weary from a lack of sleep. His mind was exhausted from studying data on the offensive and defensive capabilities of various weapon systems.

"Tell my airplane crew at Andrews Air Force Base to stand by for an immediate departure," Thomas suddenly announced to his secretary. "I'm going overseas. I should be back in two days. My destination is set forth in a sealed brown envelope in my top desk drawer. It is to be opened only at the request of the President. Is that clear?"

"Yes, sir."

General Thomas invited no reporters or assistants to accompany him on his flight. He sat alone in the spacious cabin of the aircraft. As the plane flew over the Atlantic, General Thomas still studied his map and diagrams.

They refueled in the Azores, where it was a magnificent clear night. Then as the plane proceeded across the Mediterranean, General Thomas stretched out in one of the beds in the rear, catching a few hours of sleep. When the plane touched down at an Israeli Air Force Base in the Sinai, it was early morning. General Thomas bounced out of the plane into the magnificent clear air of the Middle East.

His arrival was greeted with no fanfare. The American embassy didn't even know that General Thomas was in the country.

Zal was waiting for Thomas—a solitary figure standing next to a small battered Volvo. He was a tall man with thick gray hair. Ruddy sun-beaten skin showed through the prickles on his face. He wore a loose-fitting dark green shirt open at the neck. A cigarette was dangling from his lips.

"It's good to see you again, Al," the Israeli said. His English was broken with a heavy foreign accent.

Mordechai Zal had used his English in earlier years when he had been military attaché at the Embassy in Washington.

But now he was a retired Israeli Air Force general engaged in farming on a kibbutz.

"Well, well, Matti," Thomas said. "You look well. I appreciate you coming out here to meet me on such short notice."

"How could I refuse?"

Thomas handed Zal two cartons of American cigarettes.

"Has the last year treated you well?" Thomas asked.

"Not bad for an old goat out to pasture."

Zal drove quickly over the flat desert roads. There were no other cars in sight. Thomas could see the chain of mountains in the central Sinai on the horizon. The hot sun seared the parched earth of the desert.

The windows of the car were open. Thomas took a deep breath of the dry air. He had grown up on army bases in West Texas and Arizona. He loved the familiar sight and smell of the desert.

Suddenly Zal stopped the car on the empty road.

"Why are we stopping?" Thomas asked.

"You wanted a quiet place to talk, and I found a small agricultural kibbutz not far from here. But if you show up in your four-star general outfit, the whole world will know you were here within twenty-four hours. Change into these clothes," Zal said, tossing a brown paper bag into Thomas's lap.

Thomas put on the loose-fitting dark green outfit and returned to the car.

"Now you look like an American tourist," Zal said, "who can't afford a city hotel. We get them all the time. If anyone asks, you're my cousin Al from Milwaukee."

"But I'm a good Episcopalian," Thomas said, smiling.

"Then you're my Episcopalian cousin from Milwaukee."

Thomas liked Zal because he was a first-rate professional soldier. They could speak a common language like two physicians or engineers from different countries. Zal's mind was always clear and sharp. It worked along military frequencies —the same as Thomas's. The respect was mutual, Thomas thought.

When they arrived at the kibbutz, Zal stopped at the dining room and picked up a pitcher of coffee and two cups. Then the Israeli led Thomas to a small hut at the edge of the settlement. He poured two cups of coffee and placed the pitcher on the table. Zal lit up another cigarette.

"Well, my friend, what can I tell you?" Zal asked.

"You were in the Air Force at the time of the 1956 Sinai war, weren't you?"

"Yes. I was flying in the first group of planes that dropped paratroops behind the Egyptian lines at the Mitla Pass."

"I want to ask you about that war," Thomas said. "I understand your operation. It was clean and simple, but what happened to the British and French?"

"Well, you have to go back to the beginning. When Nasser announced that he was expropriating the Suez Canal, there were riots in London and Paris. The papers said that this was equivalent to a declaration of economic war. Then the French initiated secret discussions with the British to plan an invasion to seize the canal by military force. Both countries decided to maintain absolute secrecy to keep the information from Dulles and Eisenhower. If the Americans found out, that would have been the end of it."

"How did you people get into it?"

"The French wanted us in. The British objected and threatened to pull out."

"A carryover from 1948?" Thomas asked.

"Exactly. Well, anyhow there was finally a meeting at a château near Paris." Zal paused for a minute. "I've forgotten the name. It's not important. Ben Gurion, Dayan, and Peres flew up in secret. No one knew till after the war that they had even gone. The French brought the British around. We were like brothers with the French in those days."

"What about the plans? What were they like?"

"Pure garbage. The French argued for a swift efficient operation using boats and planes in the area. There was no need for many troops. The Egyptians didn't even have an army. We agreed. But not those stubborn British. They insisted on an armada of ships sailing from England. As you might expect, it delayed the operation and killed any surprise. That was the key—speed and surprise. Eisenhower and Dulles found out even before they landed and seized the canal. Then Eisenhower imposed that humiliating withdrawal on the French and British."

"Suppose Eisenhower and Dulles had not found out until after it was all over?"

"A fait accompli?"

"Yes."

Zal hesitated for a moment, thinking about the question.

"The British and French might still be there. Who knows?" Zal said, shrugging his shoulders.

For the next hour Thomas and Zal discussed the details of the British and French operation—the number of planes and ships, the movement of infantry, the location of paratroop drops. Then they walked to the kibbutz dining room.

"You see those tomatoes and cucumbers?" Zal asked. "Grown right here in this desert."

"What do you use for water?"

"We truck it in from Beersheba each morning."

Thomas carefully filed that answer in his mind.

After lunch they returned to the hut with another pot of coffee. Zal opened a new package of cigarettes.

"Where did we leave off?" he asked Thomas.

"You've told me what I wanted to know about the 1956 war. Now I want to ask you a very hypothetical question, Matti."

"Ask."

"This is in the strictest confidence."

"Have I ever disclosed a single word you've told me over the years?" Zal said, sounding insulted.

"I'm sorry, Matti, I shouldn't have said that."

"Okay, ask."

"Suppose that you wanted to attack Saudi Arabia and seize the oil fields. How would you do it?"

Zal seemed stunned by the question He was quiet for a few minutes. Then he started talking, slowly, thinking while he spoke.

"First, I'll tell you how I would not do it."

"Go ahead."

"I would not attack with ships and planes from the Persian Gulf on the east. You've armed the Saudis to the teeth with missile batteries aimed at your friend the Shah. The casualties would be too great."

"Then how would you do it?"

Zal lit up another cigarette and began pacing around the room, making circles around the table, and blowing puffs of smoke into the air. Suddenly he stopped, took a pencil from his pocket and started drawing a map on the table.

"At least use paper," Thomas said.

Zal found paper in one of the drawers of a small chest. When he had drawn his map, he started talking.

"I would attack from the west from the southern part of the Sinai Peninsula. I would send one wave of planes due east to Dhahran and Ras Tannurah. They would come in behind the Saudi missile defenses. You built them in concrete. The Saudis can't turn them. I would send a second wave north and east. It would pick up the TAP line that carries oil to the Mediterranean. I would follow the TAP line to Ras Tannurah, dropping paratroops to seize control of each pumping station."

"How long would the whole operation take?"

"With your equipment," Zal said, closing his eyes to focus his thoughts, "with your equipment, if you were well organized, I would think six to eight hours."

"What about casualties?"

"Negligible," Zal said. "You've been in Saudi Arabia. You

know the shape of their army and air force. Efes. Zero."

"What about the Russians? What do they have in the Persian Gulf?"

"That I don't know precisely. We depend on you for that. We only monitor them in the eastern Mediterranean."

Zal picked up the paper on which he had been drawing maps. He tore it into tiny pieces and threw them out of the window. Then he stood for a moment watching the white specks flutter in the light desert breeze.

"Let me ask you one other question," Thomas said. "This one is more difficult."

"Ask."

"Would the government of Israel be willing to let the United States use a small area of the southern Sinai for the next couple of months as a temporary military base? As far as Israel would know, this land would be used solely for training exercises to simulate desert warfare. If the United States should ever initiate any military action from that base, it will be without the knowledge and participation of Israel."

Zal started to laugh loudly.

"What strikes you so funny?"

"For so many years, since 1967, your people have said 'Give all of the Sinai back to Egypt. Give it all back.' Now you're happy we held on to some of it."

"Would your government let us use that land temporarily?"

Zal's face became intensely serious. "I don't know the answer. I don't even have a feel for it. I would be happy to go to Jerusalem tonight and take it to the Prime Minister. I'll cable you as soon as I have an answer."

"Use the special military communications system between Israel and the United States," Thomas said. "The one reserved for top secret messages and send it in code."

"If the Prime Minister approves," Zal said, "the cable will read 'Beseder,' which means okay. If he disapproves, it will be 'Lo Beseder'—not okay."

"Just like the old days," Thomas said, smiling.

"There is just one thing that surprises me," Zal said. "I guess that I had President Edwards pegged all wrong. I thought that he would never have considered even the possibility of an operation like this."

Thomas decided to ignore Zal's comment.

"How will you get to Jerusalem?" Thomas asked.

Zal sat quietly gazing at Thomas for a moment. Then he said, "An air force helicopter from the base."

"Can I hitch a ride north with you," Thomas asked, "to see Chava?"

"How long do you want to stay?"

"Until tomorrow morning."

"The helicopter will drop you at her kibbutz. It will pick you up tomorrow morning at nine o'clock and take you back to your plane."

When they drove back to the air base, it was midafternoon and the sun's rays were brutal. Zal slowed the car as a small lizard crawled across the road.

"So you're still carrying the torch for Chava?" Zal said. "After twenty-five years?"

"Why not?"

"Trying to recapture your feelings when you were graduate students together?"

"Let's just say we're trying to sprinkle middle age with a couple of happy moments."

"Trying to imagine what could have been," Zal said, laughing softly.

They rode in silence, each man absorbed in his thoughts.

"When do they retire you?" Zal asked.

"Next year, June one."

"What will you do then?"

"Let me see what the world looks like."

"You really are planning to go out with a bang!"

"Better a bang than one more lost opportunity."

The next morning the blue and white helicopter with the

Star of David carried Thomas back to the Israeli air base in the Sinai. He had a broad smile on his face as he walked quickly up the stairs and into the airplane.

As the pilot started the engines, one of the members of the crew handed Thomas a small brown envelope. His expression became very serious as he opened the envelope, slowly pulling out a thin piece of white paper. There was a single word in the center of the page: "Beseder." At the bottom was the initial "Z."

Thomas smiled with satisfaction. "Let's head back to Washington," he shouted to the pilot.

He folded the note carefully and put it into his pocket. Then Thomas went into the back of the plane and collapsed into one of the large double beds. He was still sleeping soundly when they touched down at Andrews Air Force Base.

As General Thomas arrived back in Washington, Stewart was walking toward the Oval Office. He stopped to shake hands with Sir Alec Douglas, the British Ambassador, who was leaving the room.

"A boondoggle for you, Fred," the President said, as Stewart entered the office.

Then President Edwards fired the sheet of white paper with the gold-embossed border the full length of the conference table. It came to rest in front of Stewart.

"Her Majesty's Government respectfully invites the President of the United States to attend a July Fourth pageant at Buckingham Palace."

"Douglas was instructed to tell me that this is to be a big deal," the President said. "They want to prove to the world once and for all that bygones are bygones. I can't tell if they're serious or this is British humor."

"You're not going?"

"Damn right, I'm not. I'm looking forward to a quiet Fourth at Camp David. I told Douglas I'll send a representative."

"What about the Vice-President?"

"He made a fool out of himself at the NATO meeting in Brussels. I won't do that again."

Suddenly Stewart's mind began racing in high gear. He took a small black diary from his pocket. July fourth was a Tuesday.

"I'd be happy to go," Stewart said, trying hard to conceal any emotion in his voice. "But Bill's been working awfully hard on the new SALT pact. The strain is getting to him. A few days away might revitalize him."

The President thought about Stewart's words. Black did seem tense lately. Maybe the negotiations were taking their toll.

"A good idea, Fred," the President said. "I'll send Bill Let me talk to him myself."

Stewart returned to his own office and stood at the window for a minute watching the traffic on Constitution Avenue. He was replaying his conversation with the President over again in his mind. Had he been too obvious? He didn't think so . . . Maybe too subtle? Perhaps Edwards would never follow up, never talk to Black?

Stewart was nervous. He wasn't accustomed to this type of deception. He wasn't good at it. Maybe he had made a mistake going in with Morris. Somewhere he had once read, "If you shoot a king, you better shoot to kill." He couldn't remember who wrote that—maybe Shakespeare? He wasn't even sure what it meant.

Stewart took out a key from his pocket. He glanced nervously at the closed door to his office. Then he unlocked the bottom drawer in his desk, took out a bottle of scotch, and quickly poured a solid measure in the yellow coffee mug sitting on his desk.

He slowly sipped the scotch, screwing up his courage. When the cup was empty, he pulled a package of breath mints from his pocket and popped three into his mouth. He chewed them quickly and walked to Oliver's office at the end of the corridor.

"Have you made any summer plans?" Stewart asked Oliver.

"Jesus, don't bring that subject up. Clarissa has been nagging me for weeks about a camping trip in the Blue Ridge Mountains in Virginia. She's got a bug about this back-to-nature crap."

"You'd probably like to be sitting by a swimming pool somewhere."

"Yeh, I grew up on the east side of Manhattan. I consider Central Park the great outdoors."

They joked for a few minutes about the back-to-nature movement.

Then Oliver turned serious.

"I do hope that I can get away, Fred. This job is killing my marriage. If I have another summer like the last one, she'll lock me out. And I wouldn't blame her."

There was a long pause.

"Why don't you do this," Stewart said. "Make some plans to go camping over the long July Fourth weekend. Let me talk to the Chief. It may be easier for me to clear it."

"That is one helluva good idea. If I don't get away then, I'll end up taking her down to Camp David. Not that I mind your company and Joan's, but she'll bust a gut if she has to spend three days around our leader. She calls him the great homewrecker."

"Let me see what I can do," Stewart said calmly. He had too much at stake to let Oliver broach the subject with the President. If Edwards raised the slightest objection, Oliver would back down and insist that he could pass up the camping trip.

Francine walked out to the balcony and stared at Elliott dozing gently on the chaise longue with two empty glasses on a small snack table.

"Are you free on the twentieth, Bill?" Francine asked in a loud tone that quickly ended Elliott's nap.

He rubbed his eyes with his fingers, trying to make his

mind focus. That's the day before my meeting with Morris and the others, Elliott thought.

"I need you in the evening," Francine said.

"That should be okay, what's it for?"

"Purely social. I want to give a little dinner party at Tiberio for Bill Marks and his wife. Before they make their annual summer pilgrimage to visit Marks' brother in Israel."

Elliott grunted. He only read Marks' columns in the *Times* if he couldn't avoid them. As far as Elliott was concerned, Marks was the personification of the liberal eastern establishment press. A royal pain in the ass for all government officials.

"Why are you doing this for Marks?" Elliott asked, sounding puzzled.

"I do it for him every year. He's been good to me."

Elliott's face turned bright red.

"Not that way," she said. "The *Tribune* will publish lots of things that the *Times* won't touch. They're just more conservative. From time to time, Marks sends me stuff that they won't run."

"I'm not sure that I can handle two reporters at one time," Elliott said, scowling.

"You can relax. Marks isn't like me. When he's off duty, he's off duty."

# CHAPTER

# 15

ANNE WATCHED THE WORKMEN WITH A PUZZLED LOOK ON her face. Morris had told her that he was having some repairs made in his second-floor study, which overlooked R Street in the front of the house, but Anne never dreamt that he had major construction in mind.

First they shattered the glass in all of the windows. It was replaced with a double panel of heavy bullet-proof glass. Then they stripped the walls, ceiling, and floor. They covered all of these with thick panels of aluminum. The metal paneling was then buried beneath a second layer of paneling—this one of ordinary wood.

A small electrical generator was installed. It had enough capability to supply power to the entire house in the event the outside power was terminated. Two separate beige telephones were installed with independent circuits.

The old wooden door was replaced with a thick steel door. A heavy combination lock was installed. It could be opened from either side.

The work was completed on Friday afternoon. That evening Morris inspected it thoroughly, making certain that everything had been done precisely to his specifications. He was satisfied.

Anne waited for Morris to supply some explanation. But he remained secretive and silent, never even raising the subject.

Saturday morning Green arrived at the house promptly at seven o'clock, just as Morris had asked. He was carrying a thick black notebook in his left hand.

The large house was deathly quiet. Anne was still asleep. Louise had made a pot of coffee for Morris, and then disappeared into her own room.

Morris led Green into the kitchen. The Assistant Director was clutching the notebook tightly in his hand. His shirt was damp with perspiration.

"You look tense," Morris said. "Relax, Green. Black and the President are just being cautious. I don't think there's much chance of a Soviet military action."

Green didn't tell Morris that he wasn't nervous because of the possibility of a Soviet military operation. He didn't think that was likely. He was confident that July fourth would pass without any military action by anyone—especially since the President had rejected Morris's proposal. Green was just nervous at the unpleasant prospect of being interrogated by Morris.

Morris poured two cups of coffee and pointed Green to one of the chairs at the kitchen table.

"What conclusion did you reach?"

Green started to open the notebook.

"In a single sentence. Without the notebook," Morris said sharply.

"In a single sentence. The amount of damage that the Saudis could do would be relatively insignificant."

"Good. But why?"

"The most they could do is halt the flow of crude oil by carefully placed explosives. But the damage would only be temporary. There's a company in Houston operated by a man called 'Grease Fletcher.' This outfit could repair any foreseeable damage to the oil system in seven to ten days.

They know the system. They've had experience after two explosions in Saudi Arabia in the past—one last year and one three years ago. Those were caused by terrorists, and one was major. But Fletcher's outfit repaired both of them in a week."

"Where's the point of maximum vulnerability?"

"There's no single point of vulnerability. The pumping stations are in general most vulnerable to attack. The earlier two explosions occurred at pumping stations."

Morris drained his cup and refilled it, thinking carefully about what Green had said.

The Assistant Director looked down at the table. He tried to pick up his cup. His hand was shaking so badly that he spilled more coffee in the saucer than he drank.

"Based upon what you're telling me," Morris said, "if any attack were launched, every effort should be made to seize and to defend the pumping stations quickly. Is that right?"

"Exactly. They are the key."

"Are all the details in the notebook?"

"Yes."

"And a report on Fletcher's experience as well?"

"That's there too."

"Leave it with me then. I'll read it over the weekend. If I have any questions, I'll ask you Monday."

Green was happy to leave the house. He had enough of Morris's intent manner for one day.

Then Green made up his mind once and for all. He would follow Felicia's advice. He would do what Morris asked without thinking about it.

Felicia was right, Green decided. Morris wouldn't last long. There was no use getting an ulcer worrying about him.

Green looked at his watch. It was only 7:30. He could be home in thirty minutes. Felicia would still be sleeping. He would jump into bed with her. He could still salvage something from Saturday morning.

Saturday evening the party started without Morris. He was

still in his study reading Green's notebook when the first guests arrived. He remained there until he heard two beeps on the intercom that was connected to the guard's station at the front door.

Morris walked over to the window and looked out. He could see Ahmad getting out of his Fleetwood limousine. The Iranian was walking next to a woman with long black hair and the largest bosom that Morris had ever seen. They were equal in height, but the Ambassador, thin and bony, was dwarfed in comparison.

Morris saw a second car park at the end of the street. Two men in dark business suits, resembling underworld hit men, got out and followed the Ambassador. They stopped in front of Morris's house, and stood there on the sidewalk with their hands in their pockets, trying to appear unobtrusive. Members of SAVAK, the Shah's secret police, no doubt, Morris thought to himself.

Morris waited fifteen minutes before walking down the center staircase. By then Anne was engaged in intense conversation with the Iranian Ambassador at the edge of the pool. Morris stood on the porch for several minutes studying Anne's face. My instincts are never wrong, he thought. I just hope to hell that she changes the sheets.

Morris gave Anne an opportunity to formally introduce him to Ahmad. Then he dismissed her.

"They were asking for you in the kitchen."

Anne excused herself gracefully.

Morris led Ahmad to the edge of the garden next to a large magnolia tree. The Iranian began with small talk—mostly about the two business trips that Morris had made to Iran.

Morris employed great restraint in continuing this conversation. It was obvious that Ahmad had some message for him, but the man was such a facile talker that he might never get to his message.

After fifteen minutes Morris's patience began wearing thin.

He signaled to a waiter, who brought Ahmad a glass of champagne and Morris tomato juice.

"To the Shah's health and long life," Morris said, raising his glass and hoping to prod Ahmad.

"His Royal Highness, the Shah, has asked me to convey his personal greetings to you, Mr. Morris," the Ambassador replied. "He, too, remembers you from your visits to Tehran."

"I'm flattered," Morris said, trying to sound surprised. "We had only one brief meeting."

"First impressions are important to his Royal Highness. He is an excellent judge of character."

Morris could have added that the Shah had undoubtedly received a complete report on all of Morris's activities when he was in Iran. Morris knew that he had been followed every minute he was out of the hotel; and each of the conversations in his room was recorded and transcribed.

"I have a message for you from His Royal Highness," the Ambassador said to Morris in a hushed, whispered tone. "He would like to meet with you in Tehran sometime soon—before July fourth. It would have to be you alone without any assistants."

He's not a bad messenger, Morris thought. He worked out this scheme to make his contact informal and in secret. He even managed to sprinkle pleasure with business.

Morris hesitated for just a minute. Perhaps there had been a leak from his discussions with Stewart, Thomas, and Elliott. Perhaps the Shah intended to prevent the seizure of the Saudi oil fields. If he made the trip to Tehran, it would have to be completely secret. No one could know—not even the President or General Thomas. And in that case, how could Morris assure his own personal safety? He could easily be executed by the Shah's secret police. No one would even know where to look for him.

Morris quickly pushed those doubts from his mind. The larger the prize, the larger the risks, he thought to himself.

"I would be honored by such a meeting," Morris said.

"When could you come?"

"Later this week. Beginning on Wednesday, the twenty-first. Anytime after ten in the morning."

"That will be acceptable. His Royal Highness will send a plane to pick you up at Dulles Airport. It will be there at ten o'clock on the twenty-first. Of course he expects complete secrecy regarding the visit."

"That is understood."

"And now, please excuse me, Mr. Morris. There are a number of your guests that I would like to meet."

The Ambassador walked away slowly. He left Morris gazing silently at the tree and reflecting on the possibilities that had just developed.

Tuesday evening Morris called Thomas and Stewart. Each man answered the telephone on the first ring. Each man heard an identical statement.

"We will meet tomorrow morning at six-thirty at the Burning Woods Country Club in Bethesda."

When Morris called Elliott at Francine's apartment, he heard Georgiana, the switchboard operator.

"Mr. Elliott is out for the evening. He asked me to take a message."

"That dumb son-of-a-bitch," Morris muttered to himself.

He paused for a minute. "Tell him that the meeting with General Thomas has been arranged for six-thirty tomorrow at Burning Woods Country Club."

"And who should I tell him called?"

"Tell him a colleague of General Thomas," Morris said, slamming down the telephone.

Two hours later Elliott returned with Francine from the dinner party for Marks. "I have a message for you," Georgiana said, handing Elliott a sealed envelope. He quickly tucked it into his pocket.

"What's that about?" Francine asked.

"I don't know. I haven't read it."

"Well, why don't you read it?"

"Because I have to piss in the worst way," Elliott said as he headed toward the men's room in the lobby. "Why don't you go up without me. I'll be there in a couple of minutes."

As soon as he was safely in the men's room, Elliott read the message, tore it into small pieces and flushed it in the toilet. I'm damn glad it's moving along, Elliott thought. This revenge will be sweeter than any of the others that I've enjoyed during my long career in politics.

# CHAPTER

# 16

MORRIS WAS AWAKE BEFORE THE ALARM RANG ON WEDNES-day morning. He rubbed his eyes and looked at the clock. It was ten minutes to five. He heard Anne snoring gently. She was completely buried under the covers.

He walked over to the back door, clad only in his bed-room slippers. The air-conditioned house was cool and com-fortable. Morris opened the back door slowly. It was still dark outside. The air felt like an oven—hot and sticky.

Morris plugged in the coffeepot and walked out to the pool. He swam one hundred laps, finishing as strong as he started. Then he returned to the house, drank two large glasses of orange juice and a cup of black coffee. He dressed in his study, scribbled a small note on a piece of paper, and placed it in an envelope on Anne's vanity table in the bedroom.

As Morris walked out of the house, his mind was alert, all of his senses were finely honed. This was a critical meeting.

While most of the Washington area was still sleeping, four black limousines moved quietly across the deserted roads of Montgomery County. They came from different directions, but they were rapidly converging on the same point—the Burning Woods Country Club in Bethesda.

Morris was the first to arrive at the deserted club. He waited patiently in front of the door, watching the sun rise ever so slowly on the eastern horizon. A rabbit with a bushy brown tail raced across the golf course. Two birds were playing in a tree near the clubhouse.

The others arrived a few minutes later. They assembled silently near the front door of the club. Stewart and Elliott were dressed in sports shirts and slacks. General Thomas was in his heavily decorated uniform as Chairman of the Joint Chiefs; he was carrying a large black briefcase. Morris had on a gray pin-striped suit and his crimson Harvard tie.

Morris unlocked the door and led the way along a narrow concrete corridor. Their feet made an eerie clattering sound that echoed through the empty building.

When they reached the Board Room at the end of the corridor, Morris took the chair at the end of the large rectangular table. The others took seats along the sides of the table.

"I want to start with your conclusion, General Thomas," Morris said. "Is it feasible from a military standpoint to seize the Saudi oil fields?"

There was total silence in the room. Stewart and Elliott joined Morris in staring at Thomas.

"It is feasible," Thomas said in a voice brimming with self-confidence. "I am absolutely certain of that."

Morris had a great feeling of relief and satisfaction.

"Very good, General," Morris said. "Now I would like you to present the plan for the takeover."

Thomas opened his briefcase. He took out a large map containing the area from the eastern Mediterranean to the Persian Gulf. He mounted it on the wall of the Board Room with Scotch tape. Morris could see that Thomas had made a number of markings on the map in various colors.

Thomas then reached into his briefcase and pulled out a thin silver tube. He pressed a button on the end of the tube and it opened into a pointer.

Standing next to the map, Thomas began speaking, alternating his eyes between the map and Morris. Thomas defined the critical geographic area in eastern Saudi Arabia which would have to be captured. Then he explained in detail why an attack from the Sinai Peninsula on the west was preferable to an attack from the Persian Gulf on the east.

"It will be necessary," Thomas said, "to establish a secret base in the eastern Sinai to assemble all of the planes, troops, and equipment for the attack on D-Day. Three waves of planes will take off from this base at the time of the attack. Wave A will consist of fifty B-1 and F-16 bombers. They will fly eastward at low altitudes. Their mission will be to bomb and knock out Saudi military bases, airports, large artillery, and other defensive weapons which might provide effective resistance to the attack. It will be particularly important for Wave A to knock out the anti-aircraft installations at the airports in eastern Saudi Arabia. Wave B will consist of thirty XL-120's, the smaller aircraft that land and take off vertically. We have just developed these little beauties. They will move along the large TAP line that carries oil from Saudi Arabia to the Mediterranean, dropping paratroops at each pumping station. Wave C will consist of twenty-five C-130 Galaxies. Those are the huge cargo planes. They will carry troops, tanks, artillery, and ammunition. Once these biggies touch down, an army rolls out of their belly—fully equipped and ready for action. If everything operates on schedule, the TOCO, the time of complete operation, should be eight to twelve hours. There may be scattered sniping after that twelve-hour period, but we should be firmly in control. As I told you earlier, it is my best professional judgment that this operation will succeed."

Thomas then stopped. He stood next to the map waiting for questions from Morris.

"Let me ask you first about this base you want to set up in eastern Sinai," Morris said. "How do you propose to get that land?"

"The Israelis will let us use it, provided that the operation is completely ours. They don't want any part of it."

"How do you propose to get the planes, tanks, and other equipment to that base?"

"I can borrow little bits from many different American installations around the world. You would not believe the amount of hardware that we have sitting in warehouses in Western Europe, Korea, Hawaii, and other places. There won't be a large enough dent in any one place to raise any eyebrows."

Morris thought about Thomas's answer for a minute.

"What about the men who will be sent to the Sinai for the attack?" he asked.

"I will carefully select officers who can be expected to follow my orders. Initially, they will not be told where they are going. When they arrive, they will be told that they are at a secret training camp to test the readiness of the U.S. Armed Forces for desert warfare. We can effectively seal off the troops from the rest of the world. They will not have access to a telephone, and all mail can be sequestered for delivery after the attack. They will be told of the attack only hours before the takeoff."

"Won't these men be reluctant to go?"

Thomas started to laugh.

"With all due respect, you have a typical civilian's approach. In the Armed Forces soldiers follow orders. That's the name of the game. This is an all-volunteer army. These boys joined to fight. They're tired of polishing shoes and cleaning rifles."

Thomas paused for a minute, then he continued speaking.

"We'll also have an advantage because there are already some American troops in Saudi Arabia to provide training on American planes and weapons. As soon as our first planes approach their targets, I will inform the commanding officers of those units of the attack. They should be able to neutralize Saudi arms."

"What about money?" Morris asked. "How can you get the

funds for this operation without tipping it off?"

"We have something called the Joint Chiefs petty cash fund. As the Defense Budget has grown over the years, the petty cash fund has grown. It should be adequate to handle this little operation."

Morris was impressed with the depth of Thomas's analytical skills and the thoroughness of his preparation. Thomas would be successful in any field, Morris thought. Men like Thomas were few and far between.

But Thomas could never tell from Morris's facial expression what reaction the Director of Energy had. To Thomas, Morris seemed like a great stone face, like a machine that absorbed and filed every bit of relevant information.

"Let's turn now to the Russians," Morris said. "What is their strength in the Persian Gulf?"

Thomas reached back into his briefcase. He pulled out a thin black notebook with the words "Top Secret" written in yellow on the cover. He placed the notebook on the table and began talking.

"The United States and the Soviet Union are in a situation of conventional and nuclear parity in the Persian Gulf."

"What does that mean in lay terms?"

"It means that if one side attacked the other with conventional weapons, neither would win a clear victory. It would be a standoff. The same thing would happen if one side attacked with nuclear weapons and the other responded with nuclear weapons. But, if one side employed nuclear weapons and the other side was limited to conventional weapons, then there would be a clear victory for the nuclear power."

"But how is that relevant?" Morris asked. "Both sides have nuclear weapons."

"Not quite," Thomas said, looking pensive.

"Under our system of controls, I can personally order the use of any conventional weapon. But only the President can authorize the use of nuclear weapons." Thomas's voice was bitter as he uttered this last statement.

"That means," Thomas continued, "that if the Soviets decide to go the limit in this one, they will be able to wipe out our invading force and most of our naval fleet in the area."

"That isn't a very happy thought to contemplate," Stewart said.

There were small beads of perspiration on the lawyer's forehead.

Morris glared at Stewart.

"Listen, Stewart," he said. "I'll handle the military discussion with the General. We'll be coming to your area in a little while."

Turning to Thomas, Morris asked, "How much chance is there that the Soviets would respond militarily—with either conventional or nuclear weapons?"

Thomas thought about the question for a moment. He closed his eyes and massaged his forehead gently with his fingers.

"I can recite the history of American-Soviet relations in the post-Korea period," Thomas said. "Hungary, Czechoslovakia, Cuba, Vietnam, and the rest. But I'm sure that you know all that very well. The conclusion that I have drawn from this history is that where one of the two super powers decides that its vital interests are so seriously affected that a military action is necessary, the other super power makes noise and backs down, avoiding a military confrontation. If you asked me to give you my best judgment, I would say that the Soviets would not respond militarily. But I'd be lying if I told you that I was certain of that conclusion. The ultimate decision to go or not to go is yours, Morris. You are the director of this operation. I just want you to know the risks."

Morris carefully absorbed the words that Thomas uttered. Their weight and significance were fully appreciated. Yet Morris's face remained deadpan, impassive, unemotional.

Morris had also studied the Soviet response to the British and French seizure of the Suez Canal in 1956. There the Soviets had limited their response to rhetoric—a threatening note and table pounding in the United Nations. Likewise, when the United States landed marines in Lebanon in 1958, the Soviets did not respond militarily.

A silence fell over the room as Morris thought about the General's presentation. "Can you find us some coffee?" Morris asked Stewart.

Stewart rose from the table and walked to the door. "Unobtrusively," Morris admonished.

When Stewart left the room, Morris resumed the discussion. "I will have to deal with the possibility of Soviet intervention. That will be my responsibility."

"I'm frankly as worried about the possibility of an Iranian military response," Thomas said. "The Shah is armed to the teeth."

"What would you suggest we do about that?" Morris asked.

"I have two suggestions—neither satisfactory. One is a preemptive strike against Iran at the time of the Saudi attack, knowing that we would suffer heavy casualties. The other is to enlist the help of Anderson at the CIA. He once told me that he was preparing a contingency plan to kidnap the Shah's son. It could be used in the future if action against the Shah proved necessary. Anderson has managed to place one of his agents as the Chief of Personal Security for the Shah's son. This man is an Iranian who has hated the Shah ever since the Shah helped Iraq defeat the Kurds in 1976. According to Anderson, this agent would be willing to assist in a plan to kidnap the Crown Prince. We could bargain his release in return for the Shah's promise of nonintervention."

Morris was not surprised by Thomas's kidnapping proposal. He had met Anderson a couple of times. Morris was convinced that the Director of the CIA was a cruel, brutal man. More important he was a career CIA employee who had suffered miserably during the so-called CIA reforms of the late 1970s. It was only within the last two years that the reformers had finally been ousted from the top of the agency, and the old cloak-and-dagger types like Anderson were in control once again. To Morris's mind, Anderson was capable of anything.

"You're right about one thing," Morris said to Thomas. "I don't find either of those suggestions very satisfactory. Why don't you leave the Shah to me. I will handle him."

Morris glanced at his digital watch. It was 7:36. In another two and a half hours he would be airborne to Iran.

Stewart entered, carrying a pitcher of coffee and four cups. As Stewart poured coffee for the group, Morris watched Elliott. He was very quiet this morning. Maybe he just needs some coffee to sober up, Morris thought.

"I want a set of maps," Morris said to Thomas, "like the one that you hung up and any others you have."

Thomas reached into his briefcase and pulled out a brown manila envelope. "I thought that you might ask for the maps," he said, handing the envelope to Morris.

When they were all seated again, Morris reported on the results of Green's analysis about the possible blowup of the Saudi oil fields. It was consistent with Thomas's evaluation.

"I've heard of this man 'Grease Fletcher,' " Thomas said. "He is the very best in the business. I'll have a C-130 transport alerted at Ellington Air Force base near Houston. We'll be able to take off with Fletcher's crew and his equipment with thirty minutes' notice."

"Okay. Now let's turn to the secrecy question," Morris said. "How good are our chances of keeping this operation from the President? What about at the Pentagon end, Bill?"

"You may be surprised to hear this, Morris," Elliott said sarcastically, "but I've actually done something useful."

Elliott paused, waiting for a response, but Morris ignored his comment. Then Elliott continued speaking.

"I have taken steps to formalize what had previously been an informal procedure. Under that procedure I provide daily briefings to the President on military matters unless he waives the briefing for any given day. All of the assistant secretaries and military staff assistants have been told that I am the focal point for all communications with the President. Unless I am unavailable, they are to forward nothing directly to the President. And I will be available until this operation is over. You can be sure of that."

Elliott paused for a moment. Then he continued.

"If we do get any questions from the press about movements of troops and equipment, the official explanation from the Secretary's office will be that we are engaged in a routine training exercise."

When Elliott was finished speaking, Morris realized that Elliott's initial comment had been correct. Morris was surprised that Elliott had done something useful. But Morris concealed that surprise from Elliott. He was still feeling uncomfortable about the Secretary of Defense.

"What about the plan to isolate the President?" Morris asked Stewart.

"I'm halfway there," Stewart replied. "July fourth is a Tuesday. There will be a long holiday weekend from Friday evening to Wednesday morning. The President will go to Camp David with Mrs. Edwards for the whole weekend."

"Are you sure of that?"

"Absolutely. It's already scheduled."

"Who goes with him?"

"Ordinarily I go, along with Black and Oliver. We take our wives."

"Then what good is that?" Morris asked impatiently. "With Oliver and Black there, it's hopeless."

Stewart was proceeding slowly with his explanation, hoping that Morris would appreciate the valuable contribution he had made.

"I already have Black out of the picture," Stewart said. "He'll be in England for the fourth."

"What about Oliver?"

"I'm working on that. I'm trying to arrange to have him go off with his wife on a camping trip."

"How's the weekend of the fourth fit into your schedule?" Morris asked Thomas.

Thomas took a blank piece of paper from his briefcase and began scribbling numbers.

"It will be tight. But I can do it. The later in the weekend the better. If we struck on the fourth that would be best."

"The weekend of the fourth has one other advantage," Elliott said. "This town turns into a ghost town over that weekend. It's absolutely deserted. Most of the press and the Congress are gone. It's a perfect weekend for an operation like this."

Elliott was quickly coming to the conclusion that he had the least significant role of any of the four. At first this annoyed him. But then he figured the hell with it. We'll get Edwards, and that's what counts.

"When will you know about Oliver?" Morris asked Stewart.

"I should know in another week. Is that okay?"

"It'll have to be," Morris replied curtly. "If you can't find a way to get rid of him, I'll give you a couple of suggestions. But we'll do it one way or another.

"Okay, gentlemen," Morris said in a voice filled with self-confidence. "I've heard enough. I think that the plan is feasible. I'm ready to go ahead with it. Are all of you still in?"

"Absolutely," Thomas said.

"I'm in," Stewart said.

Elliott hesitated for a moment, thinking one more time about the possibilities of prison in the event of failure.

"Yes, I'm in," he said softly.

"Very good," Morris said. "We better get moving immediately. General, you can start shifting troops and equipment to the Sinai as soon as you're ready. I will establish the study of my Georgetown house as the command center. The house is already watched by armed guards twenty-four hours a day. I want a direct telephone hookup established between that study and the base in the Sinai. I assume that this can be done using a military communications system? Is that correct, General?"

"I will have it done."

"You military people are always big on giving everything a code name," Morris said. "We'll call this 'Operation Independence.' I want to set one final meeting for the four of us —Friday evening June thirtieth, ten o'clock at my house in

Georgetown. Make sure that each of you parks a couple of blocks away. I don't want to raise any suspicions. If we hit some unanticipated snag between now and the thirtieth, we can abort the whole thing then."

As they gathered up their papers, Morris started talking in an intensely serious tone.

"I want to emphasize once again the importance of absolute secrecy. This has to be kept from wives, girl friends, special assistants, and everyone else. Lives are at stake and not just the men in those planes and tanks, but yours and mine as well. Make no mistake about that."

The session was finished. Each man had a grim expression on his face. They left the room one at a time to minimize suspicions.

Morris left first, walking quickly through the empty corridor of the club. He climbed into the back of his limousine.

"Dulles Airport, Mario," Morris barked to the driver.

Anne started to stir in bed just as Mario dropped Morris at the airport. She woke up slowly rubbing the sides of her head with her long, slender fingers. She took one look at the half-empty bottle of cognac next to the bed. Jesus, she thought, I must have had too much to drink waiting for George to come home last evening.

She opened her eyes long enough to see that bright sunlight was streaming into the room. The prospect of facing the new day depressed her, and she turned over and went back to sleep.

An hour later Anne heard a gentle knocking on the bedroom door.

"It's Louise, madam. It's eleven o'clock. Would you like some coffee?"

"Yes, please," Anne said, as she pushed herself out of bed.

She walked into the bathroom and scrubbed her face with hot water and soap, put on a dressing gown, and returned to the waiting pot of coffee.

Just as Anne was about to lift the cup, she saw a small white envelope sitting on her vanity table. It had the words "Anne Walton" on the front, scribbled in George's unmistakable scrawl.

As Anne picked up the envelope she thought to herself, There's a new first—a note from George Morris. What words did George find so essential that he had actually left her a note—something that he had never done before. If it were any other man, the note might be a message of love and passion. Or it might say, "I'm so sorry that I came home after you were asleep. I'll make it up to you this evening." But a note from George would never say anything like that.

Anne tore open the envelope. The message was short and simple:

I have to leave Washington for a couple of days. Do not try to locate me. I will return when I can.

George

Anne crumpled the envelope with rage and fired it across the room. George Morris, you dirty bastard, she thought. You didn't even have the decency to tell me where you are going. And what am I supposed to do—wait around this house until you decide to return? The hell with that. I'm not your lackey.

She walked over to the bedroom window that faced the back of the house. She saw one of the armed guards that Morris had hired walking back and forth along the side of the swimming pool. Christ, he has this house like a prison, she thought to herself.

She picked up the telephone and started dialing.

"Mario," she said, "is that you?"

"Yes, Miss Walton. I'm in the car, but I wasn't supposed to pick you up until noon."

"I want to know where he is, Mario," Anne shouted into the phone.

"I'm sorry but I don't know, Miss Walton."

"Now, now, Mario. You wait just a minute. Remember

who you're talking to. This is Anne Walton. The one who fed
you inside information on the acquisitions of General Entertainment Corp. so you could make a killing in the market on
three separate occasions. Or was it four? Don't bullshit me,
Mario. We've been through too much together in the last
several months."

There was a long pause.

"I'm waiting, Mario."

"I really don't know," the driver said pitifully. "I swear to
God I don't know."

"Well, where did you leave him?"

"Dulles Airport."

"Where at Dulles?"

"Just the normal departure area for commercial planes."

Anne paused for a moment, tapping the toe of her foot on
the carpet.

"Okay, forget it," she said weakly. "Maybe somebody will
kill the bastard."

# CHAPTER

# 17

THE GIANT AIRPLANE THAT CARRIED MORRIS TO TEHRAN resembled an ordinary Concorde from the outside. It had that frightening blue bird painted on the tail that is the insignia of the commercial fleet of Iran Air. But on the inside it was a completely different animal. It was one of the four planes that belonged to the Shah's personal fleet.

The thickly carpeted interior was modeled after one of the sitting rooms in the palace. Tapestries hung from the walls, and reclining lounge chairs were adorned with hand-carved wooden figurines covered with a gold finish.

After the plane took off, one of the Iranian hostesses, dressed in a multicolored T-shirt and matching miniskirt, tried to talk with Morris.

"I have work to do," he said, dismissing the girl.

Morris spent the first hours of the long flight studying the maps that Thomas had supplied. He went back over in his mind every detail that Thomas had disclosed. It all fit together beautifully. From a logistical point of view, the plan had no flaws.

As the long-nosed plane passed over the European Continent, Morris placed the maps and papers back in his leather briefcase with the specially designed double combination lock. He leaned back comfortably in the chair.

Then Morris turned his thoughts to Mohammed Riza Pahlavi, the Shah of Iran—the wealthiest man in the world and the only man whom Morris truly admired. Morris smiled to himself as he thought about the strange and unusual way that the Shah had acquired his throne.

In 1941, the Shah's father, Reza Khan Pahlavi, refused to permit Great Britain and Russia to use the Trans-Iranian Railroad to carry oil that was needed for the war effort. Unwilling to let their struggle for national survival be hindered by notions of territorial sovereignty, Britain and Russia promptly sent troops to occupy Iran. They forced Reza Khan to give up his throne.

At this point, Mohammed Riza Pahlavi, the Shah's twenty-two-year-old son, could have sided with his royal father out of notions of principle or family loyalty. He could have agreed with his father's cry that Britain and Russia were committing aggression against Iran. Instead the young man made it clear that if he were the Ruler of Iran, Britain and Russia would be permitted to use the railroad and to station their troops in Iran. In a matter of days the allies placed Mohammed on the throne, making him the next Shah of Iran.

Morris's recollection of the Shah's background was far more than the academic rambling of a wandering mind passing the time on a long airplane journey. Morris had learned long ago that a man's past often suggested the right combination to open the lock of a man's mind. In the case of the Shah the story of his ascendency to the throne provided critical evidence of two of the dominant characteristics of the Shah.

The first was pragmatism. The Shah was above all else a very practical man.

And the second was the Shah's intense desire to preserve his throne. This latter characteristic was particularly strong because the Shah was not descended from a long dynasty of rulers. His father had been a dirt-poor army officer who seized control of the throne. Morris could well understand the motivation of a man who had moved from extreme poverty to great wealth in a single generation.

It was one o'clock in the morning, Tehran time, when the giant Concorde touched down and disgorged its single passenger. A score of armed guards quickly surrounded the plane—each one gripping a submachine gun and looking over the airfield. The night air was hot and muggy—much like that which Morris had left behind in Washington.

Bart was waiting for Morris at the airport. A heavy-set man with a thick black mustache. He introduced himself as a special adviser to the Shah. He had been educated in England, Morris guessed—judging from his speech.

As the Lincoln Continental sped away from the airport, Morris tapped his finger against the glass. It was bulletproof —a double layer.

Bart immediately observed the gesture.

"You have no need to fear for your personal safety, Mr. Morris. You will be staying at a guest house on the palace grounds. His Royal Highness has ordered that at least one armed man will be with you at all times."

Am I guest or prisoner? Morris wondered.

"I am at your disposal always," Bart continued. "If you have any questions, you call for me."

"When do I meet with the Shah?"

"His Royal Highness thought that you would be tired from the trip. He has scheduled your interview for tomorrow at two P.M. in order to permit you to rest."

They rode in silence. Morris should have been exhausted from the long trip, but he wasn't. When he glanced through the rear window, he saw helmeted soldiers on motorcycles, following close behind. A helicopter was flying overhead.

The highway from the airport was bathed in bright sodium lights. Along the road there were modern chemical complexes rising from the earth. Next to these hallmarks of modern civilization were mud huts belonging to peasants who still farmed in the biblical way.

At the guest house, Morris asked Bart for a cup of coffee. The Iranian returned a few minutes later, followed by two men who carried a huge golden samovar on a tray.

Behind the men walked four Iranian girls, dark-haired sensuous creatures, twenty-five years old, Morris guessed. They were clad only in sheer gowns in various shades of turquoise and purple. Their dark black hair was natural. Morris could tell that in an instant.

Pointing to the girls, Bart said, "They are for your enjoyment, to pass the long night. You may select one, or as many as you would like."

Morris looked calm and detached.

"No, I don't think so. I'm quite tired. But thank you."

Bart looked totally perplexed by Morris's words. He dismissed the girls with a clap of his hands. Then he walked out of the room shaking his head.

The Iranian returned a few minutes later, this time leading a procession of four different girls dressed in sheer gowns in reds and oranges.

"If the others were not adequate," he said, "perhaps one of these will do."

Again Morris declined the offer, saying that he was tired. Bart left the room, still confused, but at least satisfied that he had done his job properly.

At precisely 2:00 P.M. the following day Bart led Morris into the private reception chamber of the Shah. It was a large ornate room, roughly three times the size of the Oval Office. The walls were decorated with huge golden ornaments and majestic tapestries were scattered throughout. The floor was covered with thick Oriental carpets handwoven in golden patterns.

At one end of the room a throne sat on a platform raised two feet off the ground. The throne was empty when Morris entered the room.

Bart led Morris into the center of the chamber and deposited him there. His departing words were "His Royal Highness will be with you shortly."

At first Morris felt that he was quite alone in that large room. But soon he noticed a series of armed guards stationed around the perimeter. They were dressed in uniforms of a dull golden color that permitted them to blend into the walls.

A few minutes later the Shah entered the room accompanied by four personal bodyguards. He was dressed in a dark blue suit, covered by a full-length purple robe.

He walked over to Morris, who was standing erect and at attention, and shook his hand. Morris thought that the Shah had aged in the two years since he had last seen him.

His hair was almost entirely gray. The nose that had always dominated his face seemed to stand out even more. As in his previous meeting with the Shah, Morris was surprised at how much shorter he seemed in person than in his pictures.

"It is my pleasure to see you again, Mr. Morris," the Shah said. "You were kind to accept my invitation. I hope that my people made you very comfortable."

"Yes, Your Highness. Very much so."

The Shah then walked slowly to the end of the room. He mounted the platform and took his seat on the throne. He motioned to one of the guards at the edge of the room, and the man carried in a large high-backed wooden chair and placed it about ten yards in front of the throne on the floor of the room and not on the platform. The Shah motioned to Morris, and the American sat down in the chair, his eyes looking up at his host.

"We will conduct this interview in English," the Shah said. "I prefer not to use an interpreter. You may speak freely. None of my guards understands English."

How could he be sure of that? Morris thought. Then he waited for the Shah to begin.

"I have asked you to come, Mr. Morris, because I want to talk with you about the new OPEC price and production policy which is scheduled to take effect on July fourth. You have an important position as Director of Energy in your government. And you are a sophisticated businessman. I was impressed with the reports that I received on your abilities when you were in Iran in the past."

"Thank you, Your Highness."

"I am very troubled, Mr. Morris, by what is happening," the Shah said. "I wanted someone to talk with who would appreciate all of the ramifications."

The Shah paused for a moment. The room was absolutely silent. Then he started speaking again.

"I have reached the conclusion, Mr. Morris, that the new OPEC policy is not consistent with my own self-interest. I have all of the wealth that I could possibly want. I have also developed my country economically, and large cash reserves are available for future development. But I am sixty-four years old, and at this point in my life I have one last desire—to make certain that my son inherits this throne with the same wealth and security that I now have. I am fearful that the new OPEC policy will set in motion a chain of events that will deprive me of that one last desire."

The Shah then stopped speaking and looked at Morris. He was being asked to respond. Oh, well, here it goes, Morris thought.

"With all due respect, Your Royal Highness, if you are really so troubled by the OPEC policy, why did you approve of that policy? Why are you going along with it?"

"Let me clarify for you, Mr. Morris, that there is no solidarity within OPEC. Iran opposed the new policy in the recent deliberations of OPEC, and I only reluctantly approved it when I realized that my opposition would have no effect at all. You must understand that I no longer have the leverage within OPEC that I did in the seventies. The leverage is all with the Saudis. Your country has permitted that to happen because you have continued to increase your consumption despite all warnings to the contrary. Now the Saudis' oil reserves are much greater than ours, or anyone else's, and they are the dominant power. The Saudis also control the votes of the bloc of Arab oil producers. At most I could get support from Venezuela, and perhaps Nigeria, and that would be all."

A very slight smile appeared on Morris's lips. It was quickly detected by the Shah.

"Why do you smile, Mr. Morris? All of my reports said that you were humorless."

"Not from humor, Your Highness. From irony. During the seventies you were the one who pushed for higher prices, and now you have concluded that higher prices are no longer in your best interest."

"Times change, Mr. Morris. As I told you, I now have all of the money that I want. I have no need to change the present order. I have been one of its primary beneficiaries."

The Shah paused for a moment. Then, without any advance warning, he said, "This initial session is concluded, Mr. Morris. Bart will give you a tour of some of the sites of our country. You and I will meet here at eight o'clock this evening for our final session."

The Shah then marched in quiet dignified steps from the room, leaving Morris bewildered. What did the Shah hope to accomplish at the evening session, and why this lengthy intermission?

Bart gathered the puzzled Morris from the center of the room. That afternoon Bart led Morris on a tour of Tehran's industrial and financial center. Two armed guards followed them at a distance of ten yards. Morris quickly observed how much sophisticated technology had been installed in the two years since he had been in the country.

They visited an air force base and watched maneuvers by skilled Iranian pilots. Morris saw the latest anti-aircraft missiles. Bart pointed out the luxurious residences of the business community. They ended the afternoon in a private dining room at the Tehran Athletic Club.

By the time eight o'clock approached, Morris was anxious to resume his discussion. Again Bart deposited him in the center of the room, and again the Shah entered a few minutes later.

"Mr. Morris," the Shah said. "I will be very blunt with you. If you were not in one of the highest positions of the American government, I would not have expected the United States to take bold and daring action in response to the OPEC announcement. But I have seen you operate in other situations. I believe that with you in a position of responsibility there is some chance that your nation will respond with military force to the OPEC policy—maybe before the fourth of July and maybe after. I will not embarrass you by asking whether that is now being actively considered. I only want you to know that I recognize it as a possibility."

Morris tried to remain absolutely still without showing any emotion in his face. He wondered whether the Shah was that perceptive or whether there had been a leak from Thomas, Stewart, or Elliott.

The Shah then stared directly at Morris. His eyes nearly pierced the American's brain.

The time for playing games was quickly coming to an end.

"You are correct, Your Highness," Morris said. "It is a possibility. Whether it would ever happen or not is something else. But let me ask you a purely hypothetical question, Your Royal Highness. Suppose that the United States did launch an attack against Saudi Arabia to seize the Saudi oil fields and no other OPEC country were attacked. What position would you take?"

The Shah smiled ever so slightly.

"A very interesting question," he said. "But you have spent the day here. What would you advise me to do?"

He's a shrewd bastard, Morris thought. I have to say it all myself—both the questions and the answers.

"I'll tell you what you should do," Morris said. "You should do nothing. You could be certain that the only attack would be against Saudi Arabia. After all, they have the greater oil reserves and the smaller military defense. Since you would not be attacked, there is no reason for you to waste your arms shooting down American planes. You are a pragmatic man. You know that one day you may need your arms for the Russians. You have that long northern border to worry about."

The Shah was listening carefully, Morris thought, paying attention to each word. Morris began speaking in a louder, self-confident tone.

"As far as the consequences of an American takeover of the Saudi oil fields," Morris said, "based on what you told me today, it would not adversely affect you if the United States drastically deflated the world price of oil for the next five or ten years by dumping that Saudi oil on the market at cheap prices. You have enough financial reserves. You don't have any great love for the Saudis, and you would be happy to leave your own oil in the ground during that period and pass it on to your son as a legacy along with the rest of the Kingdom. What better inheritance could a father leave to his son?"

The Shah seemed startled by the self-confidence that Morris was showing.

"You seem so certain of your conclusion, Mr. Morris."

"I have studied well the events of 1941, Your Royal Highness. The errors of the fathers need not be repeated by their sons."

Morris had been watching the Shah's face carefully the entire time he had been speaking, trying to understand what was in his mind. When he was finished speaking, he thought that he knew the Shah's true intentions.

"Is there anything else that you want to tell me, Mr. Morris?" the Shah asked.

Morris hesitated for a moment. Then he said, "There is just one other thing, Your Royal Highness. It has nothing to do with my advice about the oil question."

"You may speak."

"It is a matter that is none of my business, but I thought it would be of interest to you. I have heard that a man who has only one son and many enemies should sometimes change the Chief of Personal Security for his son. One can never know when someone of doubtful loyalty might penetrate to a position of trust."

As soon as Morris took one look at the fury that swept over the face of Mohammed Riza Pahlavi, he felt that his bargain with the Shah had been sealed. It had been sealed with the blood of one CIA agent.

Morris stood quietly until the Shah's anger subsided. He realized that his meeting with the Shah was over.

"I want to thank you for accepting my invitation, Mr. Morris," the Shah said.

Then the Shah pointed a single finger at one of his guards, standing nervously at the side of the room. The man jumped forward and handed the Shah a small white box. The Shah rose from his throne and walked down from the platform toward Morris.

He shook hands warmly with Morris. Then he handed him the white box.

"This, Mr. Morris, is a gift for your friend, the 'Undercover Woman,' " he said. "It is a small reward for your advice on the oil question."

Morris suddenly had an image in his mind of millions of Iranians sitting before television sets and watching reruns of Anne's weekly escape from danger. He wondered if they were shown with subtitles.

"As for the other information which you gave me, I now have no way of repaying the man who has saved my son's life. Perhaps something will suggest itself in the future."

The Shah paused for a moment. Then he continued.

"In the meantime, Mr. Morris, you may feel free to talk with my Ambassador in Washington if that should prove necessary. Ahmad enjoys my complete confidence."

The Shah turned and walked toward his own private door, leaving Morris once again alone in the center of the room.

When Morris walked into the R Street house, it was ten-thirty in the evening. Anne was sitting in the living room, sipping a cognac and sulking.

"You owe me some explanation as to where you're going and when you'll be back," she shouted. "And if you can't tell me precisely where and when, then explain that to me."

Morris was stunned by her comment for just a second. It sounded very much like something he had heard from Marjorie—many, many times.

"I had an important mission related to the survival of this country," Morris said self-righteously. "You and I are too mature for games like this."

"Oh, bullshit," Anne said, draining her cognac glass. "I frankly don't give a damn what you do. I just like to know when you'll be with me. The only women on twenty-four-hour call are nurses and prostitutes, and I don't fit into either category."

"I left you a note. I couldn't tell you anything further. You'll just have to take my word for it."

"That's not good enough anymore," she shouted.

Morris stood up and walked over to his jacket which was hanging on the doorknob. Anne glared at him, her eyes following him as he walked across the room. He reached into his jacket pocket and handed her the small white box.

"You can't buy me, George," she said. "Don't even try it. I'm not for sale."

"Oh, open it and stop blowing off steam," he said calmly.

When Anne opened the box, she could hardly believe her eyes. It was a ring with a huge turquoise stone in the center —the largest stone Anne had ever seen. The turquoise was absolutely perfect without a single line or trace. It was surrounded by twenty sparkling diamonds that were mounted on eighteen-carat gold.

Anne was stunned by the gift. She placed it on her finger, and walked around the second floor of the house looking into mirrors. Then she returned to the den and gave Morris a very gentle kiss on his forehead.

I'll give you one more chance, she thought. But my deadline is the fourth of July. You better shape up by then.

When Morris returned to Washington, General Thomas and his personal aide, Major Cox, were on their way to the large American base near Frankfurt. The trip had not been announced in Pentagon communications channels, and no one in Frankfurt was expecting the Chairman of the Joint Chiefs. A surprised tower control operator hastily said, "Permission to land is granted."

It was three-thirty in the morning when the plane touched down. A light drizzle was falling over the Frankfurt area.

"I want you to go into the base, Major," Thomas said, "and get General Ripley and General Braddock. Bring them out to this plane as quickly as you can."

While the Major was gone, General Thomas thought about the two men he had selected for the job. General Ripley—with twenty-eight years in the Army—was the Commander of the American troops in NATO. He was also a close personal friend of General Thomas from Thomas's duty in Europe. General Braddock had been a classmate of General Thomas at the Air Force Academy. They had flown together in Vietnam and had remained friends over the years.

"I apologize for the early hour, gentlemen," Thomas said, when Cox returned with the two men.

The apology was unnecessary, General Thomas thought. A commanding officer was entitled to wake up subordinates in the middle of the night for an important assignment. But these men were his friends. Their uniforms had been hastily thrown on. They still had sleep in their eyes.

"It is a matter of some urgency, however," Thomas said, with a deadly serious look in his eyes.

General Ripley could still remember the last time he had been awakened in the middle of the night by a commanding officer. It was ten years ago, during the 1973 Arab-Israeli war, when American intelligence reported that Russian troops were on their way to the Middle East. Within two hours, an American force was poised and ready to roll along this same airstrip. Then the Russians backed down—or at least the intelligence assessments changed.

The four men sat down at the large conference table in General Thomas's plane.

"Before I begin this briefing," Thomas said, "I want to emphasize that every word I tell you this morning and everything that you learn about this assignment in the future is to be treated with the highest level of secrecy. It is not to be discussed in any way with any other person not directly involved. Is that clear?"

"Yes, sir," all three men said in unison.

Thomas could tell that Major Cox, ranking well below the others, was uncertain as to whether he should be present.

"I want you here, Major," Thomas said.

Then General Thomas began his formal briefing.

"The OPEC announcement, raising prices and cutting production, has created considerable uncertainty in the Middle East. It's a fairly volatile situation. The President believes that there is a possibility that the Soviet Union might capitalize on this uncertainty and initiate some type of military action in one of the Middle Eastern countries. If this should occur, we might have to respond to that Soviet action.

Thomas paused for a moment. There was no visible reaction from any of the three. The General continued speaking.

"In view of these contingencies the President has informed me that it is imperative that we have units which are trained specifically for the Middle Eastern desert terrain. The President has therefore directed that I arrange and establish intensive training exercises in the Middle East as promptly as possible. He's doing it out of an abundance of caution. The reason for the complete and total secrecy is clear. The Soviets must not know that we are training and preparing a force to respond to possible action that they might undertake."

Thomas paused again. As he heard himself talking, he thought how credible the whole explanation seemed.

"Are there any questions thus far?"

All three men remained silent. They were accepting what he had said, General Thomas thought. This was what he loved most about the military. It was the only place left in society where you could explain something and people listened, accepting what you said without raising a thousand different questions.

"This is to be a joint Air Force-Army exercise," Thomas said. "General Ripley, you will direct the Army's participation. General Braddock, you will direct the Air Force units. This training exercise is to be conducted at a special base we will be creating for this purpose."

Thomas then spread a large map on the table and explained precisely where the base would be located. For the next hour the three generals decided which units and equipment would have to be moved to the Sinai Peninsula. They included F-16 and B-1 bombers from the Air Force; tanks, infantry, artillery, and missile units from the Army. Some of these were located in the Frankfurt area, but others were in North Carolina, New Mexico, Alaska, Guam, Korea, and Hawaii. Thomas selected many of the units based upon his personal knowledge.

"It is very important," Thomas said, "that the destination be kept absolutely confidential—kept from wives, children, Congressmen, everybody. That was the President's order. Only the four of us will know where it is."

"How can we do this if units from several locations are involved?" General Ripley asked.

"We will schedule the arrival of all units into Frankfurt for tomorrow evening under cover of darkness. All of the officers in those units will simply be told that their destination is Frankfurt for routine training exercises. Just as soon as those planes land, they will be refueled and ready to take off again. General Braddock, you are not to disclose the ultimate destination to your pilots until their airplane engines are operating on the ground ready for takeoff."

"What about the Army men?" General Ripley asked.

"They will learn the destination after arrival. They are simply to be told that these are routine training exercises that will last approximately two weeks. Under no circumstances are any wives and dependents to go."

"What about the time of departure?" General Ripley asked.

"The sooner the better," Thomas replied. "How soon can you be ready?"

General Ripley rubbed his eyes and looked at his watch. It was six-thirty on the morning of June twenty-third.

"We can be loaded and ready at 2200 tomorrow night."

"Are you certain that you can meet that deadline?" Thomas asked. "Remember we're moving a whole army."

"The Army will be ready, but I don't know about the Air Force," General Ripley said, breaking into a smile.

"Can you meet that schedule, General Braddock?" Thomas asked, ignoring the interservice banter.

"Yes, sir."

"Okay, let's set that as the time of takeoff."

Major Cox sat quietly through the entire briefing. He was stunned by the whole discussion. He was surprised that he hadn't heard about the President's concerns with the Soviets back in Washington. But then again Major Cox knew that General Thomas sometimes decided to include him in high-level deliberations and sometimes not. Those were the prerogatives of a high-ranking government official in dealing with a personal aide.

When General Ripley and General Braddock left the plane, Thomas turned to Major Cox.

"You will remain here with me in Frankfurt today and then fly with me to the Sinai tomorrow. You will remain there during the entire training exercise. I expect to shuttle back to Washington from time to time, but I will leave you there as my representative, giving you instructions about how to communicate with me directly and personally at all times. Is that clear?"

"Yes, sir."

"Oh, and there is one final thing, Major. I would appreciate it if you did not disclose your destination to your wife. I will see that she is notified that you are safe and that you will return in approximately two weeks."

There goes my July fourth weekend in Ocean City, Major Cox thought.

"Do you remember what my last instruction was to Morris?" President Edwards asked Stewart.

"You asked him to be back here by the fourth with a comprehensive energy program based upon the supply of oil that we will have after the OPEC policy goes into effect."

"Do you have any idea of how he's coming on that program?"

"None at all," Stewart said, lying easily.

"Go call him, then. Get me a progress report."

Stewart walked out of the Oval Office, heading toward his own office. He was humming softly to himself.

Stewart reached Morris by telephone at the Department of Energy.

"President Edwards asked me to call you to get a progress report on your comprehensive energy program," Stewart said in a flat tone. "The one that he asked you to prepare by the fourth of July."

Stewart's no fool, Morris thought. He's playing the call straight. He knows that we're plugged into two government switchboards. God only knows whether automatic recorders are picking this up.

"Please tell the President that I have made substantial progress. There is no need to interfere with his enjoyment of the July fourth weekend. I will present him with a comprehensive plan on the morning of July fifth. That should pose no problem because we have enough oil stockpiled to avoid any crunch until the fourteenth or maybe later."

"I will relay that message, Mr. Morris."

There was a long pause.

"Is there anything else?" Stewart asked.

"One of our research people over here has developed a new technique to burn damp wood to generate energy for cooking. It would be useful on a camping trip. If any of your colleagues at the White House are going camping, I might let them try it."

For a few seconds Stewart wondered what the hell Morris was talking about. But only for a few seconds.

"Oliver over here has talked about a camping trip for the weekend of the fourth. But his plans haven't been finalized yet one way or the other."

"Well, do let me know if he's interested. But don't wait too long."

Okay, Morris, Stewart thought, as he hung up the telephone. I'll make my move soon.

Stewart returned to the Oval Office and reported Morris's message to the President.

Edwards broke into a broad grin. "It looks like hotshot Morris is having some difficulty."

Stewart was silent.

"Morris's schedule is okay with me," President Edwards said. "We might as well enjoy the calm before the storm. I can stall the press and the Congress until after the fourth. Everybody in this town is thinking about vacations."

Here was his opening, Stewart thought.

"On the subject of vacations, sir. There is something I want to ask you."

"I already offered you that boondoggle to England, but you turned it down. It's too late. Black's going."

The President was smiling. He's in a good mood, Stewart thought.

"It's not for me. It's for Oliver. Well, it's none of my business, sir."

Stewart paused for a second. Take it slow, he thought, try to sound sincere.

"Go ahead," the President replied, sounding relaxed.

"Hank's marriage is a little rocky these days."

"You know I never get involved in the family relations of members of my staff," the President said.

He had always followed that rule. He never wanted to know how much personal grief his demands were causing.

"I know that. But Hank's wife has been nagging him about a camping trip to the Blue Ridge Mountains in Virginia. It might be a good idea to let him go the weekend of the fourth. We won't need him at Camp David. Maybe it'll make the bitch happy once and for all."

Oliver's a helluva good press secretary, the President thought, but he should be able to control his wife. The President walked over to a small brown credenza.

"Do you want a drink, Fred?" he asked, looking at his watch. "It's past five o'clock."

President Edwards put some ice in two glasses, covered it with scotch, and handed one to Stewart.

"Here's to all the unhappy wives of high-ranking government officials," President Edwards said contemptuously as he raised his glass.

Stewart was silent. He was thinking about the stormy period in his own marriage when he came to Washington with Edwards two years ago. But Joan had gradually been worn down to resignation. It was harder to do with intellectuals like Nadine Oliver.

"I guess you're right," the President said, sipping his drink. "We don't need Oliver at Camp David. Tell him it's okay. Just tell him to call in once in a while and let us know where he is."

# CHAPTER

# 18

CAPTAIN JAMES R. POLK SAT IN HIS TINY CUBICLE OF AN office at the army base in Anchorage fingering the strange message that sat on his desk. It had the usual format—dull yellow paper with blue type. The heading on the top was normal: Orders to Division R under the Direction of the Joint Chiefs.

But the message itself seemed peculiar. Polk read it again:

Prepare Company T-1402 For Immediate Departure on 6/24 at 1000. Objective: Training Mission. Destination: Not Disclosed. Warm Climate.

Captain Polk walked over to the next cubicle.

"Hey, Reilly," he shouted. "Did you get some new orders?"

"I didn't get anything," Captain Matthew Reilly said.

"Here, take a look at this," Polk said, handing the message to Reilly.

"This doesn't mean anything to me," Reilly said.

"Well, that's strange. You're the Commander of T-1403, and I'm the Commander of T-1402. Our units are the only two up here with the new Patton II tanks. Why would they be moving me out and not you?"

"It sounds to me like some more of that discrimination against you blacks," Reilly said, laughing.

Captain Polk always had a great deal of trouble handling Reilly's racial barbs. He was a product of Watts—a product of the American ghetto. He had found his place in America's all-volunteer army because he felt that he was able to move ahead on merit. He was proud of being black, but he didn't like Reilly's endless stream of slurs. Still he'd have to conceal that sensitivity from Reilly, or Reilly would increase his banter.

"Well, look at it this way, honky," Polk said. "Maybe I'm taking my boys to Hawaii while your ass sits here in beautiful downtown Anchorage."

Polk snatched the yellow sheet from Reilly's desk and carried it back to his office.

He looked again at the words "Under the Direction of the Joint Chiefs." Polk had met General Thomas about six months earlier when Thomas was reviewing the first training exercises with the Patton II. Thomas had been very complimentary that day about the organization of Polk's company. But Polk doubted that Thomas would remember him.

Polk tried to think about the work that would have to be done before they were ready to move out. He would have to push his men hard. But they could do it. Thank God it wasn't winter. The tanks were completely oiled. Nothing was dusty. The guns were clean. They would be ready to roll.

A warm climate could be anywhere, Polk thought. He fell asleep that night dreaming about the beaches of the outer islands of Hawaii. He could hear the tune from Hawaiian airline advertisements, "Fly to Our Little Island."

Thirty-six hours later the giant C-130 cargo plane that carried Polk and his company touched down in the dead of the night on a rough landing strip in the Sinai desert. When Polk left the plane, he tried to use the searchlights to identify his location. It was hopeless.

All that Captain Polk could determine was that they had stopped for refueling in Frankfurt earlier in the evening, and that he was now no more than six hours from Frankfurt, as the C-130 flies. He could also determine that the climate was hotter than hell and that the terrain was desert. As he fell asleep in his tent, the Captain felt confident about one other conclusion. It wasn't Hawaii.

Four hours later Captain Polk received an instruction to report to the field commander's headquarters. When he entered the large makeshift tent, he found a strange group of company commanders already there. They were an unusual potpourri of officers, the likes of which Polk had never seen assembled in a single place.

He could tell from the uniforms that there were other tank unit commanders from Korea and Guam. There were Air Force officers from North Dakota and Hawaii. I'll never understand this army, if I stay in it a thousand years, Polk thought.

Polk then decided to stop speculating about the purpose of the gathering. He began milling around with all of the other officers.

A few minutes later there was a great commotion in the front of the tent. Holy shit, Polk thought, it's General Thomas himself. Whatever this is, it must be big time.

As soon as the officers saw General Thomas, they jumped to attention, saluting him in unison.

Then Thomas began speaking in clear, measured tones.

"I would like to clarify to you where we are and the purpose of this mission," Thomas said. "Our location is on the southern part of the Sinai Peninsula near the east coast. The Red Sea is approximately ten miles on the east and the Straits of Tiran are twenty miles south of here. The present purpose of this operation is an intensive training exercise in desert warfare. That purpose may change later on."

Thomas looked around. Everyone was listening carefully.

"I shall be personally involved in directing this operation," Thomas said. "I shall be assisted by General Ripley, on my right, and General Braddock on my left. This is the first time we have pulled together many different units to see if they could be coordinated on a crash basis. Each of your units has been personally selected to participate in this exercise because of some special outstanding service it has performed in the past. No one was told of the mission in advance and absolute secrecy is being maintained. We do not want the Soviet Union to even know that we are engaged in an operation of this type."

Thomas could feel the perspiration breaking out on his forehead. His shirt was already soaked under the arms. It was only five o'clock in the morning. Jesus, it gets hot in this place, Thomas thought.

"There is one other thing," Thomas said. "We have ample supplies of food. We brought the usual rations on the C-130's. But water is a different matter. We will bring water in by truck every morning—as much as we can. But it will never be enough for your men in this brutal climate. All that I can say is use the water as sparingly as you can."

General Thomas was very pleased with the organization work during the first four days at the base. The morale of the men seemed good. They were excited by the chance to do something different. Coordination of units was proceeding systematically and efficiently. The temporary landing strips that had been hastily placed down for the initial landings had been strengthened and extended. All equipment had been tested and malfunctions were minimal. No critical supplies had been left behind. And most important, those Israeli water trucks from Beersheba were coming in right on schedule.

Late in the evening of the twenty-eighth, Thomas sat in his tent sipping warm bourbon and reflecting with satisfaction on how much had been accomplished. The initial phase of operation was the most difficult. Now it was done. Training exercises could begin tomorrow. Everything was on schedule.

Suddenly Thomas heard a tapping on the wooden stake in front of the tent.

"Come in," he bellowed. A junior officer entered carrying a small white envelope. He handed it to Thomas. It bore the notation "To be opened only by General Alwin Thomas."

That's from Zal, Thomas said to himself as soon as he saw the envelope. When he writes in the English language, he can never get the difference between V and W.

Thomas tore open the envelope quickly. He anxiously cast his eyes over the note:

Israeli intelligence has observed unusual movement of Soviet naval units eastward in the Mediterranean toward the Canal. At least one nuclear submarine, the *Brezhnev*, is included. We have no explanation. We will keep you advised.

Z.

Thomas walked briskly to the base communications center.

"I want complete privacy in here," he said, dismissing the officer on duty.

Thomas then picked up the red telephone, which was the tieline to Morris's house, and read Zal's message to Morris.

"What do you make of it?" Morris asked, sounding puzzled.

"I don't know. They may simply be engaged in normal maneuvers."

"What's the worst?"

"The worst is that they may have gotten word about our operation, or at least our base in the Sinai, and they are moving through the Canal to encircle us."

"What do you suggest we do?" Morris asked.

Thomas thought about the question for a minute. He could order American ships in the Sixth Fleet to move eastward in the Mediterranean. He could also order ships in the Seventh Fleet to move westward from the Indian Ocean with both converging on the Canal. That might be the prudent thing to do. After all, there were now several thousand men at this base. Their lives were at stake. But naval movements of that type might arouse Soviet suspicion, if there was none.

"We'll just watch them carefully," Thomas said. "We have the lives of thousands of men at stake. But I don't want to take any action yet. I hate to risk blowing our secrecy. There may be nothing there."

Morris considered what Thomas had said.

"Okay. We'll do it your way. But keep me posted."

"I'll call back if I receive any more information," Thomas said. "If not I'll see you Friday evening in Washington. Everything else is on schedule."

Morris set down the red telephone and walked over to the window. He had been startled by Thomas's statement that the lives of men, of living people, were at stake. Morris never looked at it from that viewpoint. To him it was a game like the type of games they had played on the computers at the Harvard Business School, simulating various kinds of decision making. Morris understood the computer better than any of his classmates. And he was willing to take greater risks than anyone else. He usually won those games.

Morris had an unscheduled visitor the following afternoon.

"Well, well, my old friend, Mr. Barton," Morris said. "I've been expecting you for some time."

Morris walked over to a humidor and pulled out two cigars. He tossed one in the direction of the white-haired Barton, who mumbled "thank you" and sat down.

"Are your new subsidiaries generating big profits?" Morris asked.

"The Bee Burgers are doing very well. All of the others too. We're only in trouble with the investment banking operation."

Morris wasn't surprised. That operation depended entirely upon his own personal involvement. He was pleased that it was in trouble now that he was gone.

"I'll come right to the point," Barton said. "You may remember that some of Global American's other subsidiaries have invested heavily in Saudi Arabia. We have a number of joint development projects with the Saudi government scattered throughout the country."

"I remember that very well," Morris said, taking a deep puff on his cigar.

"And well, Mr. Morris . . . you see . . . it's like this . . ." Barton said, hesitating.

"Don't tell me, Mr. Barton. Let me guess. You're worried that if I deal too harshly with your Saudi friends, you'll lose some of those investments. So you want me to find some way of placating Faisel. Is that it?"

"That's a perfectly reasonable concern," Barton said defensively.

Morris clenched his fists tightly. He was exercising all of his self-control. He wanted to make Barton grovel for a while and then kick him the hell out. But it would be foolish to arouse Barton and send him storming around Capitol Hill and the White House. It was better to pacify him and let him turn back to other corporate concerns. Morris would have his own revenge later on. The Saudi government—or what was left of it after July fourth—would be certain to expropriate Global American's investments. A real pity.

"Let me assure you, Mr. Barton," Morris said, trying to sound sincere, "I am doing everything in my power to deal satisfactorily with Faisel. I want to keep that oil flowing, and I think that we will be successful. Really I do."

They continued the discussion for ten more minutes with Morris continuing to assure Barton that he, too, was anxious to find a satisfactory solution to the problem. Barton left, feeling relieved.

Friday morning Miss Forrest knocked gently on Morris's door.

"No interruptions now," Morris said. "I have too much to do."

"I'm sorry sir, but it's Senator Stark. And he just won't take no for an answer."

"Oh. I'll talk to old fat-ass Stark. Put him on."

"What did you say, sir?" Miss Forrest said, not quite believing her ears.

Morris ignored her and picked up the telephone.

"Well, well, how's my favorite Senator?" he said sarcastically.

"You can cut the crap, Morris," Stark said in a grim tone of voice. "I have a very grave matter that I want some immediate clarification on. I want to know about your ludicrous and idiotic plan to seize the Saudi Arabian oil fields by military force."

All of the color drained quickly from Morris's face. Oh, Jesus, I hope that Stark hasn't found out, Morris thought. His mind was racing quickly, trying to decide what to do if Stark had stumbled across information about the attack.

"What do you mean, Senator?" Morris asked innocently.

"You know damn well what I mean. Earlier this month you presented a proposal for an operation like that to the President in the Oval Office. Don't deny that, or I'll get affidavits."

"I had frankly forgotten about that," Morris said. "That was just some thinking out loud in a brainstorming session with the President. He rejected the idea out of hand."

Morris wondered whether Stark had gotten his information from Black or Oliver, or maybe the President was trying to embarrass Morris.

"If you're telling me the truth," Stark said, "then the President has more sense than I gave him credit for. Quite frankly I was afraid that he might have adopted the idea. I know Edwards very well. He can be impulsive if he gets upset enough about something. And sometimes he takes strong action that he later regrets."

"You don't have to worry, Senator. He turned it down," Morris said again.

"I heard you the first time, Morris. But I frankly don't trust you. I intend to do some checking on my own. I want to be damn sure that there's no plan like that still floating around."

There was a long pause.

"I was planning to leave this evening for San Francisco," Senator Stark said. "But I feel so strongly about this that I'll call off my July fourth trip and stay here over the weekend if I have to."

If there was one thing that Morris did not need, it was Senator Stark snooping around this weekend.

"I hate to see you ruin your weekend for nothing," Morris said. "I'll send Green up to your office. You trust Green. You can talk to him by yourself. He'll verify what I'm telling you."

Stark was silent for a moment, thinking about his weekend plans.

"I'll settle for that. Get Green up here at two o'clock."

As soon as he hung up with Stark, Morris called Green into his office. He reported to Green on the call with Stark.

"He's your friend," Morris said. "Go place his mind at ease. So he can enjoy his weekend. Explain to him that the President turned down the idea, and it died."

"I'll be happy to do it," Green said.

As he left Morris's office, Green thought that Morris seemed slightly tense and nervous. Maybe he's just working too hard, Green thought.

At two o'clock, Green met with Stark. Green explained that Morris had presented the idea to the President, but the President killed it.

"Then it's absolutely dead?" Stark asked.

"Absolutely," Green said with conviction.

"In fact," Green continued, "the President and Black have taken a defensive position—trying to be ready if the Soviets make a move."

"Is there any reason to think they would?"

"Fortunately, nothing so far."

"I feel much better," Stark said. "I can go off and enjoy the weekend. Frankly, I wasn't willing to believe Morris. But you're an honest man, Walter. If you tell me that the idea is dead, then I can believe that it is dead."

Morris was pleased when Green reported back. The Assistant Director did some things very well.

When Green was gone, Morris turned back to the question that he had been thinking about. What would he do if the Russians had received information about the base in the Sinai, and if they were deliberately moving in that direction to trap the American forces?

Morris walked over to the window and looked out. There were already crowds of people pouring out of his own building and the other drab stone government buildings along Independence Avenue. It was four o'clock on the Friday of a four-day holiday weekend. Everyone wanted to get a jump on traffic.

Morris waited an hour before riding down the elevator to the nearly deserted underground parking garage. As he walked from the elevator to his limousine, he noticed a heavy-set man with a dark complexion. He had never seen the man before. The man was wearing a dark business suit, standing next to a car, and reading a newspaper. He looked like one of those SAVAK men who had accompanied Ahmad to Morris's house.

As Morris's car pulled out of the garage, he looked through the rear window. No one was there. It may be nothing, Morris thought.

# CHAPTER

# 19

By FRIDAY THE STUDY OVERLOOKING R STREET IN MORRIS'S Georgetown home had been converted to a command center. Large maps of the Sinai and Saudi Arabia covered two walls. Manufacturers' specifications describing the characteristics of various weapons systems were scattered along two tables.

Morris's own desk contained the two separate beige telephones with independent circuits. One had his listed number. The other phone had a number that only Thomas, Stewart, and Elliott had been given. There was a third telephone—a peculiar-looking red object—that resembled a telephone from the World War II era. That was the telephone that had been installed by army communication experts. It was Morris's direct hookup to the base in the Sinai.

Early in the week Morris made a big point of instructing Anne that neither she nor the household helpers should ever enter his study. But the instructions were superfluous. The room was always locked. When Morris was in the room, he locked it from the inside.

Anne had originally regarded the great mystery that accompanied Morris's activities in the study as a joke. More of the foolishness of a grown man who insisted on operating in the secret ways of a boy.

But when Anne saw the seal of the United States Army on the cardboard boxes containing the apparatus for the red telephone, she became alarmed. Whatever he's doing, I don't want to know, Anne said to herself.

During that entire week Anne had seen little of Morris. He returned home from the Department of Energy at six o'clock and then disappeared into his study. He emerged at nine or ten o'clock and ate something that Louise made, still mentally engrossed, with a grim, serious look on his face. Obsessed in his project, Morris was oblivious to whether or not Anne was there.

On Friday evening Anne decided she would make one more effort. She stopped Morris on his way into the house.

"Happy July Fourth weekend," she said. "Let's go away for a couple of days, George—to the country estate we rented, to the Homestead, the Greenbriar, anywhere. You've been working too hard. You need a couple of days off. It'll do us both good."

"I just don't know. There's still so much to do."

"Can't it wait till Monday? We'll just go Saturday and Sunday. We'll be back Sunday evening."

"Maybe you're right, Anne. Let me tell you later in the evening."

"What will you know later in the evening that you don't know now?"

"I'm having a small meeting here," Morris said, sounding irritated. "I told you that."

George looked Anne squarely in the eyes when he made that last statement. They both knew he was lying.

"Get Louise to put some drinks out on the dining room table. We'll help ourselves."

"Louise isn't here, George. It's July Fourth weekend. She's gone to Norfolk to visit her sister."

"Then why don't you put the drinks out?" Morris said.

"Screw you. I'm not your servant."

Red with rage, Anne raced up the stairs to the bedroom

and slammed the door. Then she stretched out on the bed and began reading scripts from last year's series of "Undercover Woman."

Anne heard them arrive at ten o'clock. They walked quietly up the stairs to the study at the other end of the hall. They were carrying glasses. She heard the ice cubes clinking against the glasses. They were talking in whispers, but she could count the voices. There were three others besides George. None of the voices sounded familiar to her.

Anne was tempted to open the bedroom door quite innocently, march downstairs, and confront them in the middle of the staircase. But she rejected that idea. Oh, who gives a shit, she said to herself.

When she heard the door to George's study slam, she walked into the bathroom, took off her clothes, and stood for a very long time inspecting her face and body in the mirror.

At the other end of the hall, Morris sat down at the head of the table and directed the others to chairs along the sides.

Morris first turned to Thomas.

"Is everything on schedule at the Sinai base, General?" he asked.

"Absolutely. We have no hitches at all at the base."

"I want to set D hour at four A.M. Tuesday, July fourth, Mideast time, which is nine P.M. Monday, July third Washington time," Morris said. "That should give you maximum daylight. Is that acceptable?"

"We will be ready," Thomas replied as he took a long drink from his glass of bourbon.

Suddenly the red telephone began buzzing. The noise jarred Elliott and Stewart.

"Who would know to use that telephone?" Morris asked Thomas.

"Only my personal aide, Major Cox. He can be fully trusted."

Morris looked concerned.

"He doesn't know the location of this end of the telephone," Thomas added.

"Pick it up then," Morris said.

When the General began listening, his facial muscles tightened. He looked tense and grim. Then he relaxed and let out a deep breath.

"Thank God for that," Thomas said. He paused for a minute. Then he continued speaking.

"Okay, Major, read the note one more time. I want to write it down."

He picked up a pencil and started writing.

Unusual Soviet movements in the eastern Mediterranean have stopped. No cause for further concern.

Z.

General Thomas read the note to the others.

Morris was relieved. Those Soviet naval movements had been worrying him more than he cared to admit.

Morris quickly snatched the note from Thomas and incinerated it in an ashtray.

"I intend to communicate with the commander of the Sixth Fleet before I leave Washington," Thomas said. "I will instruct him to watch the Soviets closely in the eastern Mediterranean. He is to report to me any unusual activity. If it looks like they are starting through the Suez Canal to encircle us before we take off on the fourth, I intend to blow up some tankers in the Canal and seal it off. The commercial countries will be pissed at us if we do that, and I hope to avoid it. But it's a last resort."

"The critical question is what the Russians will do after they receive word of the attack," Elliott said.

"I have a plan to handle that," Morris replied.

"What about Iran?" Thomas asked.

"You don't have to worry about the Shah," Morris replied.

"On the subject of Iran," Stewart said, "you should be aware that Anderson at CIA thinks that SAVAK, the Shah's secret police, has increased its presence in Washington during the last week. It may just be to suppress the Iranian students and take action against them in this country. On the other hand, they may suspect that something is happening."

"Don't say any more about Iran," Morris said angrily to Stewart. "I already told you. I am handling that subject."

Morris took a sip from his coffee and walked over to the window. His guard was carefully patrolling the sidewalk. There were no signs of other activity.

"What happened with Oliver?" Morris asked Stewart.

"Mission accomplished. Late tomorrow morning, Oliver and his wife are leaving for their camping trip in the Blue Ridge Mountains."

"And Black still goes to England?"

"Early tomorrow morning." Stewart paused.

"Then at noon," Stewart continued, "Joan and I go by helicopter to Camp David with the President and Mrs. Edwards."

Morris didn't tell Stewart, but he was impressed. The President's counselor had done a good job.

"Does the President usually have a drink in the evening when he's at Camp David?" Morris asked Stewart.

"Always one or two scotches before dinner and one or two glasses of Grand Marnier after dinner."

"Are you sure about the Grand Marnier?"

"Absolutely. Once we ran out of it at Camp David. I had to call two marines to bring some up from Washington."

"Are you listening carefully?" Morris said to Stewart.

Stewart nodded his head.

"Okay. Tomorrow morning I want you to go out to a drug store and buy some chloral hydrate syrup. It's a widely sold sedative. Nothing exotic."

Stewart was listening carefully. He was still nodding.

"On Monday evening," Morris continued, "I want you to

add the chloral hydrate directly to his first Grand Marnier, which should be around nine o'clock. You don't have to worry about the President detecting the chloral hydrate. It's an orange liquid just like Grand Marnier. Its odor and taste will be drowned out by the Grand Marnier. If you follow the dosage on the bottle and add it to the Grand Marnier, he should quickly become drowsy. He'll sleep until ten o'clock Tuesday morning, maybe even longer. It won't have any adverse effect on him. During that time you can sit next to the switchboard and handle any suspicious calls. Do you understand all that?"

"Very well," Stewart said.

Then Morris turned to Elliott.

"Where are you going to be over the weekend?"

"Tomorrow I'm going to be in town. There's a party at the Club in the evening. Then Sunday I'll go up to my yacht on Chesapeake Bay with Francine. We'll spend Sunday, Monday, and Tuesday on the Bay."

"Bang her once for me," Stewart said, laughing. Thomas smiled, shaking his head. Elliott was grinning from ear to ear.

"Okay, knock it off," Morris said, sounding like a warden. "We've got work to do."

That's probably the best place in the world for Elliott, Morris thought. In the middle of Chesapeake Bay.

Then Morris turned to Thomas. "When are you flying back to the Sinai?" he asked.

"As soon as I leave here I'm going to Andrews. My plane is standing by. I'll stay in the Sinai until the end of the operation. I want to make certain that everything is in place. And I want to direct it myself."

Morris sat for a moment quietly sipping the last drops of his cold coffee.

"I'm flying over with you tonight," Morris said. "I'm not cut out to sit by this phone all weekend. I want to see things first hand tomorrow. Just a short inspection. Then I'll fly back. I should be back in the early hours of Sunday morning."

Morris stopped to see if Thomas had any objections.

The General didn't mind at all. He was very proud of his Sinai camp.

"When I get back, I'll call each of you," Morris said, pointing to Stewart and Elliott. "I'll let you know if everything is in order. Be near the phone Sunday between eight and ten in the morning. I know the number at Camp David, Fred. And I assume that you'll be at Francine's Watergate apartment, Bill. Is that right?"

"That's right," Elliott replied.

Morris remembered his last call to Elliott.

"For God's sake, Elliott, be near the phone this time," Morris said.

Thomas, Elliott, and Stewart sat still while Morris went back over all of the logistics one more time in his mind. There was one final communication that the group should have.

"General Thomas," Morris said, "I will be carefully watching the Washington scene on Sunday and Monday. If no complications develop, I will call you at precisely eight forty-five Washington time Monday evening and say to you 'Happy Independence Day.' Once you hear that, you may order your planes to take off. But do not have them take off before you receive that call. Is that clear?"

"Very clear, George."

"I will also call you, Fred, with the same message so that you know to move ahead," Morris said. "There will be no need to call you, Bill. You'll be on your boat."

Morris paused for a minute. Then he continued.

"Incidentally, Fred, once you've given him the chloral hydrate, unplug all the radios and televisions at Camp David if you can without raising any suspicions. I want to cut off communications as much as I can with the outside world."

Morris asked if anyone had any questions. There was no response.

"I guess that's it," Morris said. "We're finished."

"We should make a toast to the successful completion of Operation Independence," Elliott said, raising his glass.

"A good idea," Stewart replied.

"Jesus Christ," Morris shouted, with a scowl on his face. "You two aren't back in a fraternity house. We don't need sentimental bullshit like that."

Morris started gathering up a pile of papers.

"Eliott, you leave first and walk west on R Street," Morris said. "Stewart, you wait two minutes and walk east on R Street. General, will you wait for me by the swimming pool in the back. I have one small matter to take care of. It won't take me long."

When the other three had gone downstairs, Morris walked quietly down the hall to the bedroom. He opened the door slowly. He didn't see Anne, but he heard water running.

She must be in the bathroom, Morris thought. He pulled a small suitcase from his closet and piled some light clothes into it.

"I can't go away with you this weekend, Anne," Morris shouted in the direction of the bathroom. "I have to leave Washington again on urgent business. I should be back Sunday."

Suddenly the water stopped running. Anne emerged from the bathroom wearing the same silk blouse and skirt that she had worn when they first traveled to Washington in mid-April. Large round sunglasses were resting on her head. The blouse was deliberately open at the neck to expose a portion of her well-rounded breasts.

"You don't have to worry about coming back Sunday," Anne said. "I've declared Independence Day tonight. It's only four days early. Why don't you wish me a happy holiday?"

"What do you mean?" Morris asked, looking puzzled.

"I mean I'm leaving you, George. My bags are packed and sitting by the front door. I'm just waiting for the cab to come."

Anne was pleased. She had spoken her words calmly and with dignity just as she had intended. Her tone reflected the type of detachment that she had learned from Morris.

Morris just stood there silent, bewildered, looking at her.

Suddenly he realized that when he sold out to Barton, he had had the chance to break the old pattern—the determined drive for success at any cost. He could have taken Anne and dropped off the carousel quietly, even respectably. But he hadn't. Or maybe he couldn't. He didn't know which. He wasn't philosophical. He didn't even care. It was too late now.

Maybe after the operation with Thomas was over, they could pick up the strands, Morris thought. No, he was just kidding himself. He would never look back.

She was waiting for him to speak. He wanted to ask her to stay, to tell her that she helped him overcome the loneliness. Maybe he even loved her. He wasn't sure. He wanted to break the old pattern; but he couldn't. He didn't say anything at all.

"Why don't you ask me what I'm doing when I get back to L.A.?"

He remained silent.

"Well, as long as you asked," she said, "I'll stay fairly loose. I would even be happy to see you again if you ever decide to move back to a more normal place like Beverly Hills."

A horn was honking on the street.

"That must be my cab, George."

He walked over and kissed her gently on the cheek. His lips were cold. They had no feeling, no emotion.

She squeezed his hand once firmly and walked out of the room.

From the top of the stairs, she called back, "Whatever you're doing, George, I hope you succeed. I really do for your sake."

The Metropolitan Opera performed *Tosca* on Friday evening. Ahmad loved to watch Maria in that role. He refused to leave until the final curtain came down.

But once it did, Ahmad raced out of his seat. He left a

note for Maria with an usher. "I'll meet you back at the hotel in about an hour." Then he bolted from the hall and into his waiting limousine.

"The Waldorf," Ahmad said to the driver.

Faisel was waiting for the Iranian when he entered the suite.

The Saudi was fully dressed, quite sober, and alone. Not bad for 11:30 on a Friday evening, Ahmad thought.

"Would you like something to drink?" Faisel asked.

"Yes. Some cognac. Please."

Faisel poured cognac into two large glasses. As he handed one to Ahmad, the Iranian thought that he detected a trace of nervousness in Faisel's face.

"I asked for this meeting at the Shah's instruction," Ahmad said.

Faisel waited anxiously.

"His Royal Highness has had differences of opinion with your government over OPEC pricing policies in the past," Ahmad continued, "but His Royal Highness wants to end those differences once and for all time. We are prepared to do more than reluctantly follow OPEC's July fourth pricing policy. We will enthusiastically support it."

Faisel was relieved. Morris and the Americans had been so quiet lately that he was beginning to feel apprehensive. He was worried that the Shah had made some type of deal with the Americans—something he had not contemplated.

Faisel refilled the two cognac glasses to the top.

"Here's to the unity of OPEC," Faisel said.

"I'll drink to that," Ahmad replied.

The two men spent the next hour talking in Faisel's suite.

When Ahmad left at one-thirty, Faisel sent a cable to his Minister of Defense in Riyadh.

I have met with the Iranian Ambassador. There is no cause for concern.

# CHAPTER

# 20

BILL MARKS EMERGED FROM THE SPARKLING BLUE WATER of the swimming pool with a broad smile on his face. As he walked along the edge of the pool, he gazed at the mountains that ran to Jerusalem in the north. The sky was picture-book blue without a single cloud.

Marks fell into a chaise longue, singing an old limerick that he remembered from his youth. He could only recall the first six words: "In China they never eat chili . . ."

"What are you so happy about?" his wife Sarah asked.

"Oh, I could get used to this life very easily," Marks said. "It beats killing myself as a reporter in Washington."

She laughed. "You tell me that every time we come to Israel on a vacation. But let's face it. You'd be bored in two weeks if you became a member of the leisure class."

"Maybe so," Marks said, trying to visualize that prospect.

As he dozed in the chaise, Marks thought about his brother, Dan, who had come to Israel to live in 1948, when they were both at the end of their teens in Boston. Now that his own children were in college, Marks and his wife had developed a good plan. They came to visit Dan and his family every summer.

There was a large commotion at the end of the pool, but Marks was too lazy to open his eyes.

"What's all that noise?" he asked.

"Just the whole kibbutz descending on the pool. That's all. Remember it's Friday. The farmers quit work at noon."

Marks looked at his watch. She was right. It was Friday, June thirtieth. He had lost track of the days.

"Then my teamster brother should be back soon," Marks said, laughing.

"What's so funny?"

"If you won't let me retire, then I'll switch places with him next month. I'll haul the fruits and vegetables to Beersheba every night, and he can go be a Washington reporter."

Marks thought about Francine and his other friends in the Washington Press Corps. They'll all take off for the weekend. Francine will be rolling down the Bay in Elliott's yacht.

A few minutes later a large burly man with a mustache and wild bushy hair quietly approached Marks from the rear. He picked up the dozing Marks and the rubber mat on his chaise and threw them both into the pool. Sarah roared with laughter.

"That's my brother, King Kong," Marks said, as he climbed out of the pool. "Put on a suit and join us."

"Are you crazy? I'm going to sleep. I've been driving for the last twelve hours. I'm shot."

Then Dan added, "Why don't you walk me up to the house, Bill? I want to talk to you."

As they walked along the narrow dirt path, Marks asked, "Did you get all of your fruits and vegetables delivered?"

"I did better than that," Dan said. "I even heard something that might be of interest to you."

"What do you mean?"

"I pulled into Dora's for coffee like I always do about eight o'clock. It's a truck stop near Beersheba. I saw about ten large tank trucks pulled off to the side. They looked bare. No markings or identification. Now I'm a little curious by nature, right?"

"You're just plain nosy."

"Well, anyhow I get to talking to some of the boys. Where are you going, and this and that."

"And?"

"And it turns out that these boys are hauling water down to an American base in the southern Sinai. Do you know anything about that?"

Marks was startled.

"I've never heard about a base like that. In fact about a month ago the President made a big deal of the fact that no Americans are stationed on Middle Eastern soil."

"Well, I never saw anything in the Israeli papers about it either. So I says to these boys, how long have you been doing this? They tell me only about a week. But the pay is great."

"You sure these guys weren't B.S.ing you?" Marks asked.

"No. I know these boys. They're good boys."

Marks was quiet for a minute trying to find an explanation.

"Where is this base?" Marks asked. "Did they tell you?"

"About ten miles in from the Red Sea, and twenty miles north of the Straits of Tiran."

They walked into the small wooden cottage that Dan and his wife lived in on the kibbutz. Marks was disturbed and brooding about his conversation with Dan. That just can't be right, Marks thought. What the hell's going on? The United States doesn't have a base in the Sinai. I would have heard about it before.

"How long a drive is it to that spot in the Sinai?" Marks shouted to Dan, who was heading toward the shower.

"About six hours over difficult roads," Dan replied, his voice booming over the sound of the running water.

Marks thought about his promise to Sarah that this trip would be pure vacation—no research for articles or any other business. They had rented a Fiat to tour the Galilee beginning next Monday.

"I'm driving down tomorrow morning," Marks said. "I want to see it for myself."

"You're not going down alone," Dan shouted back. "The driving's too hard. It's not like your turnpikes and beltways."

"That's ridiculous. Stop pulling the big-brother routine. You drive six days a week. I have no intention of making you drive on your one day off."

"Either we drive together, or I remove one tire from your car tonight," Dan said, drying himself.

"Okay. Okay," Marks said. "Don't hock me any more. We drive together. We'll leave at four-thirty in the morning. Just do me one favor. Please. Tell the women that we're going off to Tel Aviv to see a soccer match. I promised Sarah that I wouldn't do any work on this trip."

"I'll do that."

Marks walked back to the swimming pool still engrossed in thought. Is it possible that this base could have something to do with the OPEC July fourth program, he wondered. That's consistent with the length of time it's been here. I can't believe that Edwards would go for something like that, Marks said to himself.

Just as he was about to enter the pool area, Marks turned around and started retracing his steps along the dirt path. Instead of walking back to Dan's cottage, Marks walked to the Central Administration Building of the kibbutz. There was someone who could get some information. Marks looked at his watch. It was still Friday morning in Washington.

"I want to send a telegram," Marks said to the secretary in the Director's office.

"Write it out on this paper," she replied, throwing a blank pad in his direction.

Marks sat down and printed carefully:

*Francine:*

Please ask your friend Elliott if U.S. has any bases in Sinai. Will explain later. Wire back immediately.

Bill Marks

Marks realized that sending the telegram to Francine at her Watergate apartment was a long shot. She might already be gone for the weekend. Still she was close to Elliott. Maybe she could get something.

Marks and his brother set out the following morning just as the sun was beginning to rise. For the first half hour Marks was behind the wheel. Dan was shouting furiously. "Speed it up. You drive like an old woman. We'll never get there."

Finally Dan said, "Pull this damn thing over to the side. I can't take it any more. Let a professional do the job."

After Marks stopped the car, Dan took the wheel, and they roared across the desert. Dan had a pretty good idea of where the base was from the water trucks. It had to be accessible to trucks of that size. There weren't too many areas of that type.

When it was close to noon, Marks saw a strange and incredible sight rising out of the desert. In the middle of nowhere he suddenly saw tanks and planes with United States markings. Marks rubbed his eyes, thinking it was a mirage. "Holy Moly!" he shouted. He simply couldn't believe what he saw.

"Those are our planes and tanks?" Marks asked Dan in a tone of disbelief. "Not yours? Is that right?"

"Well, they have stars with five points and not six, and the letters say 'U.S.' What else can I tell you?"

As they drove a little farther, they saw men in American uniforms, some marching, some running, and others just walking around. They saw tents with the large letters "U.S. ARMY" painted in white on the green canvas.

Suddenly a small jeep cut into the road in front of the Fiat and another behind it. Four soldiers with white "M.P." symbols on their sleeves and helmets jumped out of the jeeps armed with rifles and bayonets.

"Identify yourselves," one of the soldiers shouted to Marks and Dan.

"I'm Bill Marks, a reporter with *The New York Times*. I'm an American citizen. This is my brother Dan. He's an Israeli."

Marks pulled a press badge from his wallet and showed it to the soldier. He took the card from Marks and walked back to his jeep. Marks watched the soldier talking into a two-way radio, but Marks couldn't hear what he was saying. It seemed to Marks that the conversation was taking a very long time.

Then the soldier walked back to Marks and Dan.

"Come with me, in the jeep," he said. "Leave your car here."

"What the hell is this?" Marks shouted. "I'm an American citizen. I have constitutional rights. You can't tell me where to go—and certainly not on foreign soil."

The soldier ignored Marks' words.

"We better go with them," Dan said, taking one look at the other three soldiers who were nervously holding the triggers of their rifles. Dan was a veteran of four wars. Unarmed, he had no intention of challenging the soldiers.

The jeep carried Marks and Dan to a tent marked "Operation Headquarters." There it stopped abruptly.

The two brothers followed the officer into the large tent. It was empty. They were seated on hard wooden folding chairs. The three armed M.P.'s followed them into the tent and were watching them carefully.

Marks could hear faint voices outside of the tent.

"No, I don't know what to do with them," one voice said.

"Let's wait until General Thomas gets back," the other one said. "He's due back at fifteen hundred hours. Why don't you interrogate them in the meantime?"

Boy, oh boy, Marks said to himself when he heard the reference to General Thomas. We must have really stumbled onto something big.

Two hours later Thomas arrived with Morris. General Ripley raced out of the Headquarters tent with a distraught look on his face. He quickly explained what had happened with Marks and his brother.

"Jesus, we didn't need a reporter snooping around," Thomas said. "Where are they now?"

"In your tent," Ripley answered. "We didn't know what to do with them."

"Wait for me at Headquarters," Thomas said, dismissing Ripley.

When Ripley had gone, Thomas turned to Morris with an intensely serious look on his face.

"I'll tell you what we should do with them," Thomas said. "We should take the bastards out into the desert and shoot both of them. No one would never know what happened to them."

Morris thought about it for a moment. He had no qualms of conscience about following Thomas's suggestion. There was no way that he would let some nosy reporter interfere with the operation. Not now.

On the other hand, maybe Morris could use Marks for his own benefit.

"I have a better idea, General," Morris said. "Let's keep them here, out of communication with the outside world, until the operation is over. Once it's over, we'll let them go."

"But then Marks will write a story describing what he saw."

"Let him do it. The operation will be successfully completed. You and I will be national heroes. Any article that he could write will only be good press for us. It will confirm the notion that we worked a great miracle for the country. It will help to generate a legend about us."

Thomas couldn't find any flaw in Morris's reasoning.

"I guess you're right," he said reluctantly. "They can't hurt us after it's over. I'll have them put in a remote tent and guarded around the clock."

During the next three hours Thomas toured the entire base

with Morris at his side. Thomas explained to Morris what each piece of equipment was and how it would be used.

"I'm going to talk to you like I talk to the President when I give him a tour of a military installation," Thomas said.

That statement brought a broad smile to Morris's face.

Occasionally Thomas found small items that bothered him —some tanks that were clogged with sand or a pot hole in a landing strip that needed repairs. He gave prompt and direct orders for corrective action, explaining to Morris in lay terms what those orders meant.

"Do you understand that, Mr. President?" Thomas said once to Morris.

Then he caught himself. "I'm sorry for that slip, George."

"Don't worry about that at all," Morris replied, sounding pleased. He could still remember his boyhood dream of wanting to be President.

They walked silently for a few more minutes, each man absorbed in his own thoughts.

"We're doing a great deed for the country," Thomas said, self-righteously.

Morris ignored the comment. But the General persisted.

"Don't you try to articulate a justification to yourself?"

"I'm not philosophical. I don't need it."

"But you must have some ideas about why you're doing it."

"I just do things. I don't think about why."

"You're doing it for yourself," the General said, kicking a small mound of sand. "You're not motivated by patriotism. I know that. You want it for yourself."

The two men walked along in silence. Morris was scowling.

"I don't mind," Thomas said, fearful that he had angered Morris. "Really I don't."

They stopped to inspect a storage tent holding ammunition.

"At least we don't have to worry about this stuff getting wet," Thomas said. "It hasn't rained here in the summer in centuries."

When they completed the tour, Thomas said to Morris, "As

far as I'm concerned, all preparations are completely on schedule. We will definitely be ready to go at four A.M. Middle East time on Tuesday, nine P.M. Washington time."

"Remember my instructions," Morris said. "No planes take off until I call at eight forty-five with the message 'Happy Independence Day.'"

"I remember those instructions very well," Thomas said. "I'll have someone take you to your plane."

As Morris was about to climb into the jeep, he stretched out his hand to Thomas. Thomas shook it firmly.

They stood there for a moment shaking hands and staring at each other. They were both so taciturn and inward, so contemptuous of small talk, and so hostile to sentiment that neither man said anything to the other. They simply stood there shaking hands and looking at one another.

Their eyes told it, though. Their eyes expressed the peculiar respect that each man felt for the other, the good fortune that each one felt because his path had crossed with the other at a critical point in time, and the concern that each man had deep down, despite his self-confidence, for the success of the dangerous and risky operation that had been planned. Neither man was religious. Neither could invoke the blessings of God.

"This year it will be a happy Independence Day," Thomas said, as he let go of Morris's hand.

Bill Elliott finished munching on the frozen donut that comprised his Saturday breakfast. He took a few more swigs of coffee to clear his head and looked at his watch.

Almost ten o'clock, Elliott said to himself. Francine must have left at the crack of dawn to cover Black's departure to London. I better get my ass moving, or I'll miss my starting time at the Club.

As Elliott walked through the lobby, he heard Georgiana, the switchboard operator calling him.

"Mr. Elliott," she shouted. "Please come to the desk."

When he reached the desk Georgiana took the earphone

from her ear and handed him a Western Union envelope.

"This arrived for Miss Rush last evening," she said. "The night clerk must have forgotten to send it up."

Georgiana pointed to the time stamp on the envelope to verify her story.

"I just found it about ten minutes ago," she said, "and I haven't had a chance to send it up. Do you want to give it to her?"

Elliott looked at the light brown envelope, trying to conceal his feeling of pride. It's probably one of her boy friends, he thought, displaying his jealousy because I've moved in.

"Thank you, Georgiana," Elliott said, taking the envelope. "I'll give it to Miss Rush."

As he walked through the door, he heard Georgiana call, "Have a nice weekend, Mr. Elliott. I leave at two today, and I'm gone until Wednesday."

When Elliott reached the street, he stepped into his waiting limousine. As the driver sped away from the Watergate apartment and eased on to Rock Creek Parkway, Elliott took a pocketknife from his jacket and carefully slipped open the envelope of the telegram.

Elliott was surprised to see that it wasn't about love and jealousy after all. It was from Bill Marks. Jesus Christ, Elliott said to himself when he read the telegram. Marks may be able to blow open the whole thing.

Beads of sweat formed on his forehead. His face was flushed, and he was in a state of near panic by the time the car sped past the Washington Zoo.

I better get control of myself, Elliott thought. Morris will know how to handle this. But then he suddenly recalled that Morris was in the Sinai, and any efforts to locate him would probably raise more problems than it solved.

I'll just have to wait for Morris's call tomorrow morning, Elliott thought. There's nothing else to do.

Elliott tore the telegram and its envelope into thousands

of tiny pieces. He opened the car window and released half of the pieces, watching them flutter away in all directions in the summer breeze. Elliott repeated this act a few minutes later with the remainder.

Then he began softly mumbling to himself, "And all the King's horses and all the King's men couldn't put Humpty Dumpty together again."

At noon on Saturday Janet was sitting at the swimming pool of her apartment.

"Telephone call for you, Miss Koch," a lifeguard shouted.

She dropped her book, *Further Reflections on Advanced Computer Design*, and walked quickly to the phone. That must be Morris she thought. Who else would call me on a holiday weekend?

Disappointment registered on her face as soon as she picked up the phone. It was only Philip Jordan, Morris's personal attorney in Los Angeles.

"What's going on back there?" Jordan asked.

"What do you mean?" Janet replied, sounding puzzled.

"Well, Anne flew back to L.A. last night. For good, she says. She won't tell me what happened. I called George, but he refuses to talk. Says he's too busy. You're the only one I could call."

Janet paused for a minute, digesting what Jordan had said.

"I'm sorry I can't help you," she replied. "I don't know anything about it."

"I'm not being nosy. They're both good friends. I just want to know what happened."

"I really can't help you, Mr. Jordan," Janet repeated as she hung up the phone.

A very interesting development, Janet thought. Her mind began racing, automatically assigning probabilities to each of the possible factual developments.

Then she hurried down to her apartment and called Arden's

for a miracle treatment. This time, she decided to change her image. There was a possibility, she thought, not great—maybe one in ten—that with Anne gone, Morris might turn to her. And if he did, she wanted to be more than the operator of the Morris 6000.

# CHAPTER

# 21

FRANCINE WAS JUST BEGINNING TO ENJOY THAT LAST GOOD hour of morning sleep, the one between nine and ten o'clock, which she only managed to capture on Sunday mornings, when Elliott gently kissed her on the nape of her neck.

She moved across the bed trying to escape, but he pursued, whispering into her ear, "Francine, do you have your protective device?"

"I'm always protected," she muttered, half asleep, hoping that he would go away.

Elliott began caressing her until she was fully awake. Then he whispered into her ear, "I knew that you weren't sleeping."

"In your case, this just proves the revitalizing effect of a good night's sleep," she said.

Elliott was getting ready to respond verbally when the telephone rang on the night table next to the bed, shattering the calm of the morning. On the first ring Elliott quickly stood up in the bed and announced, "I'll answer it in the living room."

He jumped on to the floor, raced out of the bedroom, and slammed the door behind him.

Jesus Christ, Francine thought to herself, that must be some important call. He never answers the phone in this apartment.

She picked up the receiver on the pink Princess phone next to the bed very gently to avoid any clicking noise. Then she held the receiver to her ear.

Francine could hear a man shouting into the phone.

"What the hell took you so long to answer, Elliott? I told you to be by the phone between eight and ten."

She recognized that voice immediately. It was lover boy himself, George T. Morris.

Elliott was out of breath and puffing from his sprint to the living room.

"I'm sorry, George. I answered as quickly as I could," Elliott said, speaking in a soft voice.

"I called to tell you that everything is ready to go. No problems at all."

"Don't hang up," Elliott said. "There is one urgent matter that I must report to you."

"Make it fast."

"Yesterday morning the woman at the desk, here at the apartment, handed me a telegram for Francine from Bill Marks in Israel. The telegram arrived on Friday, but it was never delivered to Francine."

"What did it say?"

"Marks told her to ask me if the United States has any bases in the Sinai. He said that he would explain later, and he asked her to wire back immediately."

"I hope that you had the sense to dispose of the telegram," Morris said, talking quickly.

"I'm no fool, Morris. Give me some credit. It was torn into thousands of little pieces and released into the wind in Rock Creek Park."

That bastard, Francine thought.

There was a pause in the conversation.

Morris was thinking quickly. From the timing, Marks must have sent the telegram before he and his brother made their trip. Maybe someone else knew where they were going. Or maybe not. There was nothing to do about it now.

"Don't worry about the telegram," Morris said. "Go have a good time on your boat."

"But aren't you concerned?"

"I told you to forget it. Now forget it," Morris said, sounding angry.

Elliott hung up the phone. As soon as Francine heard it click, she put down her own receiver and burrowed under the covers, pretending that she had gone back to sleep.

She could hardly believe what she had heard. What the hell is going on? Francine said to herself. Either I'm losing my mind, or Elliott and Morris are participating in some kind of a clandestine operation that involves an American base in the Sinai. But we don't have any bases in the Sinai. Or at least none that I know about.

Whatever it is, there must be one helluva good story here, Francine thought. And I'm going to get it.

She felt a thud in the bed that told her that Elliott had returned. She also detected the aroma of lime-scented cologne that Elliott had applied before returning.

"Who was that on the phone?" she asked innocently.

"It was for me. Someone who wanted to sell me some stock."

"On Sunday morning?"

"He thinks it's a hot issue."

"That's bullshit, and you know it," Francine said. "Now tell me who called you and what he wanted."

Elliott was breathing heavy. He tried to snuggle up to Francine, but she pulled her body away.

"Come on, Franny," he said softly. "I want you so badly this morning."

"Well. I want something this morning too. I want to know about that call."

"That's not fair," he moaned.

"That's too damn bad," she said, getting out of bed. "When you give me what I want, you'll get what you want."

She washed her face and emerged from the bathroom

wearing only a T-shirt. It had the word "UP" written on the front in blue and a red arrow pointing skyward on the back. The T-shirt only came to her navel.

"You can look, but you can't touch," she said. "When you're ready to play ball, I'm ready to play ball."

"What are you doing?" he asked.

"I'm fixing breakfast. What the hell does it look like I'm doing?" she said as she walked toward the kitchen.

She fixed a pot of coffee, warmed some frozen Danish in the oven, and poured some orange juice from a carton. While the water for the coffee was heating, Francine refined her plan to get into Elliott's brain.

When the brown color of the coffee appeared in the top of the percolator, she pulled the mildly warm Danish from the oven and shouted, "Breakfast is ready."

Elliott entered the kitchen wearing a red silk robe that Anita had given him for his birthday last year. Francine was still clad only in her T-shirt.

"We're eating in the den," she said, resting a piece of Danish on top of the juice glass. Carrying the glass and the coffee cup, she marched out of the kitchen. Elliott followed behind.

She sat down in the center of the large den couch, leaving Elliott a wingback chair facing her.

They ate breakfast in silence. Francine had her eyes riveted on a tiny spider that was trying desperately to make its way across the blue-painted ceiling. Elliott kept his eyes squarely on Francine.

When Elliott finished the last piece of Danish, he said to her, "Isn't this ridiculous? We're grown people."

"Don't tell me about grown people," she responded. "You went to law school. I'm talking about a simple quid pro quo. But if the answer is no, then it's no," she said, walking from the den and shaking her bare buttocks at him.

"What are you doing now?" he asked.

"I'm packing some food for the boat. Remember we were planning to stay on the Bay Sunday, Monday, and Tuesday?

I realize that your boat is well stocked with booze, but I like to eat too," she said, patting her stomach. "It's a normal bodily function."

They rode in silence along Route 50 to Annapolis. Elliott was behind the wheel driving at 65 or 70 miles an hour, cursing under his breath. Francine sat in the front seat with her feet on the dashboard thinking about what activity Morris and Elliott could be involved in that related to the Sinai.

When they arrived at the Yacht Club, it was almost noon. It was a miserably hot and humid day—typical summer weather for the Washington area.

"You really should change the name of this boat," Francine said as she stepped onto the forty-foot Hatteras. "Don't you think it's a bit much to still call it *The Anita*?"

Elliott ignored her remark.

"I'm going inside to put on a bathing suit," she said. "Why don't you get a boy to help you haul all that food and other crap on board."

They spent the afternoon winding their way up and down narrow streams and inlets along Chesapeake Bay. Francine lay on the deck most of the long, hot afternoon in her print bikini, sunning herself and acting indifferent or downright hostile to Elliott. She had a permanent scowl on her face. If he won't open up, then I won't open up, Francine thought.

Elliott for his part sat in the skipper's chair steering the ship. He had his captain's hat pulled down low on his forehead, and he was bearing a stiff upper lip. Periodically he pointed out some landmark or other, but his comments received no response. I am definitely not doing well with women, Elliott thought.

As the sun started to dip slowly in the west, Francine walked over to Elliott.

"Let's bury it and have a nice dinner, Bill. What do you say?"

"I think that's a good idea," Elliott said, sounding relieved.

"I'll pull up along side the Naval Academy and drop anchor there."

Chalk up one round for me, Elliott thought, as he watched Francine go below.

She emerged a few minutes later carrying a large dish of cold fresh shrimp and champagne in an ice bucket.

When Elliott dropped the anchor, she set up a portable table in the back of the boat with two chairs.

"You pop the cork, Bill," she said in a sweet voice, handing him the bottle.

He sent the cork flying into the Bay, and then he filled two glasses.

"Here's to a happy July Fourth," he said.

"I'll drink to that."

"Your taste is excellent, Franny."

"Dom Pérignon. Nothing but the best."

I learned something from Anne Walton's party, Francine thought.

"Tell me how you spent July Fourth as a boy," she asked.

"Oh, come on. That would be a waste of time."

"No. No, really. I'd like to know."

She refilled Elliott's glass, and he started to talk about his family life in downstate Illinois.

As the last rays of the sun disappeared behind the gray stone buildings of the Naval Academy, Elliott was talking about family picnics, county fairs, the mating of horses, and the feeling up of high-school girls.

Elliott laughed as he told funny little family anecdotes, and Francine laughed with him. The evening air was still hot and sticky. His mouth became dry as he talked, and he sipped champagne.

She went down below and returned with another bottle and a dish of cashews. Elliott continued talking, and she continued refilling his glass.

When Elliott had finished two full bottles of champagne,

he was slurring his words. His eyes were glazed; and they were only half open. Then Francine made her move ever so gently.

"Tell me about George Morris, Bill," she asked. "What's he really like?"

"I hate the son-of-a-bitch."

"Why do you hate him?"

"Because the bastard doesn't have a sense of humor."

"What does he do?"

"Why, Friday evening I said to Morris, let's make a toast, and he said that's for fraternity boys."

"What a killjoy," she said sympathetically.

"You're damn right. Fred Stewart agreed with me."

"Fred's a good man," Francine said. "What did you and Fred want to toast?"

"We wanted to toast the success of our operation."

"What operation?"

"We're attacking Saudi Arabia," he said, "and seizing their oil fields."

Then he paused. Francine could hardly contain herself. Don't quit now, Bill, she said to herself. She refilled his glass.

"Who is attacking the Saudi oil fields?"

"We are. The U.S. Army led by General Thomas. And we're going to teach those A-rabs a lesson. You better believe it."

"When is this attack taking place?" she asked.

Elliott was quiet. He was leaning back in his chair. He seemed half asleep.

"I can't remember, Franny. I'm so tired. So tired."

"Try to remember, please."

"July the Fourth, Happy Independence Day."

"Whose idea was it? Was it the President's idea? Or did Morris convince the President to go along?" she asked.

It never occurred to Francine that President Edwards had not ordered the military operation.

"I'm so tired, Franny. So tired."

With those words Elliott fell off his chair and landed on the deck of the boat in a heap. She could hear him snoring . loudly in the dark night air.

"You sleep well, Bill," she said. "You've given me what I wanted."

Francine was ecstatic. She jumped up and down on the deck of the boat.

"Holy shit!" she shouted. "This is what Bill Marks stumbled onto. It all makes sense—the telegram, and the Morris call."

"I've got the news story of the century. This is bigger than Watergate. I might even get the Pulitzer Prize."

She checked her watch. It was nine o'clock. I can still make the morning papers, she thought. She could already see the headline—"President Orders Secret Attack of Saudi Oil Fields"—with the Francine Rush byline.

Suddenly Francine realized that she was stranded on a boat in the middle of Chesapeake Bay. She had never operated a boat in her life, and the skipper was dead drunk and sound asleep on the deck. Her joy turned to absolute panic. Her warm perspiration became a cold sweat.

She tried to cajole Elliott into waking up, but he wouldn't budge. She put damp towels on his head. She poured the cold water and half-dissolved ice cubes from the champagne bucket into his pants. But nothing helped.

"You can't do this to me," she shouted in vain at the sleeping Elliott.

She looked around in the Bay. She couldn't see another boat.

Well, there just aren't too many choices, she said to herself as she grabbed the captain's hat from Elliott's head and put it on her own.

Clad in that hat and her print bikini, Francine climbed up into the skipper's chair and started trying buttons. She quickly found the switch for the boat's spotlight. It sent a bright beam of light out into the darkened waters. That's at least a start, she thought. As she looked out, all that she could see were some funny round objects sticking up in the water with white numbers painted on the front. Those must be markers of some kind, she thought.

Suddenly she remembered the anchor. She raced to the back of the boat. Struggling mightily she pulled it up and flung it on the deck, slime and all, narrowly missing Elliott's head. The sweat was pouring down her forehead and into her eyes.

She raced to the front of the boat and started trying buttons, keys, and knobs. "Come on, baby, be good to Franny," she pleaded. A few minutes later she heard the putt, putt, putt of the engines.

She grabbed a knob and pulled it one way. The boat lurched backward. She pulled the knob the other way, and the boat started forward. She turned the wheel and it swerved to the side.

"Francine, you're a mechanical genius," she shouted, as the boat gathered speed.

She could feel the spray on her bare shoulders. She trembled with excitement. Hey, this is fun, she thought. It's like losing your virginity. It's only painful in the beginning. After that—pure pleasure.

The next problem, Francine quickly perceived, was to bring this thing in for a landing. She could see an inlet coming up on the right with a lot of lights. That must be a marina or yacht club, she thought. She steered the boat sharply to the right, cutting her speed.

She was making good progress, heading straight for the marina. Suddenly the boat came to an absolutely dead stop, hurling Francine out of the chair. She hit her head on the instrument panel. She could feel drops of blood oozing from her forehead.

She picked herself up, slightly dazed, and looked around.

I'm only about a hundred yards from the shore, she thought. She tried all of the controls again, but the boat just wouldn't move.

"Oh, shit," she wailed. "I must have run it into a shallow area, and we're stuck in the fuckin' mud."

She sat down on the deck for a moment, thinking about her options while her head cleared. Then she rose quickly, picked up the captain's hat, and walked to the back of the boat. She placed the hat on the stomach of the still sleeping Elliott.

"I'm sorry to leave you like this," she said. "But friendship is one thing and a Pulitzer Prize is another."

Then she stood on the end of the boat, held her nose with her left hand, and wiped the blood with her right. She shouted "One, two, three," and jumped into the chilly waters of the Bay. Through a combination of swimming and wading in the shallow mud bottom she made it to dry land.

There she was greeted by a swarm of mosquitoes and gnats. Then Francine alternately ran and walked along the grassy mud of the shore for another two hundred yards to "Martha's Marina."

She found Martha sitting behind the cash register of the snack bar—a kindly old lady who took one look at Francine's bloody forehead and the mud caked on her legs and offered to help.

"You want me to call the police?" she asked. "He beat you up pretty bad."

"The telephone. Can I use your telephone?" Francine asked, catching her breath.

"You can use it, young lady."

Francine looked at the clock on the wall of the snack bar. Five minutes to ten. Here's one of the advantages of a morning newspaper, she thought. You can find the editor-in-chief in his office at ten o'clock in the evening.

"I want Skip Roberts," she shouted to the switchboard operator at the *Tribune.*

There was a long pause. Finally she heard "Roberts here."

"Skip. It's Francine. I've got the story of the century for you."

He started to laugh.

"I'd like to have a quarter for each time I've heard that." Francine got furious.

"Don't be a shit," she yelled. "I busted my ass for this one."

Martha looked up from the cash register with a disapproving expression on her face.

"I'm not kidding you, Skip. This one is bigger than Watergate."

"Why don't you just give me a little hint," he said.

She took one look at Martha listening carefully to every word.

"I can't talk now. I'll get downtown as soon as I can. But wait for me."

"I'll wait for you, I promise."

"And hold me a big space on the upper right-hand corner of page one, and plenty of room for a big headline."

When Francine hung up the phone, she looked at Martha with her most innocent expression.

"One more call, Martha, please," she begged.

"Just one more," Martha said, completely alienated by Francine's language.

"Oh, you're wonderful. What's the closest cab?"

"The Bay Cab Company, 624-5000."

Ten minutes later a taxi pulled up at the marina.

Francine picked up an empty brown paper bag from the counter of the snack bar. Then she raced into the street.

"The Washington Tribune building in downtown Washington," she shouted, getting into the cab.

The driver took one look at Francine in her wet bathing suit, with dried blood on her forehead.

"You got money to pay for a fare like that?" he asked.

"I got one hundred dollars in twenties right here, mister," Francine said, pointing to the brown paper bag.

"Get in then," the driver said, shrugging his shoulders.

# CHAPTER

## 22

SKIP ROBERTS TOOK ONE LOOK AT FRANCINE AND SHOUTED, "What in the hell happened to you?"

"I look that bad?"

"Worse. Go wash up and find a charwoman's outfit or something so you can get out of that wet suit. Then we can talk."

"While I do that," Francine said, "I've got something for you to do. There's one irate cab driver sitting in front of the building."

"How much is it going to cost me this time?"

"Only forty-two fifty. The tip is up to you."

When they sat down in Roberts' office ten minutes later, Francine told him the whole story.

Roberts listened carefully. A look of disbelief appeared on his face early in the story. And it remained there till the end.

When she was finished Roberts said, "I can't buy it."

"What do you mean, you can't buy it?"

"I mean I can't accept the story based on what you told me. It's all hearsay and speculation. There's no fact. Get me one verified fact, and I'll believe it."

She stormed out of Roberts' office cursing under her breath.

Fifteen minutes later she returned.

"Okay, big shot," she said. "I got your fact. I called the *Times* in New York and got Bill Marks' vacation address in Israel—some kibbutz in the desert. I called up the kibbutz and talked to the Director. He told me that Marks and his brother left the kibbutz on Saturday morning. They haven't returned. His wife's going out of her mind."

"What's that prove?"

"It proves that Marks and his brother must have found this base. They're holding him there to prevent any public disclosure of the operation."

"Maybe they were kidnapped by Arab terrorists. Or maybe their car broke down in the desert. That's no proof."

I could kill the son-of-a-bitch, Francine thought. If he lets this one go.

Roberts continued thinking about Francine's story and the call to the *Times*. He had been a reporter once himself. You develop a sense about these things. There may be something here.

"You may just be right," Roberts said pensively. "But I won't run the story until I give the President a chance to deny it."

"What's Edwards ever done for us?"

"That's not the point. You're telling me to run a story that the President of the United States is planning a secret military attack on Saudi Arabia. I have to give the President a chance to deny it."

Francine sat silent, looking depressed. There was dried blood on her forehead and her legs were stiff.

"Go write your story," Roberts said. "I'll call Camp David."

"It's done."

"What do you mean it's done."

"I borrowed a pencil and paper from the cabbie and wrote it in the back of the cab."

She tossed onto Roberts' desk four pages of blank taxi manifests. He turned them over. There was handwriting on the back—the sloppiest handwriting he had ever seen.

"You really are too much," Roberts said, as he pulled out his government telephone directory. He started pressing buttons.

Stewart was sitting next to the switchboard. He picked up the phone on the second ring.

"Camp David. This is Fred Stewart."

"Stewart. It's Skip Roberts at the *Tribune*. I'm sorry to bother you people so late but I have an urgent matter to raise with you."

Roberts then explained to Stewart what Francine had reported to him. He read Francine's story to Stewart, stumbling over the handwriting.

Stewart listened carefully, tapping his fingers on the table. Beads of perspiration appeared on his forehead. He almost wet his pants.

"We're convinced of the facts," Roberts said, sounding confident and holding his breath. "But we want to give you people a chance to deny it."

"At this moment I am not authorized to make any response," Stewart replied in a very official-sounding tone of voice.

There was a pause. Stewart was thinking.

Well, well, Francine was right, Roberts decided, smiling broadly.

"I will promptly consult with the President," Stewart continued. "Then I will respond to you formally. I trust that you will permit us to have thirty minutes for this consultation."

Roberts looked at his watch. It was 11:45. If he knew by 12:15, they could still make the early edition.

"You may have the thirty minutes," Roberts said.

Stewart put down the phone, then frantically dialed Morris's number at the Georgetown command center.

"All hell has broken loose," Stewart said in a terrified tone.

"Take it easy, Fred," Morris said calmly. "Get hold of yourself and tell me what happened. Then we'll decide how to deal with it."

Stewart repeated what Roberts had told him. Morris's computer brain began racing furiously even as he listened.

When Stewart was finished talking, Morris was ready with his response.

"There's no point denying the story," Morris said. "Francine has the facts, and she has enough verification."

Morris paused for a moment. Then he continued talking.

"Will Roberts accept you as a spokesman for the President?"

"I think so. He always has in the past."

"Wait about fifteen minutes. Then call Roberts back. Tell him that you have talked extensively with the President and that you are authorized to state that his facts are essentially accurate."

Stewart began to wonder what Morris had in mind.

"Then tell him," Morris said, "that the President has asked Roberts to recognize the terrible loss of American lives and danger to the national security that would be caused by the *Tribune*'s publication of this story. Tell him that in view of these facts, the President is requesting that the *Tribune* exercise voluntary restraint and not publish the story. Remind him that *The New York Times* used precisely this type of voluntary restraint when it declined to publish information that it received about the Bay of Pigs invasion before that invasion took place."

"You think that will work?" Stewart asked, sounding dubious.

"That's an asinine question. It's all we've got. Stop worrying about whether it will work, and concentrate on making certain that it does."

"I could kill that drunken bastard Elliott," Stewart said.

Morris felt the same way. His instincts had told him at the beginning that Elliott would blow it one way or another. But he had kept marching along anyhow. Still, what choice did he have? Without Elliott there could never have been an operation.

"We knew what we were getting into with Elliott," Morris said, calmly trying to reassure himself as well as Stewart. "That was just a risk we had to take. The key point is that they still think the President has ordered the attack."

As Stewart hung up the telephone, he thought to himself, Nothing ever seems to bother Morris.

The Camp David house was absolutely quiet. The President, Mrs. Edwards, and Joan were asleep.

Stewart walked to the kitchen. Without even thinking about it, he was walking softly on his toes. He poured some scotch over ice in a large water tumbler. Then he stepped outside the back door. The evening mountain air was cool. Only crickets shattered the silence.

One of the marines on duty walked over to Stewart.

"Is everything okay, sir?"

"Oh, yes, very good, Corporal. I'm just getting a deep breath of this air. It's not like the city."

Stewart hoped that the marine would respond. He wanted someone to talk with to pass the fifteen minutes. But the Corporal knew his orders. He remained silent.

"Where are you from?" Stewart asked.

"Colorado—near Denver."

"Then this is like home for you."

"Yes, sir."

"I go hiking in the Smoky Mountains," Stewart said.

Stewart took another long sip on his drink. Then he looked at his watch.

"Well, good night, Corporal," Stewart said. He walked into the house, finished his drink, and returned to the switchboard.

Stewart followed precisely the script dictated by Morris. Roberts listened carefully without interrupting.

When Stewart was finished, Roberts was silent for a moment. Then he said, "Now, I need a few minutes to think about it. I'll call you back with our decision."

His voice sounded tentative and uncertain. I think he bought it, Stewart said to himself.

Roberts then explained to Francine what Stewart had said. "Don't do it, Skip," she begged. "Don't give in. We've got the story of the century."

Roberts didn't respond.

"Don't let them con you," she said. "Edwards is trying to con you. We don't owe Edwards anything. We . . ."

Suddenly Roberts exploded.

"Can you just sit there and shut up for five minutes," he shouted. "Just let me think without all that jabbering."

It was a helluva time for Mrs. Warner to be in China, Roberts thought. The decision should really be made by the publisher and not by the editor-in-chief. But there wasn't any choice.

Roberts put his head into his hands and closed his eyes. Francine watched him carefully.

A couple of minutes later he opened his eyes and put down his hands.

"I'm not going to publish it," he said to Francine.

"You've got no guts!" she shouted angrily. "You're a disgrace to the profession."

"It's not that simple," Roberts replied, his mind made up. "If I publish, the President will probably have to call off the invasion. Isn't that right?"

"I suppose so," she replied bitterly.

"But Edwards has already made the decision that the seizure of the Saudi oil fields is in the national interest. I might agree with that decision or disagree with it. But what right do I have to take that decision away from him? He's the duly elected official with that authority."

"What about your responsibility to this organization?"

"Home delivery is our bread and butter. How many more papers do you think we'll sell with this story than we will without it? Relatively few. Nobody's even in town to buy the paper."

Francine was thinking about her Pulitzer Prize that had just walked away. Roberts could read her mind.

"As far as your own fame and fortune, Francine, hell, everybody in Washington already knows who you are."

She looked totally despondent. "I still think that you don't have any guts."

"When you become the boss of this operation, you can run it your way. Right now I'm the editor-in-chief, and it's my decision. I made it."

"Oh, bullshit."

"I'll tell you what. I'll let you do the first byline story about the invasion right after it takes place."

"Big deal. Every other paper in the world will have the story then."

Roberts picked up the telephone and called Stewart at Camp David. When Stewart heard the decision, he thanked Roberts on behalf of the President and hung up the phone. Stewart breathed a large sigh of relief and called Morris to report the good news.

Francine meantime picked up her wet bathing suit and the four pages of taxicab manifests from Roberts' desk.

She walked out of the door looking disgusted. Suddenly her legs started to ache. She felt a great throbbing pain in her head, and she was tired, very tired. Francine wanted to go home and sleep, to sleep for a very long time.

# CHAPTER

# 23

ON MONDAY EVENING MORRIS SAT CALMLY AT THE DESK IN his study, watching the slow sweep of the black second hand on the wall clock. The large R Street house was deathly quiet —as it had been since Anne's departure.

The excitement that Morris had felt inside was gone. It had been replaced with a cold, unemotional efficiency that characterized Morris's success in the business world. Morris had passed from the world of the living to the world of machines—a finely honed computer with wires and transistors that was programmed to succeed.

At precisely 8:45 he picked up the red telephone on his desk. There was silence for a couple of seconds. Then he heard a voice at the other end say, "Thomas here."

When Morris's ears heard that sound, they instantly sent a signal to his brain, confirming that the voice indeed was that of General Alvin Thomas.

Then Morris announced in a dispassionate tone: "I want to wish you a Happy Independence Day, General."

"And a Happy Independence Day to you, sir," replied Thomas.

As soon as he uttered those words, Thomas set down the

red telephone. He shouted to the officers standing outside his tent.

"All systems are go. Prepare for takeoff at 0400."

Fifteen minutes later the first of the F-16's in the attacking force roared down the runway on the temporary makeshift airstrip. The takeoffs continued at ten-second intervals. First there were the F-16's and B-1's in Wave A that would fly eastward to pinpoint-bomb selected targets. Then there were the smaller aircraft in Wave B that would drop paratroops at the critical pumping stations on the long pipelines; finally there was Wave C, the large, slow C-130 transports, that held the men like Major James R. Polk—a great sea of humanity huddled together with their weapons in the musty heat of the darkened planes.

Some of those men were battle-hardened veterans of Vietnam—those who survived emotionally and physically the horrors of the jungle. Others were among the volunteers who had swollen the ranks of the all-volunteer army as jobs had become scarce in the civilian economy. Both groups had been stirred to their boots when General Thomas had announced the new objective of the operation six hours earlier.

Five thousand miles away from that airstrip in the Sinai, Morris picked up another telephone on his desk—one of the two beige telephones.

Morris immediately began pressing buttons on the telephone. He had committed the number to memory. He listened carefully to the voice answering the telephone.

"Mr. Ambassador, this is George Morris. I want to meet with you at my house on a matter of great importance."

"I will be there at ten o'clock," came the reply.

Morris called his chief of security, who sat at the front door on R Street, to inform him of the visitor who would be arriving. Then he looked out of the window at the street below. It was completely deserted. It would remain that way until Tuesday evening when the holiday weekend ended.

Morris returned to the desk and picked up the beige telephone again.

When the phone call came, they were just concluding dinner—the President and Mrs. Edwards, Stewart and Joan.

One of the marines on duty walked into the dining room and announced, "Telephone call for Mr. Stewart."

Stewart excused himself quietly and walked down the long hall to the deserted living room. As he picked up the phone, his eyes twitched slightly. "Stewart here," he said nervously.

"I just wanted to wish you a Happy Independence Day," Morris said. "Please call me with a report later in the evening."

"Understood," Stewart said, quietly placing the receiver in the cradle of the telephone.

Stewart placed his right hand in the side pocket of his slacks. His fingers, warm and moist, tightly clasped the small plastic bottle that he had filled with chloral hydrate earlier in the evening. He walked back to the dining room, trying to appear nonchalant.

The President was sitting alone at the head of the table.

"What was that about, Fred?"

"Oh, nothing, sir. My secretary called to say that she had a death in the family and would not return until late next week."

Then Stewart hastily changed the subject. "What happened to the girls?"

"They're going to watch a movie downstairs. One of the old Hitchcocks. I told them we'd pass it up."

There was a pause as the President took one final sip of his coffee. Stewart was watching him carefully. He didn't suspect anything. The President walked over to the humidor and selected two cigars.

Then he announced to Stewart, "Fix a couple of glasses of Grand Marnier and join me outside on the terrace."

Stewart walked to the bar at the end of the hall. He poured the Grand Marnier quickly, spilling some on the wooden surface. With trembling hands, he removed the small plastic bottle from his pocket and poured its contents into one glass—the one on the right. Remember that, Stewart said to himself, the President's glass will be in my right hand.

When Stewart reached the terrace, he could see the flame from the President's match as he lit his cigar. Stewart handed a glass to the President and picked up the cigar and the matches that were waiting for him. He sat down in the wooden rocker next to the President.

He struck the match once, but it wouldn't light. Another match, still nothing. My fingers must be perspiring, Stewart thought. Take it slow, he said to himself. The next match lit.

They sat there in silence for ten or fifteen minutes—the burning tips of their cigars glowing brightly in the darkness. The evening air of the mountains was cool. A slight breeze made the trees tremble and wafted the scent of fresh pine toward the house.

"It's a strange position, the American presidency," the President said, sipping his drink.

Oh God, he's in the mood to lecture about American government, Stewart thought, recognizing the tone of voice.

"How do you mean, sir?"

"Whoever occupies this position has so much power at his disposal that it's almost frightening. In some respects I can rule more absolutely than King John ever could before Runnymede."

"Isn't that a bit of a strong statement, sir?" Stewart said. "After all, we have the Congress and the people to account to."

"But it's all accountability after the fact—after the decisions are made," the President replied. "At least in the area of foreign affairs and military matters. Oh, I remember how we had a lot of yelling after Watergate and the war in Vietnam, but we've continued to increase the power of the presidency since that time. And our institutions of government are even more vulnerable now than they were then."

Stewart leaned forward in his chair quickly when he heard the President talking about the vulnerability of our institutions of government. But he's sipping his drink. He couldn't possibly suspect anything.

The President sniffed the Grand Marnier. Then he took another drink, leaned back in his chair, and began blowing large puffs of smoke in the air. Stewart looked at him through the corner of his eye.

Most presidents needed companions like Stewart—men who were content to be "yes" men, awed by being close to power, and no intellectual challenge to their leader. Someone to share the Grand Marnier and the cigars that the American people provided, someone to fetch their sexual companions when that was necessary, someone to drop to their knees with them in prayer at a time of great crisis.

As Stewart watched the President sip his drink, he thought to himself, it's not too late. He could still expose the whole plan, place all of the responsibility on Morris, and avoid some of the damage. He thought about it one final time.

No. There was no turning back, Steward concluded. He was finished being the President's "boy."

A few minutes later the President yawned.

"I'm worn out from a long day. I'm going to turn in early. Tell Mrs. Edwards not to disturb me."

"I'll be happy to, sir," Stewart said, as he watched the President disappear into the house.

Stewart sat outside for a few more minutes. Then he walked downstairs to the movie room and gave the message to Mrs. Edwards.

Stewart lingered in the back of the room to watch a few minutes. It was *Vertigo,* a movie about dizziness at great heights, which Stewart had seen several times. It was his favorite among all of the Hitchcock movies.

Stewart left the room and walked quietly up two flights of stairs, passing the lone marine who stood on guard at the door to the President's bedroom. He took a quick glance at the bottom of the door. It was dark in the bedroom. The entire second floor of the house was quiet.

Stewart walked to his own bedroom and placed the small

plastic bottle behind an air-conditioning unit. Then he returned to the switchboard.

"I'll relieve you for a few minutes," he said to the marine on duty.

"Thank you, sir," came the reply as the marine took a pack of cigarettes from his pocket and walked out of the room.

Stewart dialed Morris's number quickly. Morris answered on the first ring.

"It's done," Stewart said.

"Excellent," Morris replied, and he replaced the receiver.

Morris looked at the clock on the wall. It was five minutes to ten. The transfer of power was completed. For the next twelve hours he would be the President of the United States.

Morris walked over to the window and stood there waiting. Five minutes later the Ambassador approached the house, flanked by the two SAVAK men, who silently took up positions on the front steps next to Morris's guards.

He greeted his guest at the front door. Morris was a little nervous when he shook the Iranian's hand. He wasn't quite sure why. The two men marched silently upstairs to the study.

"I have an urgent message for His Royal Highness," Morris said. "I want to inform him that an action of the type that was discussed in Tehran has been commenced. It poses absolutely no threat to His Royal Highness or to the people of Iran."

Morris looked at Ahmad, waiting for some response, for some assurance that the conclusion he had reached in Tehran about the absence of Iranian intervention was correct.

"Your message will be delivered at once," the Ambassador said in an unemotional tone, sounding like a professional messenger—a Western Union courier.

Morris sat still, waiting. He thought that he had sealed a bargain with the Shah. He could see the expression of agreement in the Shah's face when he had given his analysis. And then the gratitude when he had told the Shah about the threat to his son. Even the gift for Anne.

There had to be something else from Ahmad. Some small sign. But there was nothing.

"You have my telephone number," Ahmad said. "I will remain very close to that telephone. You may call me there at any time."

Morris wanted to say something to Ahmad. But he didn't. He rose and quietly shook the Ambassador's hand.

When the Iranian left, Morris suddenly had a sick feeling in his stomach. The color drained from his face. What if he was wrong? What if he had misread the Shah and drawn the wrong conclusion in Tehran? Or worse, what if the Shah had manipulated him to draw the wrong conclusion? The bargain had been easy to strike. He realized that at the time. Perhaps too easy.

Suppose that the Shah had helped to lull the Saudis into a false sense of security. Now he had his war machine poised and ready to go. He could wait until the American F-16's and B-1's had wreaked their damage over Saudi Arabia and turned west to return to the Sinai. Then as the lumbering C-130 cargoes approached, the Shah could unleash his F-15 Eagle fighter aircraft. The American planes would be like clay pigeons. An entire army would be slaughtered in the air.

Morris could visualize the mangled ruins, parts of airplanes mixed with the metal of tanks and artillery. And everywhere the seared flesh of human bodies.

And how would it end? Not with American flags on top of those Saudi oil rigs. Not with a ticker-tape parade for Morris along Broadway. Rather with the Shah of Iran in control of both sides of the Persian Gulf.

Morris looked at the red telephone. He could call General Thomas. But what good would that do? The planes had been in the air for more than an hour. And Morris doubted whether Thomas would agree to change any of the plans.

Thomas would probably be right. The risks were great; but the stakes were high.

For the first time in his life Morris was frightened.

# CHAPTER

# 24

THE FIRST AMERICAN F-16'S ROARED EASTWARD ACROSS THE desert at low altitudes to avoid radar detection. They flew out of the darkened western sky and into the brilliant sunrise.

Undetected, they reached their primary targets—the airports, anti-aircraft installations, and military bases. Then they struck with a furious efficiency, bombing and strafing their targets, pinpointing their devastation and destruction to those small areas on a map that General Thomas had identified with small black circles.

The surprised Saudi military never had a chance to activate their anti-aircraft guns or to start the engines of their planes. F-16's with American markings were bombing and destroying F-16's with Saudi markings that sat on the ground.

The heaviest bombing was concentrated in the area of Dhahran, the oil center. It was this same area that Italian planes had bombed in October 1940.

The smaller aircraft in Wave B swept over the TAP line, swooping down vertically at each pumping station. American soldiers rushed out of the planes to seize control of the stations—most of which were not defended.

At some stations the American attackers faced startled Saudi soldiers. With the element of surprise, the Americans quickly killed the first Saudis to open fire. The rest were then taken prisoner.

Following the prearranged schedule the F-16's and B-1's turned around and headed back to the Sinai. Then the giant C-130 transports lumbered eastward, fully exposed to the Shah's Air Force if he chose to send his planes east. But there was no movement in the eastern sky over the Persian Gulf. Only silence and a brilliant sunrise.

Unchecked, the C-130's landed quietly at Ras Tannurah and Dhahran—at airports that sat in shattered silence after the devastation of the attacking planes. As soon as they touched down, the hatch doors were thrown open. Out of their wombs rolled tanks, artillery, and hundreds of helmeted soldiers in drab, olive uniforms.

They moved quickly. Each man knew precisely what his assignment was. In a matter of minutes Captain Polk and the other tank commanders had their units rolling out of the airports in the direction of key targets.

By this time the awful wailing of air-raid sirens could be heard everywhere. Soldiers from the Saudi army were now awake. They swarmed out of their barracks, grabbing rifles. They left the anti-tank weapons and bazookas in the storehouse. These were much heavier and difficult to operate.

At first the Saudi soldiers raced through the streets unopposed, yelling "Death to the Jews," and firing their guns into the air.

Captain Polk encountered the first Saudi soldiers about two miles from the airport in Dharan. They were no match for the heavily armed Americans who had the element of surprise.

Captain Polk stood in the turret of his own tank shouting directions to the men in his company. The roar of loud gunfire was heard at frequent intervals as the tanks opened fire with their machine guns and tore apart the soldiers at the head of the pack. The dead and dying lay together in large piles along the road.

The soldiers in the rear quickly dropped their weapons and

raced into the nearest houses, where scores of frightened eyes looked through the narrow openings behind the slats of closed green shutters.

Captain Polk's orders were to avoid any civilian casualties if humanly possible. So once the advancing column of Saudi soldiers had disappeared, the Captain ordered his men to hold their fire as tanks rumbled down narrow roads to silence the scattered pockets of Saudi resistance. There were no anti-tank ditches, and the Patton II's moved quickly through the deserted city. They were followed by jeeps carrying American soldiers armed with submachine guns. The terrible wailing of air-raid sirens continued to pierce the air. Before long the Americans had mopped up the remaining enemy opposition.

As Captain Polk approached a Saudi military supply base, he could see American soldiers standing in front waving an American flag. These were military advisers who had been sent by the Pentagon months earlier as part of a routine program to train Saudi soldiers in the use of American weapons. As soon as they had received General Thomas's order, they moved to seize control of the weapons that they were providing training for. These weapons, including anti-tank missiles, would never be used by Saudi soldiers against the advancing American troops.

Suddenly a series of violent explosions rocked the earth as bombs were set off by Saudis at one of the pumping stations. Huge torches of flame could be seen throughout the city. Large clouds of black billowing smoke filled the sky.

Captain Polk led his unit in the direction of those explosions. They were met with fierce fire when they reached the area. Saudi soldiers were concealed at the top of a water tower, manning an anti-tank gun. They opened fire, striking the tank next to Polk's with a direct hit. It exploded with the impact, sending the remains of steel and human limbs flying into the air. Polk shouted "Fire," and the Saudi gun was destroyed.

Within two hours the entire Saudi army collapsed. Here and there an isolated sniper fired from a building while American soldiers pursued. But hundreds of Saudi troops threw down their arms in the street and surrendered to the Americans.

White handkerchiefs could be seen hanging from the windows and doors of boarded-up houses and buildings. The sirens had stopped.

Captain Polk pulled his tank up to the front of the main Administration Building of the Saudi oil industry headquarters in Dhahran. The building was deserted and quiet. He assumed a defensive position in front of the building, protecting what had suddenly become the property of the United States government.

A strange, eerie silence settled over the whole city. The Captain looked at his watch, but it was unnecessary. The sun was directly over Polk's head. It was nearly twelve o'clock, Saudi Arabian time. The operation was complete.

Captain Polk radioed his position to General Ripley, who in turn provided it to General Thomas back at the base in the Sinai.

Thomas smiled broadly when he heard the message. He walked over to a large map of the city of Dhahran on the wall of his tent and marked down Captain Polk's position and the time.

Thomas then picked up the red telephone. It was five o'clock in the morning when Morris heard that peculiar buzzing noise in his study.

He was wide awake, standing next to a map that showed the Persian Gulf with Saudi Arabia on the left side and Iran on the right. There were empty coffee cups scattered around the room.

Morris raced over to the phone. He held his breath waiting for Thomas to speak.

"The military operation has ended," Thomas said with

pride. "Everything was completed as planned. Our troops are on the ground and in control."

"What about the Iranians?" Morris asked tensely.

"All is quiet on the east. The Shah decided to stay out of this one. You did your job well."

Morris gave a large sigh of relief.

Thomas continued. "Our troops are still manning the Saudi missile systems that point eastward. But if the Shah didn't make any move earlier, he's not coming."

"Is the damage to the pipelines great?"

"Minimal," Thomas replied. "We can wait a couple of days before getting Grease Fletcher over here. Let things calm down a little."

"What about the Soviets?" Morris asked.

"Nothing yet."

Morris congratulated Thomas. Then he walked down the stairs, two at a time, and fixed a martini. He stood there alone in the middle of the living room raising his glass.

"Here's to the Shah of Iran," Morris said aloud, though there was no one there to hear him.

At least his instincts hadn't misled him. He hadn't misread the Shah. And the Shah kept his end of the bargain.

Morris returned to his study and picked up the beige telephone. Despite the hour someone at the Soviet Embassy answered on the first ring.

"I want to speak with Ambassador Kuznov," Morris said. "You may tell him that George T. Morris is calling."

There was a pause. Then the voice at the other end of the telephone said, "I'm sorry, but Ambassador Kuznov is not available."

"Tell him that I am speaking for the President of the United States," Morris said calmly. "I have the authority to talk with him about the present situation in Saudi Arabia. I want to meet with him at the Embassy. I can be there in ten minutes."

There was another pause. Morris could hear the sound of voices in the background—talking Russian. He couldn't understand a word. A few moments later the English voice returned to the telephone.

"The Ambassador will see you, Mr. Morris."

Morris called down to his security desk to alert his driver. Then Morris picked up the beige telephone and made one more call. Again there was an answer on the first ring.

"Well, well. It's my old classmate from Harvard Business School, Yaman Faisel," Morris said. "I'm so surprised to hear that you are awake at five A.M. and even answering your own telephone. You must be expecting some important news from home."

"What do you want, Morris?" Faisel shouted angrily.

"I only wanted to wish you a Happy Independence Day," Morris said, placing down the telephone before Faisel could respond.

Morris then walked down the stairs and climbed into the limousine that was waiting in front of the house. The car sped across R Street to Wisconsin Avenue and then down to M Street. The streets were empty. The sodium lights shone brightly against the dark sky. They roared across K Street, catching each green light.

When he entered the Soviet Embassy on Sixteenth Street, Morris saw a flurry of activity. Harried ministers, with half-open eyes, were shouting orders in Russian to their deputies. A heavily armed guard met Morris at the door and escorted him to the Ambassador's office. A contingent of four were seated around the conference table in the Ambassador's lavish office.

Morris had met Kuznov once at a diplomatic reception. After that meeting Morris had made a detailed study of Kuznov's background. He assumed that the Russian had done the same.

Morris did not recognize the names or the faces of the

other three men with Kuznov. They must be low-level diplomats, he thought.

As soon as the introductions were completed and Morris sat down, Kuznov began shouting.

"Mr. Morris, we have tracked the movement of planes eastward from the Sinai to eastern Saudi Arabia on the Persian Gulf. We have also received reports of extensive military activity in Saudi Arabia in the last several hours. I assume that your government has received the same reports. It is my duty to warn you that the government of Israel has gone too far this time. We will not sit back and tolerate this type of Zionist aggression. We will respond against Israel, and we will respond with force."

Morris waited quietly until Kuznov was finished speaking. Then he dropped his own bomb—calmly and dispassionately.

"Mr. Ambassador, with all due respect to Soviet intelligence, the Israelis had nothing to do with the action in Saudi Arabia. This was a military action taken by the United States government to seize the oil fields of Saudi Arabia. It was taken for reasons that have to do with our own self-interest. I have come to inform you of this fact and to tell you that our action will not pose a threat in any way to the Soviet Union."

Kuznov was absolutely stupefied when he heard Morris's words. He could not believe his ears. He rubbed his eyes slowly, both from fatigue and to make certain that he was truly awake. One look at the horrified expressions on his colleagues' faces confirmed for Kuznov that he had correctly understood Morris. The Soviet Ambassador began tapping the tips of his fingers on the table.

"This is pure insanity on the part of your government," Kuznov shouted in an angry menacing tone. "We will not tolerate naked aggression of this type. You run the risk of a terrible nuclear holocaust."

"You waste your time threatening me," Morris replied. "We both know that you are no more than a messenger to relay information to and from the Kremlin. When I leave here, you will immediately send on what I have told you. I ask only that you pass on one other item as well."

"What is that?" Kuznov asked.

"Please tell your government that we know that they will be oil importers in the very near future. They will then be subject to the same type of action that OPEC took against the United States. If the Saudis did it to us, they can do it to you."

"I don't understand," Kuznov said. "How will your action in Saudi Arabia affect our situation as oil importers?"

"We are prepared to offer you long-term supply contracts at $2.50 a barrel."

Morris was pleased at how facilely he had assumed the use of the imperial we, in speaking for the entire United States government.

Morris continued, "We believe that your own self-interest dictates that you accept such a long-term supply contract rather than engaging in rash conduct that would be detrimental to the cause of peace and economic stability in the world."

"But how can we trust you to hold to your promise of $2.50 a barrel?"

He's awfully dense, Morris thought.

"Developments in recent years," Morris said, "establish that the two super powers have very similar interests on issues relating to natural resources even though we have different interests on other issues. What I am saying is that we would be a more dependable supplier of oil to your government than the Saudis."

When Morris was finished speaking, he looked carefully at Kuznov, trying to see if his words had made any impression. Impossible to tell, Morris thought, as he stared at the same expression of fury and anger that Kuznov had displayed since Morris arrived.

Morris left the Embassy and rode back to the house. He

had not slept in twenty-four hours. He was starting to feel the strain. He fixed a fresh pot of coffee to drive off the fatigue.

Morris sat down at his desk and mentally reviewed everything that had happened. It was all precisely on schedule.

At six-thirty, the telephone rang. It was Stewart. He had a frantic sound in his voice.

"The White House switchboard girl, Agnes, has just called me," Stewart said in a trembling voice. "She relayed the text of a note that has been received from the Soviet Premier. I wrote it down on a piece of paper."

"What did it say?" Morris asked, taking a deep breath.

"It goes, 'Mr. President, we demand that the United States take steps by 9:00 A.M. Washington time to begin the complete withdrawal of all American forces from Saudi Arabia. Unless this demand is met, the Soviet Union will be required to take any and all necessary measures to crush this aggression through the use of force. You will bear the responsibility for the consequences.' "

As Stewart finished reading, the language sounded familiar to Morris. Suddenly he recalled that the language of this note was almost identical to the one that the Soviet Union had sent to Britain and France at the time of the Suez Canal seizure in 1956.

"Does anyone know about this note—other than you and the White House switchboard girl?"

"No," Stewart said. "She called here immediately."

"What is the situation at Camp David?"

"All quiet. The President is still sleeping. If the chloral hydrate works, he shouldn't be up until sometime around ten o'clock."

"Will there be any televisions or radios on between now and ten?"

"Unlikely. The marine guards will not turn any on. Joan and Mrs. Edwards sat up watching movies till four o'clock. I don't expect to see them until noon."

"Okay, Stewart," Morris said, pausing for a moment to clarify his thoughts. "Take that piece of paper on which you wrote the note, tear it into small pieces, and flush it down the nearest toilet."

"Why do you want me to do that?" Stewart asked, sounding puzzled.

"My guess is that the Soviets are bluffing, just as they were in 1956 and just as they were at the time of the Cuban missile crisis. But we have to hope that the President doesn't find out about that note until after the nine o'clock deadline. Otherwise, he'll give in to the Soviet threat and order an immediate pullout from Saudi Arabia. Once the nine o'clock deadline passes and nothing happens, he will know that the Soviets were only bluffing."

"And you are prepared to call their bluff?" Stewart asked, in a very frightened tone of voice.

"Exactly."

"And if you are wrong?"

"I haven't been wrong yet," Morris replied, very calmly, in a voice brimming with confidence and flushed with victory.

# CHAPTER

# 25

HENRY OLIVER DIDN'T SLEEP WELL MONDAY NIGHT. IT WAS his third straight night in a tent. When he woke up at six-thirty on Tuesday morning on the hard ground of the Blue Ridge Mountains, his back was sore. He could hardly move his right arm, and he had the stale taste of homemade Virginia wine in his mouth.

That woman is going to kill me, Oliver thought. I hope to hell her intellectual infatuation with nature passes soon.

He forced himself to an upright position and then announced to his half-sleeping wife, "I'm driving down the road to use the telephone."

It was better to tell her before she woke up, he thought. Otherwise she'd bitch, "You're calling the White House again. I thought it was a vacation."

She was probably right. He did call in too much. But he was compelled to make routine calls three times a day just to see if there were any emergencies that needed his attention.

When Oliver called the White House from the roadside phone booth, he was ready to joke with the switchboard operator.

"It's Thomas Jefferson," he said, laughing. "Wishing you a happy Fourth of July."

"Mr. Oliver," Agnes said in an intensely serious tone, "you will not want to joke when you hear the message that I have just relayed to Mr. Stewart at Camp David."

"Read it to me."

Oliver listened in disbelief as Agnes read the Russian note that was still sitting on her desk.

"Jesus Christ," Oliver said. "What in the hell is going on?"

Oliver was silent for a moment. His body stopped aching. He tried to figure out what was happening. He had no ideas at all.

"Connect me with Camp David," Oliver shouted.

He heard some clicking on the line. Then a few seconds later, he heard Stewart's voice.

"What in the hell is going on, Fred?"

"Why, nothing at all. It's very quiet here," Stewart said, trying to remain calm as he heard Oliver's frenzied voice.

"Agnes on the White House switchboard has just read me one helluva frightening note from the Soviet Premier. What's going on in Saudi Arabia?"

Stewart broke out into a cold sweat. Try to do it like Morris would, he thought.

"She must be yanking your chain," Stewart said, trying hard to laugh. "She's joking with you for the holiday, and you fell for it. Why don't you go back to your camp and have a good time. You can pull her leg when you get back."

"Maybe so."

Oliver hung up the phone, convinced that Stewart was right. He started back to his car. After all, he knew of no recent developments of the type that would have to precede such a note.

As Oliver reached the car, he still felt uneasy about the whole thing. He wasn't quite sure why. He walked slowly back to the phonebooth and began dialing again.

"Agnes," Oliver said, "Stewart tells me that you're joking about the note. If you tell me that's true, I'll forget it. But I have to know."

"I'm not joking, Mr. Oliver. I swear it. I have the note right in front of me. I've been shaking like a leaf since I got it."

She sounds absolutely terrified, Oliver thought. If she's putting me on, she's one helluva good actress.

"Agnes," Oliver screamed, "if you're joking, I swear to Christ that I'll fire you and keep you from ever working anywhere. You and those two kids of yours will starve."

She started to cry with loud wailing sounds.

He listened in silence for a moment. His hand was damp with perspiration. It stuck to the telephone.

"Okay, okay," Oliver said. "You're telling me the truth. Connect me back with Camp David."

Again Oliver heard the clicking, and again Stewart answered.

"Fred, old buddy," Oliver said. "I decided that you were right about Agnes. I'm sure she was joking. She's pretty good, though. I have to hand it to her. She had me going for a while."

There was a pause. Stewart didn't want to overplay his hand. He was waiting to see what else Oliver would say.

"I just want to talk to the Chief about something else," Oliver said innocently. "Can you get him for me?"

"I'm sorry, Henry, but he's still asleep. He had a late night. Give me a message? I'll give it to him."

"I don't want to bother you. Why don't you let me talk to one of the marines on duty."

"They're all outside now," Stewart said.

That last statement couldn't possibly be true, Oliver thought. There was an absolutely firm order that at least three marines had to be in the house at all times when the President was at Camp David. That order was never disregarded.

"Well, forget it," Oliver said. "I'll talk to him later."

When Oliver hung up the phone, he was scared to death. At this point I know three facts, Oliver thought. There are American forces in Saudi Arabia, the Russians have given us a 9:00 A.M. ultimatum, and Stewart has managed to put the President in a state of incommunicado. To Oliver it sounded like a military takeover of the government. Oh God, it couldn't happen here, he thought.

Oliver stood next to the roadside phonebooth thinking about what to do. His heart was pounding. He began taking deep breaths, gasping for air. He stepped behind the phonebooth and urinated on the damp ground.

"Get control of yourself," Oliver said aloud.

Then he went back into the phonebooth and called Agnes on the White House switchboard. He identified his precise location and gave Agnes strict orders.

"I want a helicopter to pick me up as quickly as possible."

"Yes, sir, Mr. Oliver," she said. "I'll do that at once."

Stewart didn't intend to wait around Camp David to see if Oliver believed his story or not. He was too scared for that. As soon as he put down the telephone, he walked out of the house, heading toward one of the limousines sitting in the driveway with keys in the ignition. He was walking slowly, trying to appear calm and nonchalant, in order to avoid raising the suspicions of any of the marines on duty.

Stewart thought that he would never be able to summon the courage to start the car. But he did somehow. Then he drove quietly down the long driveway, waving to the marine at the guardhouse who lifted the gate. He was out of the Camp David complex before the helicopter even picked up Oliver.

By the time Oliver arrived at Camp David, he already imagined a score of possible scenarios—one worse than the other.

He raced up the stairs of the house.

"Where's Stewart?" he shouted to the marine on the porch.

"He just drove away."

"And the President?"

"I haven't seen him yet this morning."

Oliver ran into the house and up the stairs two at a time to the President's bedroom at the end of the corridor. I hope to hell he's still alive, Oliver thought. He looked at his watch. It was already five minutes to nine.

Oliver passed Mrs. Edwards' bedroom. She was snoring loudly.

He raced into the President's room. Thank God he's still breathing, Oliver thought. He was still sleeping soundly.

Oliver began shaking the President hard, trying to wake him up. Stewart must have drugged him, Oliver decided. He brought cold towels from the bathroom, and slowly President Edwards regained consciousness.

Oliver looked at his watch. It was already nine o'clock. There was no use rushing now, he thought. We'll all have a chance to see if the Russians were bluffing.

Oliver put the still groggy President under a cold shower. When he was sure that the President could stand up on his own, Oliver frantically called the White House switchboard.

"Any message from the Soviet Ambassador?" Oliver asked.

"Just this minute received one," Agnes said.

"Read it."

"It goes, 'Dear Mr. President. We are demanding an emergency session of the U.N. Security Council. We intend to condemn this aggression with a verbal attack in the media beginning at once. We do not oontemplate any military action at this time.' "

Oliver breathed a large sigh of relief. They were only bluffing. Thank God for that.

"Is that it?" he asked Agnes.

"No, there's one more sentence. It says, 'Your offer of crude oil at $2.50 per barrel has been noted.' "

"Read that sentence again," Oliver said, sounding puzzled.

"What does that mean?" he said aloud when he heard it again.

Oliver hung up the telephone and looked at the President drying off.

"What in the hell is going on here, Oliver?" the President asked. "I thought you were camping."

"I was hoping that you could answer that question, sir. But I don't think that's possible."

Oliver then explained to President Edwards everything he

had learned that morning. When he was finished, both men stood puzzling about the details of what had happened.

"We better get back to the White House immediately. We can piece it out better up there," the President said to Oliver. "Tell them to get that helicopter fueled up. And get hold of Black. Tell him to get home."

As Oliver raced out of the door, the President shouted another order.

"Try to reach Anderson. He should be at his home or CIA headquarters in Langley. I want him at the White House when we get there."

As he was halfway down the hall, Oliver heard the President shout, "And get out of those camping clothes. Put on one of my suits. It will be baggy, but you'll look a damn sight better than you do now."

When Oliver reached Anderson by telephone, the CIA chief was furious. Before Oliver could even open his mouth Anderson shouted, "What have you clowns done without cutting me in?"

"We didn't do anything, Andy. I swear it . . . really we didn't . . . we're trying to find out what happened ourselves. How did you hear about it?"

"As of nine o'clock all of the media had it. They're quoting the Soviet Foreign Minister."

"We're coming back to Washington by helicopter. The Chief wants you at the White House when we get back."

"I'll be there."

When he hung up the telephone, Oliver knew that a mad scene would be waiting for him in the Press Room at the White House.

Oliver's worst fears were realized. The President escaped into the privacy of the Oval Office where Anderson was already waiting. But the Press Room was Oliver's domain. It was a confused scene jammed with reporters shouting anxious questions. The glare of the bright lights from the television cameras nearly blinded the press secretary.

When Oliver looked around the room, he could see some of the White House regulars like Francine Rush, but there were many other new faces. They must be substitutes for regulars who are away for the weekend, Oliver thought.

Unpleasant as it seemed, Oliver knew that he would have to make at least a pretense of answering half a dozen questions.

As Oliver talked, Francine listened carefully and watched him closely. He was a man normally composed and calm, with his white teeth flashing. He was an immaculate dresser with tight-fitting tapered slacks.

But Francine observed that today Oliver was sweating and distraught. His breath smelled from stale wine, and he was wearing a suit that Francine recognized to be the President's.

Francine's mind began racing furiously. Oliver's words would be heard by the whole world, she thought. The Press Secretary would have been here dressed in his finest if he had known in advance that he would be on television on such an important subject. Since he wasn't dressed that way, it was safe to assume that he didn't know in advance about the press conference. And if Oliver didn't know in advance about the press conference, then it was safe to assume that the President didn't know in advance about the attack because Edwards would surely have tried for maximum coverage.

Suddenly Francine pieced it all together. Holy shit, she thought, the boy wonder of Wall Street did it on his own. He did it without the President. He did it with Thomas, Elliott, and Stewart. The President never even knew that there would be an attack.

Francine started to smile. She had to be right. Black was in London, and Oliver had really been camping. The President would not have ordered an attack at this time.

Francine also realized that she was the only person in the world besides the four conspirators who knew the real story. Oh, mamma mia, she said to herself. I can see that Pulitzer Prize again.

Oliver concluded his remarks and headed toward the door that would provide him with a sanctuary from the insanity of the Press Room. It would permit him to escape to the calm, if puzzled, atmosphere of the Oval Office. Reporters were pursuing him, trying to get in one last question.

Francine positioned herself right next to that door. She was wearing a powder blue T-shirt with a picture of Pike's Peak on the front and a short denim skirt. She had a brown leather handbag over her shoulder. She was holding a stenographic pad, a book, and a magazine in her hand.

Oliver opened the door slightly and started through it. Then Francine made her move. Like a tackler on a football team, Francine forced her body against Oliver and went through with him. As Francine crashed into Oliver, she threw him off balance and knocked him on the floor on the Oval Office side of the doorway. Francine landed on top of Oliver with her stenographic pad, book, and magazine flying in different directions. Oliver could hear the laughter coming from the reporters. He quickly kicked the door shut to insulate this humiliating scene from the gaze of the television cameras.

"What the hell are you doing, Francine?" Oliver shouted. "You know damn well that press people aren't allowed on this side of the door. I have no time for games."

"I don't have time for games either," Francine said. "I know the entire story behind the attack."

She paused for a minute, waiting for a quizzical look to appear on Oliver's face. When it did, she continued. "That's more than you or your boss knows."

"I don't know what you mean."

"Don't bullshit me, Oliver. You're wearing his suit. I know that you people don't know what the hell's going on. But I do."

Oliver was silent. The two of them were sitting on the floor.

"Well, do you want to know or not?"

"Okay, go ahead and tell me."

"Are you crazy? I don't talk to anyone below the President. Screw you, buddy."

"Wait here," Oliver said. "I'll walk down and see if he'll talk to you."

Oliver rose to his feet, leaving Francine on the floor.

"You could at least help me pick up my stuff," she said. "You did knock me down."

Oliver reached over and picked up the book and magazine. Francine picked up the stenographic pad and her purse.

"*Cosmopolitan*," he said. "It figures."

"Look at the book, big shot," she said.

"*The Book of Job, A Modern Interpretation*," Oliver said, looking at the green cover and sounding puzzled. "I didn't realize that you were a student of the Bible."

"I have to do something to pass the time while I cool my heels waiting for handouts from you. Anyhow, it's old-time religion. There's a lot of lust in the Bible."

"That's more like it," Oliver said.

Then he noticed the bruise above Francine's eye.

"What happened to you? Did big Bill hit you?"

"You'll hear the whole story if you ever get your ass moving," she said.

"Okay, I'll be right back."

Francine paced the floor anxiously waiting for Oliver. He returned five minutes later.

"The Chief will see you," he said. "Anderson from the CIA is in there too. I just hope to hell that you have something. I went out on a real limb to get you in."

"I'll repay you some day," she said, giving him a sexy smile.

"Forget it," Oliver replied, leading her down the hall. "I couldn't stand the repayment."

"Yeh, you probably couldn't handle it," she mumbled.

When Francine entered the Oval Office, she thought that she was attending a wake. The President was seated behind his desk looking glum and serious. Anderson was leaning back on a sofa with a grim expression on his face.

"Sit down, Miss Rush," the President said, pointing to a chair near his desk.

"And please, no notes," he said, motioning toward the stenographic pad in her hand.

Francine placed the stenographic pad, the book, and the magazine on a brown credenza under a portrait of Lincoln. She sat down slowly, making certain that her short skirt covered as much of her legs as possible. After all, this was the Oval Office.

The President waited patiently until she was comfortable. Then he said, "Okay, Miss Rush, tell us what you know."

With that signal Francine began speaking. She talked for the next half hour. First she repeated the entire story that she had told to Skip Roberts on Sunday evening. She described in detail the conversations that Roberts had had with Stewart. Finally, she explained the conclusion that she had reached in the Press Room.

"Simply stated, gentlemen," she said, "George T. Morris has organized and executed the seizure of the Saudi oil fields with the assistance of General Thomas, Fred Stewart, and Bill Elliott. There is absolutely no doubt about it."

When Francine was finished speaking, the President's face was absolutely white, like death itself.

She sat quietly waiting for some comment. He made none. Slowly the pale look faded as shock and disbelief gave way to anger and fury. Francine saw such a look of hate in the President's eyes that it frightened her. She glanced away, looking at Anderson. His face, too, was filled with rage and fury.

"That bastard, Morris," the President said in a harsh and threatening voice. "That dirty bastard."

No one responded to the President's comment. He repeated it again and still one more time.

"I should have known better than to trust Morris," the President snarled. "They warned me that he was an egomaniac, only interested in himself, in his own power."

"You couldn't have known," Oliver said weakly.

The President ignored his comment.

"I thought I could control the bastard. I thought I could use him. That he would respect the office . . . but he didn't . . . he doesn't respect anything."

Then the President got up from his desk and walked over to the window. He was walking very slowly, muttering to himself.

"And as for that disloyal son-of-a-bitch, Stewart. After everything I've done for him. That's some gratitude."

President Edwards stood there for several minutes staring at the emptiness of Constitution Avenue. The room was absolutely silent. Suddenly he turned around.

"Thank you very much, Miss Rush. I appreciate it that you came to me with this story rather than merely publishing it in the paper."

Francine could tell that her meeting was over. She quietly picked up her stenographic pad and left the room. Anderson and Oliver were intently studying the face of their leader. Neither man moved when Francine shut the door behind her.

An hour later Francine knocked gently at the door of Mathilda Hardy, the President's arrangements secretary.

"Mathilda, I'm awfully sorry to bother you," Francine said. "But I had a meeting in the Oval Office with the President a little while ago. I forgot my book and magazine in there. Could you please get them for me?"

"I would be happy to," Mathilda replied. "The men have all gone out of there. They're upstairs now. What do your things look like?"

"The magazine is *Cosmopolitan*. That's no big deal. But the book is *The Book of Job, A Modern Interpretation*. It's a rare book. I would hate to lose it. I left them both on the brown credenza under the Lincoln portrait."

"Wait here. I'll get them for you."

A few minutes later Mathilda returned with Francine's book

and magazine. Francine thanked Mathilda, took the book and magazine from her, stuffed them into her brown leather bag, and walked quickly out of the White House.

Francine crossed Lafayette Park walking briskly with a broad smile on her face. She began humming a tune as she walked directly through the path of a water sprinkler, sticking out her tongue to catch a few drops of water for her dry mouth. Francine passed an unshaven seedy-looking man on a park bench who was muttering to himself. She handed him five dollars. "Go buy another fifth," she said.

Francine crossed H Street and walked into the Hay-Adams Hotel. The wood-paneled lobby was deserted because of the holiday weekend. She walked down the staircase to the Ladies Room on the lower level.

Francine looked around carefully inside the Ladies Room. She checked each of the toilet stalls. It was empty. She locked the door behind her.

Twenty minutes later Francine walked out of the Ladies Room at the Hay-Adams. Her face was wan and pale. She had a look of fear in her eyes. Francine gazed behind her to see if she was being followed as she climbed the stairs to the lobby. She clutched her brown leather bag tightly.

Satisfied that she wasn't being followed, Francine crossed the short pathway from the hotel to the street with deliberate measured steps. I don't want to raise any suspicions, she thought. She collapsed into the back seat of a cab waiting in front of the hotel.

"Georgetown, please," Francine said to the driver in a hoarse whisper. "The corner of Wisconsin Avenue and R Street."

# CHAPTER

# 26

As Francine walked along R Street approaching Morris's house, she was carefully watched by the guard on duty in the front. She tried to walk casually, like a tourist out for a summer stroll, swinging her brown leather bag.

Once Francine was in front of the house, she turned sharply and raced up the stairs, eluding the guard on the street. Another guard stopped her on the front porch.

"Do you have some business here?" he asked, seizing her by the arm.

"Yes. I came to see Mr. Morris."

"Is he expecting you?"

"No. But he will see me."

The guard looked at the cut above Francine's eye and the terrified look on her face. He tightened his grip on her arm.

She saw the telephone sitting on the guard's desk.

"Call him," she said. "Tell him that it's Francine Rush, and it's urgent."

As the guard picked up the telephone, Francine suddenly realized that Morris might simply refuse to see her.

"No. Let me talk to him myself," she pleaded.

The guard handed Francine the phone. She held it with trembling hands.

"George," she whispered, "it's Francine Rush. I must talk to you at once. It's urgent."

When Morris heard her voice, a look of disgust came on his face. It was his finest day, his greatest victory, and now he had to be bothered with this pest.

"Francine," Morris said. "This really is the wrong day for your nonsense. I just have too much on my mind. Go away."

"George. It's no nonsense. I swear to God. It's a matter of great urgency."

He was silent.

"Please," she said. "If you don't find my visit worthwhile, I'll never bother you again. I promise."

He was still silent.

"If you let me in, I won't try any funny stuff, no games. I swear it."

Francine heard no response from Morris. All the color drained from her face and she began screaming. "Please let me in . . . I'll behave . . . I swear it . . . I'm scared to death . . . Oh God, I'm scared."

Then she began sobbing into the telephone.

"Let me talk to the guard," Morris said.

When the guard hung up the telephone, he escorted Francine into the house. He led her into the living room where Morris was waiting.

Morris looked like a man who was dressed for a coronation. He had just showered and shaved. He had a clean, fresh look. He was wearing a blue silk suit with a polka dot tie. He had on a new white shirt and those cufflinks from his April fifteenth swearing in—eighteen-carat gold with an American flag engraved in the center.

Francine was startled for a moment by Morris's appearance. She had spent the morning with men who were unshaven, wearing the crumpled suits that they had grabbed when someone said, "There's a crisis, get to the White House." Henry Oliver was even wearing the President's suit. But here was Morris dressed for a visit to the Royal Palace.

"What are you dressed for?" she asked Morris. "Where are you planning to go?"

Morris looked at his watch. It was close to one o'clock. They'll be calling soon, Morris thought. There's no harm in telling her now. He might even gain some satisfaction from it.

"My dear Miss Rush," Morris said, "You are looking at America's newest national hero. I am waiting for the President to call, summoning me to the White House to decorate me with honors for my accomplishment. I have just saved the country from a national disaster. Now I will enjoy the gratitude of two hundred twenty million Americans."

Morris said his words with quiet dignity. Francine could hardly believe her ears. He is actually serious, she thought.

Then Francine started to laugh. At first it was a slight chuckle. But the more she thought about the events of the past forty-eight hours, the louder she laughed. And by the time she was finished it was a raucous laugh and large round tears were flowing down her cheeks.

"What in the hell is so funny?" Morris asked.

"Nothing That's the whole point," Francine said, turning intensely serious again. "This is one time that your computer brain has come up with a wrong answer. It has made a mistake—a terrible mistake."

Morris could tell that she was serious.

"What do you mean?" he asked.

She reached into her purse and pulled out the green book—
*The Book of Job, A Modern Interpretation.*

"It's all in here," she said, handing the book carefully to Morris.

He opened it, looking very puzzled. He leafed quickly through the first fifty pages. Then he saw what Francine had been alluding to. Between pages 50 and 200, the centers of the pages were cut out. There was a large rectangular hole at that point which had been precisely fitted with a small battery-powered tape recorder.

"You're not the only one who can use the advantages of modern technology," she said.

"Where did you use this recorder?" Morris asked in a demanding tone. "Here in my house?"

"Don't flatter yourself. I managed to leave it in the Oval Office at the White House about an hour ago."

"Play it," he said, anxious to hear what she had recorded.

"I will, George, but first some background."

Francine then described in detail her activities during the preceding forty-eight hours—even explaining the bruise above her eye. He listened quietly and impassively.

When she was finished, he said, "Play it," pointing to the tape recorder.

"Okay. I've heard it once already. I'll skip to the critical part. The people present were the President, Oliver, and Anderson, the head of the CIA. You know all of them. You will have no difficulty recognizing their voices."

She pressed a button. Morris could hear the sound of the tape being rewound until Francine reached the point she was looking for. Then she placed the book on a small marble coffee table.

"Okay. I'm ready," she said.

Morris sat down on the sofa behind the coffee table. Francine sat next to him and pressed a button. The tape started playing:

President: Maybe I should pull those troops out of Saudi Arabia just as quickly as I can. What effect would that have on my popularity in the polls, Henry?"

Oliver: I don't know, Mr. President.

President: Oh, for God's sake, Oliver. You're the press secretary. Give me your professional judgment. Express an opinion for once. I need it.

Oliver: My best judgment is that the people will be absolutely euphoric when they fully grasp the fact that the United States has seized the Saudi Arabian oil fields by force. They'll love it. They'll dance in the streets. It will be like 1945 over again. The early reports that I've seen confirm my judgment.

President: Do you think he's right, Andy?

Anderson: Absolutely. Let's face it. We haven't had a winner in thirty-eight years. You can't count Korea and I wouldn't even mention Vietnam. The people will realize that with cheap Saudi oil, the country's energy crisis will be over for many years.

Oliver: There will be some Congressmen like Stark, who will be furious because they weren't consulted, but most will be happy to be out of the energy mess. Also there will be some liberals and intellectuals who will be upset by the attack, but they will be a small minority.

There was a silence on the tape. Then the voices started again:

President: From what you two are telling me I can't pull those troops out. If I do, I'll be a national villain. I might as well flush my chances for reelection down the drain.

Anderson: I think that's right.

President: That bastard Morris has presented me with a fait accompli. I'm stuck with it. I can't pull out of Saudi Arabia.

Morris smiled broadly. That's precisely what I was hoping for, he thought.

Oliver: What about the possibility of a Russian or Iranian military response?

Anderson: The Russians have confined themselves to rhetoric, and we can handle that. The Shah has surprisingly but happily been silent. I don't know why, but we can't complain.

There was a pause, then Anderson started talking again.

Incidentally, I lost one of my best agents there about a week ago. He was the Chief of Security for the Shah's son. His head turned up in one place, and the rest of his body in another.

President: There is only one terrible blemish on this otherwise happy picture.

Oliver: What's that?

President: If this invasion is as good as you two say, I sure as hell want to take full credit for it.

Oliver: Go ahead. Just act as if you ordered the whole thing. Everyone assumes that you did anyhow.

Anderson: With all due respect, Henry. You're being a little naïve. The whole story will come out sooner or later. And probably sooner. Hell, Elliott will probably get drunk and shoot off his mouth tomorrow. People will spread the story at cocktail parties. You know this town.

President: When the story comes out, I'll look like a horse's ass. It will be clear that Morris took the Presidency away from me without me even knowing it. That dirty bastard. I'll be the biggest fool in the history of the Republic. I've been cuckolded politically. I couldn't control the government.

Anderson: It's worse than that. Until it does come out, you will be subject to blackmail by anyone who knows the story. And you saw a good example of Stewart's integrity last night. Fred's not above blackmail.

President: Let's arrest the bastards—all four of them. We'll charge them with criminal conspiracy and treason. They'll all get good long jail sentences. I want to punish them all, Stewart for his disloyalty, and especially that bastard Morris.

The expression on Morris's face became intensely serious.

Anderson: You can't afford a public trial. Then you really will look like a fool not only at home but abroad. You could forget about your whole foreign policy and reelection. A public trial would be worse than cocktail party gossip.

President: Then what in the hell do we do?

There was a long pause on the tape. Morris heard a noise that sounded like the shuffling of papers. Then the voices started again.

Anderson: You have only one viable option. You must dispose of the participants in this plot permanently and efficiently. You have to prevent this story from coming out. You have no choice.

President: What do you suggest?

Anderson: In the two years that I've been the head of the Agency I have recruited a small elite force for foreign assassinations. It's something that the agency always had until the post-Watergate nonsense of the late 1970s. Some of these men are stationed at agency headquarters and others are in Western Europe. They could move immediately. It's my recommmendation that we use them.

Oliver: Is that really necessary? Isn't that a bit extreme?

Anderson: Do you have any other viable alternative?

Morris leaned forward, closer to the tape, listening intently. His face was frozen. None of his muscles moved.

Oliver: I guess I don't have any other suggestion.

Anderson: The decision is, of course, yours, Mr. President.

President: How many people are we talking about? I mean how many people know that I didn't order and direct this operation?

Anderson: There are four—Morris, Thomas, Stewart, and Elliott.

President: Is that all?

Anderson: Oh, no. I'm sorry I forgot. There is one other.

President: Who?

Anderson: That bitch of a reporter for the *Tribune* who was here before.

President: You mean Francine Rush.

Anderson: Yes.

There was another long pause. Francine looked absolutely terrified.

President: Andy, you have my order to dispose of all five of these people. I have a constitutional duty to protect the integrity of this government. I am not interested in how you carry out my order. That is your responsibility.

Anderson: I assure you that your order will be executed promptly and efficiently.

The voices stopped on the tape.

Francine was paralyzed with fear. She couldn't even raise her hand to turn off the machine.

"Okay. I've heard enough," Morris said to Francine. "Let's get moving."

But she never heard him. She just sat on the sofa suspended between the conscious and the unconscious. She had a dazed look on her face. Then she dropped her head to the table, burying her face in her hands.

Morris watched her for a few seconds. Then he sprang to his feet and raced to the telephone in the corner of the room. His fingers pressed the buttons on the telephone as quickly as his brain could make them work. He was dialing the telephone number of the Iranian Ambassador.

# CHAPTER

# 27

TWO YEARS LATER, CAPTAIN POLK AND HIS COLLEAGUES celebrated the Fourth of July in Saudi Arabia. As of that date, President Edwards, who had been reelected in a landslide, was still sticking to his decision that the United States troops would not be withdrawn from Saudi Arabia. The Independence Day celebration could have been a bit of a drag with the Moslem ban on alcohol, but the United States Army obliged with a whole planeload of Kentucky bourbon.

Walter Green had been appointed Director of Energy on July 6, 1983—two days after the attack. Green immediately dispatched Grease Fletcher to Saudi Arabia to repair the damage to the Saudi oil fields. Green then began rummaging through his files. He quickly found what he was looking for: a copy of the five-year plan for achieving independence from foreign oil that Morris's computer had developed before the OPEC announcement.

With the help of the continuous flow of cheap Saudi oil under the control of the United States Army, Green was able to begin implementing the Morris five-year plan in the two years after the seizure of the Saudi oil fields. He had every hope of continuing its implementation for the next three years. The period immediately after the attack was not without tragedy, however. General Thomas returned to Washington for a hero's welcome on July fifth. However, two days later, when he went to visit his wife at the Boston Psychiatric Hospital, his car was struck broadside by a trailer truck on the Massachusetts Turnpike. Both Thomas and his driver were killed instantly.

The General's body was returned to Washington for a full hero's burial at Arlington National Cemetery. President Edwards declared a national day of mourning in tribute to the military genius who directed America's Fourth of July War.

On July ninth, William Elliott's body washed ashore near Oxford, Maryland, on the Chesapeake Bay. The Secretary of Defense was an apparent victim of one of the numerous boating accidents that occur every year on July Fourth weekend on Chesapeake Bay. The Coast Guard recovered Elliott's boat, *The Anita*, in early August.

Later that same month, the badly decomposed body of Frederick Stewart was found in the Smoky Mountains of northeast Tennessee. Stewart's empty wallet was lying near the body. The police suspect foul play, perhaps a group of primitive mountain men. But they still haven't been able to develop any good leads as to the killer.

As for Morris and Francine, an air controller at Dulles Airport spotted them racing across one of the runways on the afternoon of July fourth. They were heading toward a Concorde which was registered in the name of the Shah of Iran.

The air controller actually saw the couple board the plane prior to its takeoff. When last seen by the controller, the plane carrying Morris and Francine disappeared into the blue sky enroute to the power and riches of Iran.

One month later, the *Washington Tribune* reported that Janet Koch had appeared at the Iranian Embassy in Washington to obtain a visa for an extended visit to Iran. Then in mid-August, Comp-Systems, Inc., a California manufacturer of computer hardware, applied for an export license to ship advanced computer parts to Tehran. An industry expert concluded that the Morris 6000 was being constructed in Iran.